# RELUCTANT GUARDIAN

## THE OTHERWORLD GUARDIANS, BOOK 1
## ELISHA BUGG

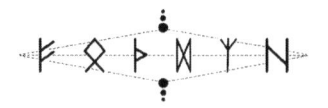

Copyright © 2019 Elisha Bugg
All rights reserved.

No portion of this book may be reproduced in any form without written permission from the publisher or author, except as permitted by U.S. Copyright law. Small quotes may be used for the purpose of review.

This is a work of fiction. Any similarity to actual persons, living or dead, or actual events, is purely coincidental.

Cover and interior design – Inkwolf Designs

Follow author at:
Twitter: @ElishabWrites
Instagram: elishabuggwrites
Facebook: ElishaBWrites
Tiktok: elishabuggauthor

www.elishabugg.com

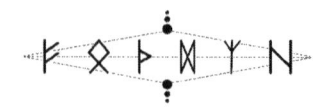

*To Michael, for always being there to support me and listen to my rants as I try to get my words on the page.*

*Also, to all the ladies in the Creative Central Facebook group who have helped and supported me in this journey.*

# Chapter 1

This was the last place Thane wanted to find himself. He didn't want to come, but Edwin had been insistent. So, instead of searching for his friend and mentor who was taken by hunters over twenty years ago, Thane found himself surrounded by hundreds of people he didn't know and didn't care to.

This place was a nightmare. His entire journey from the entrance to the main hall, people trod on his feet, shoving into his sides and generally getting in his way.

Thane growled deep in his throat, rubbing his fingers over his throbbing temples that pulsed with the beat of the music. Why Edwin had decided to meet him at a masquerade party full of teens and college students was beyond him.

Roaming deeper into the massive house, Thane's eyes watered from the overpowering odour of cheap perfumes and sweat mixed in the air. He forced himself not to breathe too deeply, afraid he'd choke as the air around him grew heavy. He couldn't wait to get out of here and continue on his hunt, but that wasn't going to happen anytime soon, not if Edwin had his way. The old man always tried to get him to stay. Why would this time be any different?

Thane huffed, coming to a stop in front of a large table filled with sweets and alcoholic beverages. Deciding to indulge himself, he poured a drink of unnaturally dyed red liquor and lifted the flimsy plastic cup to his nose, inhaling deeply. Cherries and vanilla. Such a sickeningly sweet smell. What was the worst that could happen? He shrugged and gulped it down, gagging as it hit the back of his throat.

"Disgusting," he grumbled, wrinkling his nose as he poured a second cup. Anything to numb himself from this experience.

"Where is he?" Thane muttered to himself, crossing his arms over his chest and tapping his foot on the floor as he took another sweeping glance of the busy room. The sound of feminine giggles and whispers travelled to his over-sensitive ears, drawing his attention to the other side of the room. If he closed his eyes and concentrated hard enough, he could hear their words and the excited flutter of their hearts.

Let them look. None of these women would approach him; they never did. He could smell the scent of their attraction, feel their eyes lingering on his body causing every hair to stand on end, but his dark appeal wasn't enough for them to overcome their fear of him. A fear he saw in their watchful eyes that kept them at a distance as they danced and gossiped.

Thane turned to face a particularly loud group of women he could hear above the others. Each of them gasped and shied away hiding their scarlet faces beneath elaborate masks. Thane rolled his eyes and looked away. None of it mattered to him. He would rather they didn't speak with him. Some of these women may be attractive, but they were human, possibly even hunters. He didn't want them anywhere near him. The only reason he'd come was to find out why

Edwin needed him to rush back to this place he used to call home.

Tired of the stares and the whispers, Thane returned to the refreshment table and chose something a little less sickly than before.

He froze his hand pausing mid-air, causing the dark liquid to spill over the rim of his cup. There, above the harsh perfumes and other odours he'd been so desperately trying to avoid. A scent deliciously sweet and fruity drifted to his nose on the chilly breeze that came from the open patio doors. Thane closed his eyes and turned toward the mouthwatering aroma, inhaling deeply, letting the alluring fragrance fill his lungs— Honeysuckle. It was like ambrosia crafted by the gods, making his mouth water and his body hum as it coaxed him forward.

"Thane. There you are," a familiar voice called from behind, breaking him free of the trance the scent had put him under. Thane turned to face the very man he'd been waiting for and smiled as he approached.

"It's good to see you, my boy. I'm grateful you came."

Thane was shocked at how much the man had aged. His normally golden blond hair had become silver, making him look distinguished. His amber eyes faded to a pale yellow, yet they still held that spark of mischief they always had.

"How could I refuse when you practically begged me?" Thane teased, resting his hand on Edwin's shoulder, squeezing it tight. "It's good to see you too, old man."

"Less of the old, thank you," Edwin smiled and passed him yet another drink.

"What do you need me for so urgently?" The sooner he helped Edwin, the sooner he could leave this place and all the bad memories it brought back.

"I can't explain here, Thane. It's not safe," Edwin paused, looking around the room as though searching for something or someone. "I'd like you to familiarise yourself with the place. I need to find a friend, to introduce you to."

Thane grumbled, the sound coming out more like a growl.

Edwin always did this. Stalled for time, forcing Thane to stay longer than was necessary. Only this time, Thane might crack. He clenched his fists, grinding his teeth to rein in the beast within.

Edwin paid no attention to him. Instead, he passed Thane a mask and smiled, pulling his own regal cat mask down over his face. Thane raised a brow as he accepted the gift, rubbing his fingers over the soft leather, admiring the subtle shades of blue that blended flawlessly with the black. A wolf.

"Why bother now? Almost everyone here has already seen my face?"

"The hunters live here, Thane. This party is a sham. An excuse to scout for new members," Edwin whispered, leaning in close as he adjusted his suit. "We need them to believe we're the same as everyone else here. Besides, it suits you."

Thane exited the room, leaving Edwin to his agenda while he began to roam the halls, familiarising himself with the building like he'd been asked. He would rather leave the party now to find out why he was here, but the old man had insisted on finding his friend first. Who could this person be? Why would Edwin be close to someone at a hunter's party?

Thane stomped through the halls, his muscles tense and his jaw clenched shut. How long did he have to be here? He wanted to get away from all these people. From this town that held nothing but painful memories. He should be searching for traces of Lucas, not here; not at a hunter's party. He longed to be in the open, running in the woods. The cool dirt beneath his paws, the scent of pines drifting to his nose as he roamed free and wild.

Thane closed his eyes and took a deep breath, soon wishing he hadn't when the noxious perfumes cloying in the air nearly choked him; all hints of that honeysuckle scent vanished.

He pushed his way through the crowds, grumbling with each step before he spotted another member of the Guard in the distance. The alliance created to protect the Lore from hunters and humans, both Edwin and himself were a part of. There was no mistaking Tynan with his wavy, surfer blond hair that brushed the collar of his shirt and that wide grin that made women melt. He was a charmer, a real ladies' man, not at all fussy when it came to claiming someone for the night.

Thane took a step toward him, ready to ask why they were both here when he noticed the young girl; his view of her partially blocked by Tynan.

She was a pretty little thing. Long, raven black hair and big blue eyes, but she was human. Thane scoffed and wrinkled his nose when he saw Tynan stroking the girl's face, touching his fingers to her lips and whispering in her ear. The girl stood no chance against his charms. Thane shook his head, muttering under his breath as he turned and walked away.

Several guests turned to glare at him as he barged his way through, but none of them dared to stop him or say a word.

He paused. That same honeysuckle scent from before drifted to his nose. Faint, but definitely there.

Instinct took over, forcing his feet to move without any conscious thought.

With each step, the fragrance grew stronger, spurring him forward as his pace quickened. The sensation of something pulling at him surged through his body, the animal within now wide awake, guiding his feet. The pull became more powerful, a feeling unlike anything he'd ever felt before.

His heart raced. His long strides made it appear as though he were running through the halls, shoving other guests out of his way. He needed to find the source of this overwhelming feeling coursing through him. His body ached and his throat burned as he struggled to catch his breath. He wanted to stop, fearful of what would be waiting for him around the next bend, but the animal was in control now, urging him forward, becoming impatient and needy.

Thane collided with a soft body and heard a loud thud as it hit the floor. He looked down to see a young woman in a heap before him.

"Sorry," he apologised, rolling his eyes as he reached down to help her up. "I wasn't looking where I was going."

"It's all right. I wasn't paying attention either," the woman replied, looking up at him through thick black lashes; her voice like music to his soul. She reached out, her emerald eyes locking with his as she took a hold of his hand.

The contact took his breath away as a jolt of electricity surged through his body, straight to his groin. He pulled her to her feet, continuing to stare at her in disbelief. That nagging sensation that lured him through the halls, vanished. The beast within him now still, silent and content for the first time since he'd arrived back in town.

Was it searching for her? Impossible. She was human. Possibly even a hunter.

It may not be unheard of for a shifter to take a human mate. Hell, his best friend had. But Thane would never trust a human again, not when they had destroyed his home and taken everything from him. Only, when he looked at the woman in front of him, his heart clenched. How could this beautiful creature be his enemy?

His eyes drifted lower to her black dress that was tight around her middle, pushing her breasts forward until they looked like they might spill over. He would be only too happy to catch them if that should happen. Her creamy skin screamed for him to taste; to touch.

He shook his head vigorously. What was he thinking? He couldn't lose himself to his desires. Not with her.

Thane forced his attention back to her face, and away from

a body that was beginning to reawaken the beast, but it did little to douse the fire building in the pit of his stomach.

Her hair was down, just the way he liked it, shimmering like fine silk. The long, rich, burgundy waves framed her face and he longed to run his fingers through it. Faint freckles dotted over her button nose and high cheekbones, drawing his attention as she gave him a nervous smile.

He almost broke. Those full red lips were so tempting and inviting. He leaned forward to taste them, catching himself before he made contact.

Never in his existence had he been so captivated by a woman.

There were a lot of beautiful women here, but none of them held his interest. Not like her. No, there was more to her than a pretty face, something stronger that called to him and made the beast wild.

Who was this woman?

He looked down at her, noticing she too had been affected by their contact. Her heart raced, making her chest rise and fall quickly, drawing his attention once again to her generous bust.

Thane went to leave, needing to put some distance between them when he noticed her rubbing her arm.

"Did I hurt you?" he asked, clearing his throat as he continued to watch her. Why it bothered him if he'd hurt her, he didn't know. He'd been pushing people out of his way all evening, but with her, things were different. He felt guilty.

"No, no. I'm fine. Really," she insisted, pulling a mask over her face.

Like his, hers was shaped into a wolf. The delicate lace lay in stark relief against her pale skin.

He leaned toward her to examine the mask more closely, stopping mere inches from her face. Her dazzling emerald eyes looked so familiar as they doubled in size with fear and something else. Desire perhaps. The rich scent of honeysuckle filled his nostrils, making him close his eyes and take an indulgent breath.

"Interesting mask," Thane commented, reopening his eyes to lock with hers.

"Thank you. A friend gave it to me."

Her face burned red beneath the mask as he traced the edges with his index finger.

She leaned in close and pressed up on her tip-toes, brushing her moist lips against his in a fleeting kiss.

"Sorry. I don't know what came over me. I've never—"

He cut her sentence short, pressing his lips back against hers, deepening the kiss.

She moaned into his mouth, spurring him on and sending another jolt to his groin. He needed to stop, needed to control himself. But she felt so right. Like he'd been waiting for her for years.

He curled his hands into tight fists, his sharp nails digging into his palms, forcing himself to step back and break free of the kiss and the passion that consumed him.

# Chapter 2

Anya raised a shaky hand to her still-tingling lips.

*What was that?* She'd never kissed a man first, especially not like the one she now watched race through the halls away from her; but an overwhelming urge to kiss and touch him forced her to act.

What a fool. She thought he'd desired her too, mistaking that look in his eyes for a hunger matching her own; when in fact it was something else.

As he disappeared around the bend in the distance, she couldn't help but think she'd offended him. But why had he returned her kiss?

She leaned back against the wall, tracing her kiss swollen lips with her fingers. Even now she could feel his lips pressing firmly against her own. Could feel the faint stubble that dusted his chin tickling and scratching her face as he deepened the kiss further.

She looked down at the hand she'd touched his with and

frowned. The feeling of electricity buzzed beneath her skin, spreading up to her wrist. She touched it with her other hand and gasped. Tiny pinpricks erupted up and down her arm making her vision blur and her ears ring loudly. She closed her eyes and inhaled deeply, trying to gain control of her racing heart.

"Anya," someone called from down the hall, breaking her concentration on her breathing.

"Anya," the call grew louder.

She reopened her eyes and stared down the corridor, searching for a face she recognised in the cramped space.

"There you are," her friend shouted, her voice loud and shrill to Anya's still ringing ears. "I've been looking for you everywhere. I was beginning to think you'd abandoned me."

"Sorry, Keri," Anya replied with a forced smile.

Something wasn't right. A simple kiss shouldn't have affected her so drastically.

Who was that man?

Anya took one last glance down the corridor in the direction her mystery man had fled and sighed. Would she ever see him again?

Trying to keep up with Keri as they made their way to the main hall was impossible.

Keri barged her way through, elbowing and shouting at those who got in her way. Anya was the opposite. Quiet, slipping into gaps as they appeared, ducking and weaving in between, excusing herself when she did bump into anybody. Not that they noticed. It was packed. They probably didn't even realise she'd touched them with how close they stood together.

In the distance, Anya spotted Keri's head bobbing up and down as the gap between them increased. She tried to pick up her pace, squeezing her way past, but it was no use. Keri's blonde head disappeared.

Anya reached the end of the corridor and paused, looking left and then right. Which way could she have gone? There was no sign of her anywhere.

She bit down on her lip and clung to her necklace, hugging herself close.

Not again. She'd already gotten lost once tonight; she didn't want to be alone again.

What she wouldn't give to be home now, curled up on the sofa with a good book rather than surrounded by people she didn't recognize.

She'd hoped to see a few familiar faces, but the only one she knew, she'd just lost in the crowds. What was she going to do now?

Anya squeezed tighter on her chain and took a deep breath. It was no use. She'd have to make a decision. She took a right, hoping to catch a glimpse of Keri up ahead, or at least find a room less cramped and loud than the halls.

"Anya?" Keri called from behind, forcing her to spin around and bump into a boy next to her, who corrected her footing and smiled down at her. Only he wasn't smiling at her face. No, he was looking down at her chest, his wide-eyed grin a dead giveaway as he leaned in closer, an overpowering aroma of vodka seeping from his open mouth.

Anya hugged herself tighter and hurried toward Keri, glad she'd turned up when she had.

"You're white as a sheep. What's up?"

"I thought I'd lost you again," Anya admitted, tugging on her dress in a vain attempt to cover herself as she looked back at the boy who still watched her, nudging and whispering with his friends.

"Stop it," Keri insisted, swatting her hand away. "You'll stretch the dress."

"You're smaller than me. This dress is too tight, and people keep staring at me. I knew this was a bad idea."

"They're just jealous, so stop squirming."

Anya forced a smile but continued to fuss with the dress despite Keri's protest. According to her, none of Anya's clothes were suitable for a masquerade ball.

If it was a few years back, it wouldn't have mattered. Their sizes were similar. Now, Anya was curvier, filling the dress to the maximum. It was a surprise she could even breathe. Keri was taller, standing almost a foot higher than her. Normally it bothered Anya how short she was against her friend, but right now, she was grateful. The dress was already short, stopping halfway up her thigh. If she'd been as tall, it would barely cover her behind.

"Stop fussing," Keri scowled over her shoulder. "You're not going to make a good impression if you don't stop fidgeting."

"I'm sorry, but I'm really uncomfortable."

Keri shook her head and grabbed a hold of her hand, pulling her through a large archway.

Anya's mouth fell open in awe.

The hall they'd been searching for was massive, taking her breath away.

A swarm of people filled the room, their masked faces glowing ice blue in the moonlight shining in through the high glass ceilings. The familiar scent of mulled wine filled the air around her as candles burned on each table scattered around the room. A beautiful Celtic song played in the background, loud but not deafening like most of the other rooms around the house. It was almost peaceful here.

"Keri," a male voice called from behind them.

Anya turned around quickly causing her head to spin. She steadied herself on a nearby table and closed her eyes as a wave of dizziness washed over her.

Reopening her eyes, she came face to face with a stranger.

"Who's this?" he asked Keri, continuing to stare at her

beneath her mask.

Anya could feel her cheeks burning as he leaned even closer, not caring a bit about her personal space. His nose almost brushed hers, his warm breath tickling her face.

She thought he was going to kiss her like the man upstairs, only she didn't have the urge to kiss him.

He was quite handsome with his short, light brown hair spiked up on his head in an almost military fashion. She wondered whether it would be prickly beneath her fingers. His dark eyes were like chocolate, twinkling when he flashed her a dashing smile which lit his whole face; she couldn't help but smile back. Yes, this stranger was handsome, but he didn't make her heart soar or her stomach flutter.

"That's Anya. She's the friend I mentioned to you the other day, the one who's just moved back," Keri replied, walking passed them to another man who approached, throwing her arms around his neck in a display of affection.

"Oh? My name is Hugh. It's a pleasure to meet you." He took her hand and placed a kiss on her knuckles with an old-fashioned charm. "What's wrong?" he asked, crossing his arms over his chest when she snatched her hand away and cradled it against her, rubbing as pain spread up her arm.

"S-sorry. I think I hurt myself earlier when I fell."

"Wait. What? You didn't tell me you fell over."

"You didn't exactly give me much of a chance," Anya muttered, still clinging to her arm.

To her surprise, Hugh burst out laughing and moved even closer, draping his arm across her shoulders like he'd known her for years. "She can get a bit carried away, can't she?"

"Hey. I'm right here," Keri scowled, punching Chase's chest playfully. "Aren't you going to defend me?"

"You're tough enough to look after yourself. You punched that guy earlier because he pinched your arse."

"He had it coming. But that's not the point."

Hugh shook his head as Keri and Chase continued to bicker and turned to face Anya with a smile on his face. "Would you like some ice?"

"Pardon?"

"For your hand."

"No, no. I'll be fine. Thank you."

"Alright. Let me take a look," he insisted, not waiting for her to agree. He took her hand, causing her to bite down hard on her lip to keep from screaming. The metallic taste of blood filled her mouth and the edges of her vision began to fade. She shook her head and fought against the feeling she was falling. She snatched her hand back and rubbed her sensitive skin.

"Hurts that much, huh?" he asked, brushing his thumb over her lip, causing her to shudder and wince.

Anya brought a hand to her now stinging lips and gasped, noticing the blood that stained her fingers. Had she really been biting so hard?

Her pulse beat loudly in her ears, her heart racing. Hugh spoke again but she couldn't make out the words. Everything around her sounded muffled as though she heard it through a wall of water. Hugh reached out his hand and placed it on her shoulder in an attempt to gain her attention, supporting her as she swayed on unsteady feet, but the contact felt like a branding iron against her skin. She clenched her fists tight, creating moon-shaped dents in her palm as the feeling of flames spread their way across her arms and torso. Her whole body burned as though encased in fire.

Anya moved away from him, aiming for the open patio doors.

With each step, her throat constricted tighter, her breath coming out choppy and laboured.

What was this feeling?

Sweat shimmered on her skin as she pushed her way

through the crowds, her hands trembling as she neared the doors.

Strong arms wrapped around her waist from behind in an unbreakable cage, holding steady as her head lolled to the side and the world around her faded black.

Anya awoke to a different kind of heat wrapped around her as she was held against a large, firm chest.

The wind swept over her fevered skin, blowing her long hair across her face, tickling her nose and sticking to her glossed lips. She craved to brush it aside, but her limbs felt heavy and lethargic, the steady beat of this stranger's heartbeat lulling her back to sleep. She fought against it, shaking her head and cracking open her eyes to look up at the man carrying her.

Who was he?

Not a single street light was lit, his features shrouded in darkness. Except for his eyes, shining bright like sapphire orbs.

This must be a dream. His eyes couldn't possibly be glowing.

Another gust of wind blew across her face; the scent of musk and pine filled her nostrils, making her inhale deeply.

She tried to sit up in his arms, only to be pushed back again with a sigh.

Her eyes watered and blurred, the darkness creeping in once again. She tried to fight against the pull, but it wasn't enough. Her vision faded to black.

Anya's eyes flickered open for a second time, the familiar sights and scents of home greeting her.

She sunk deeper into the worn-out sofa and sighed.

She'd never fainted like that before. What was wrong with her?

Covering her eyes from the burning light above her, she moaned and rubbed her aching head. Only she wasn't alone like she'd first thought.

Goosebumps erupted over her flesh everywhere his eyes lingered, sending an uncontrollable shiver down her spine. Not a pleasant feeling like she'd imagined it would be to have someone stare at her so intently.

She turned to face the room, searching for him, forcing herself into a seated position, her eyes still blurry with dizziness.

"I wouldn't do that just yet if I were you," he groaned, pushing to his feet and taking a step toward her. "You still look pale. I don't want you to faint on me again."

Her cheeks burned red. What a fool she must have looked. Everyone probably thought she was drunk.

She forced herself to focus on his face as he drew closer.

His eyes caught her attention first, seeming to glow in the dull light like they had outside. She froze to the spot unable to break eye contact, feeling like prey to a hungry animal. Then she noticed that strong square jaw, dusted in stubble and marked by a dark scar that cut across his sensual mouth.

The mystery man from upstairs. He'd been the one to catch her, bring her home and wait for her to awaken. Her face reddened. How pathetic she must look.

He opened his mouth to speak, only to close it again and look away.

"H-how did you know where I lived? Where's Keri?" she asked when he walked past her, pausing to lean against the wooden frame of the door as she spoke.

"Edwin," he replied, choosing not to answer her second question.

"You know Edwin?"

"Yes."

She made a sound of frustration under her breath when she realised he wasn't going to elaborate further. Why was he making it so difficult? This man was infuriating, yet she couldn't stop herself from craving him. Just the sight of him filling her door frame, propped against the wood made her mouth water and her fingers tingle with the need to touch.

He was huge, easily over six foot and at least two hundred pounds of solid muscle. His legs like tree trunks, straining against the tight confines of his black trousers. She could easily see the ropes of muscle across his chest and stomach defined beneath his thin white shirt.

Finally she forced her attention away from his body and up to his face. She blushed and licked her lips as she remembered the kiss they shared.

He watched her every move, his nostrils flaring and his deep blue eyes glowing brighter than humanly possible.

Unease crept over her skin, but she continued to watch him. That same feeling of goosebumps erupted over her as a shiver made its way down her spine.

"You need rest," he said, his voice rumbling in his chest, his eyes on her skin, burning.

This was a man she should be cautious of. But when he looked at her with those amazing, yet terrifying eyes, it was hard to remember why.

# Chapter 3

It wasn't wise to leave her alone after she'd fainted, but Thane couldn't stay around her any longer, not with her scent of lust flowing to his nostrils begging him to finish that kiss.

He stepped out into the cool air and rested his head against the wooden door behind him.

How is it possible for this girl to be affecting him like this, making him lose control?

He growled and stepped down from the porch.

There was something different about her, something that called to him like nothing else. The wolf clawed at his insides, fighting to be free. With each step, it fought him to turn back. To confront her. To take her. He growled louder, furious with fate for sending her to him now.

"A human," he scoffed, glancing back over his shoulder.

He couldn't allow himself to be driven mad with lust over a female, let alone a human one who could very well be a hunter.

No. She couldn't be. Edwin wouldn't know a hunter like he seemed to know her. But then, why was she there? Why were any of them there?

Thane clenched his fists, turning his knuckles white and punched a nearby wall. The plaster cracked, exposing the brick beneath as the cloud of dust settled on the floor. But it wasn't enough. No matter how much he told himself it was a bad idea. No matter how much he insisted she couldn't be his, the wolf fought to return to her, hungry.

The sweet scent of her lingered on the breeze forcing him to turn, expecting to see her behind him. She wasn't. He sniffed the air once more and frowned. It was coming from him.

Thane turned and began to run toward Edwin's in search of answers. Taking a quiet route on the outskirts of town, he sprinted through thick woods on the path that would lead to the old man's backyard. Still he fought every instinct not to run in the opposite direction, his muscles aching as he pushed them harder, fighting against the wolf inside, sweat gleaming on his skin under the moonlight.

He dodged and weaved through trees, easily manoeuvring past branches and trunks. Leaping over a fallen log, his body erupted in black fur that shimmered dark blue in the light shining through the broken canopy of trees. His bones and muscles rearranged themselves under his skin as he landed on four paws on the other side. His canines grew into fangs, dripping with saliva, blue eyes glowing wildly as he searched his surroundings before taking off once again.

The trees became sparse. The strong aroma of flowers and bushes tickled his nose. He didn't remember the journey from the town being quite so quick.

Looking up at the house before him, Thane couldn't help but compare it to the hunter's bleached home.

Edwin's house was beautiful, blending in with its wooded

surroundings. Everything about it natural, from the stone walls and wood panelling to the handcrafted furniture. Even the water and electricity were sourced from nature. A complete opposite to the large, unnatural, and modern house the hunters called their own.

As Thane stepped through the backdoor, into the kitchen, he transformed back into his human self. The transition from man to beast, and back again, had never bothered him. From a young age, he'd learnt to control the change with ease, and as he grew older, the process only became faster and less painful. Now he could change in a matter of seconds, the feeling almost a pleasure.

He continued through the kitchen, helping himself to some of the food laid on the table. A pair of jeans draped over the back of one of the chairs. Clearly, Edwin was expecting him.

Thane entered Edwin's study, brought there by the scent of apple and cinnamon; a scent everyone who knew the old man associated with him due to his obsession with the unusual concoction.

Still pulling on his jeans, and fastening the buttons, Thane spotted Edwin seated at his desk, leaning over a pile of papers.

"I take it Miss Shaw arrived home safely?" he asked, never bothering to look up from his work.

"No, Edwin. I left her in a ditch somewhere once I had my way with her," Thane paused, waiting to gauge Edwin's reaction. He didn't even flinch. "Of course I took her home. I even waited for her to wake before I left."

"She was alright?"

"Fine. A little wobbly. Not that I understand why you care. She's human," he scoffed, crossing his arms over his bare chest as he leaned against the bookcase behind him.

"Not all humans are the same. You of all people should know that. Just look how close you and Amelia were."

"She was different," Thane growled, irritated that Edwin would bring her name up now. "She earned my trust over the years."

Finally looking up from his papers, Edwin mirrored Thane's stance as he leaned back in his chair.

Much like himself, Edwin was a large man, but when he looked at Thane like that, there was no mistaking this man was head of the Guard.

"What's the problem, Thane? Don't you like the girl?"

"This has nothing to do with whether I like her or not. I just don't get why you felt I should deal with it. Why would you think she's safe with me?"

"You may have a fiery temper, Thane. But you'd never hurt an innocent girl, whether you were in a rage or not."

Thane grunted. He knew how bad he got when the animal took control and his human mind was lost. Things ended bloody. Many of the Guards feared him, and so they should. He scared himself sometimes. Even Edwin struggled to hide his fear when Thane lost his temper.

"Besides. When you ran across the room to catch her as she began to fall, I saw the fear in your eyes."

"I only caught her because I felt responsible. I told you I knocked into her upstairs. It's probably why she fainted," Thane replied through clenched teeth, stepping toward Edwin, pounding his fist down onto the table in front of him.

Thane knew he was lying to himself, but he couldn't admit he was unable to take his eyes off her. All the signs she was about to faint as panic consumed her forced him to step into action. He couldn't just let her fall in the middle of the room. He wasn't a monster. Not yet.

"Why am I here, Edwin?" he asked, pinching the bridge of his nose between his thumb and fingers. He didn't need reminding that he couldn't stop thinking about her. Even now she was at the forefront of his mind when all he should be worrying about was why he was here.

"The hunters are recruiting again, Thane. Their numbers

are flying out of control but I don't know how they're getting the people," Edwin replied, rummaging through the stacks in front of him. "In the last month, they've recruited over thirty new members in a ten-mile radius."

"How is that possible?" Thane asked, slumping down into the chair next to him, taking the piece of paper Edwin offered.

"That's what I can't work out. They must be using scare tactics or showing humans proof of our existence. That's why I need you."

"Why not tell me this sooner? If I'd have known at the party, I could have—"

"It wasn't safe to talk there."

"Then why ask me to meet you there in the first place?" Thane growled, scrunching the paper in his fist.

He knew there had to be a reason why Edwin planned to meet him there. Nothing Edwin did happened by chance. But why a hunter's party of all places? He didn't understand.

"I knew that Anya would be attending and I wanted to keep an eye on her, make sure she wasn't sucked into a trap."

How could this girl be of importance to him? What reason could there be to care whether one human girl joined the hunters when they were recruiting dozens more?

"I swore to protect her and I will. That is all you need to know right now."

Thane pushed out of his chair, causing it to crash against the floor.

"Remember, Edwin. You were the one who asked for my help," he snarled, heading for the exit. "Keeping information from me isn't the way to win my loyalty."

Thane stormed from the house. He'd hoped that talking with Edwin would take his mind away from the girl and that he'd have the answers he was looking for, but all he felt now was a combination of rage and curiosity.

There had to be more to this girl; a reason Edwin was determined to protect her.

One way or another, Thane swore he'd find out.

ᚠ ᚩ ᚦ ᛘ ᛏ ᚾ

Anya couldn't sit still. Her body ached for a release she didn't understand.

Everything around her seemed new and different, as though seeing it for the first time.

She was used to meeting large and intimidating men from her time around Edwin, meeting his friends and colleagues, but every instinct inside warned her that the stranger she'd bumped into was different.

She found herself texting Edwin, asking him to pop round before she'd been aware her phone was in her hand.

"No taking it back now," she grumbled, flinging her phone onto the sofa, and heading to the kitchen to pour herself some hot chocolate. She needed something to help calm her nerves.

A loud knock hammered on her front door, making her jump out of her skin, spilling chocolate powder all over the floor. She sighed loudly, placing the jar on the worktop and headed for the door.

"That was fast," she called, pulling open the door, expecting to come face to face with Edwin. The man in front of her was nothing like him.

Edwin was a kind and gentle man, who had always treated her like family. He always smiled and helped those in need. She loved him like the father he'd been to her. This man certainly didn't look friendly.

Her heart raced as she watched him, clenching tightly on

the chain around her neck when he moved forward, stepping into the light that poured from her open door.

His long, thin, and angular face curved into a cruel and menacing smile, drawing her attention to a deep, pale scar that cut across his features. His left eye appeared white, as though sightless, yet it followed her as she took a step back, her hands trembling.

"Good evening, Miss Shaw. My name is Richard Grosvenor, Hugh's father," he smiled, but it didn't reach his eyes. His tone sounded dead like the eye he watched her with.

"When he told me what happened, I had to come and check you were alright."

"I-I'm fine," she stammered as her muscles tensed and her body shook uncontrollably. "Thank you for asking. But you didn't need—"

"I make it my business when somebody faints at one of my parties," he interrupted, taking another step toward her, the smile on his face disappearing when she clutched at the door handle. "Who was it that brought you home?"

"I don't know."

"Come now, dear, I'd like to thank the man properly," he replied, tapping his foot on the floor. She thought she saw his hands clench briefly, but the movement was so quick, she wasn't sure whether she'd imagined it.

"He never told me his name."

"Oh," he paused, looking behind him as though he heard a noise.

When he turned back to her, his good eye had faded to a lighter shade of brown, almost resembling the other. "Hugh seemed quite taken with you. Be sure to let him know when you're feeling better."

Anya nodded, hoping that if she agreed, he would leave. He didn't need to know that she had no intention of seeing Hugh again.

"Such a pretty girl," he whispered, raising his hand to her face and stroking a long, slender finger down her cheek. He cupped her chin and tilted her face to the light. "Shame about those eyes."

She could hear the pounding of her heart in her ears as she cringed and tried to pull away from his bony fingers.

Finally he released her, his lips curving into that same hollow and menacing smile as before.

"I'll see you again, my dear," he called over his shoulder as he walked away, the click of his boots tapping on the floor echoing inside her head.

Anya loosened her grip around her necklace and released a long, slow breath to ease the tension in her shoulders.

Never had she met someone who terrified her like that. She just prayed she would never have to see him again; knowing instinctively that she wouldn't be so lucky.

# Chapter 4

Anya awoke to the morning sun filling her small room.

She sat up and flung her legs over the side of the bed. Her head pounded and her limbs were heavy, yet she felt restless and fidgety.

She looked around the room, searching each corner and dark space. Her stomach fluttered and her heart raced, but nothing jumped out at her.

She was used to nightmares; she'd had them for as long as she could remember, but something about last night's dream had felt so real.

Shaking her head, she looked up at her reflection in the tall mirror hung on the back of her door and cringed. "What a mess," she grumbled. She looked like the undead. Her eyes sunk into her skull, surrounded by large, black circles. Tangled and unruly curls framed her face and stuck to her lips.

Teasing a comb through her knotted hair, she tried to tame

it into a ponytail, deciding it would be a good idea to go for a run before soaking in a nice warm bath. There had to be a way of burning up all of this unexpected energy and she did love to run in the morning, before all the hustle and bustle of town.

Anya stepped outside and shivered as the early morning chill bit at her skin.

The sun was low in the sky, painting the horizon yellow as day began to break. The smell of dew and rain combined in the air, mixing with the fog that still clung to the tops of the trees making her breath mist in front of her.

She forgot how cold spring mornings could be. Tugging her jacket tighter, she rubbed her hands up and down her arms and began to run.

Anya paused, placing her hands on her knees and inhaled deeply to catch her breath.

It hadn't taken her long to reach the other side of town and now she finally felt more like herself.

She hadn't been running for months. Edwin used to take her all the time when she was younger. He seemed to enjoy it more than she did, always turning it into a game and challenging her, pushing her to the limit. She missed the exhilaration, the adrenaline and the content feeling welling up inside of her like it was now. Maybe if she asked him, he would run with her and give her the motivation she needed to start it up again.

Standing up straight, an uneasy feeling crept up her spine, causing the hairs on her arms and neck to stand on end. Someone or something was watching her. Their eyes burned a hole in her back.

Anya turned around and glanced up and down the streets. Nobody was there lurking in the alleyways and nobody was making their way to work or out shopping. But she couldn't shake the feeling of eyes on her.

She took a long gulp of water from the bottle concealed in the pocket of her trousers and decided to head home. Quickly.

That feeling grew stronger still, as though whatever was watching her drew closer.

She began to jog, hoping it was all her imagination, despite the urge to run, to hide. She pushed herself harder, making her muscles scream and her lungs burn, all the while hoping that she wouldn't come face to face with whatever danger was following her.

She'd almost made it home when a loud noise sounded behind her.

Frozen to the spot, her heart raced and her already sweaty body trembled. Slowly, she glanced over her shoulder. A small tabby cat burst from the alley, causing a loud crash that made her jump out of her skin.

"Stupid cat," she sighed, blowing out short breaths to steady her rapidly beating heart as she played with her necklace between her fingers.

Suddenly a firm hand came down on her shoulder from behind. She jumped even higher, barely holding onto the scream trapped in her throat.

"Are you alright, my dear?"

Anya didn't hesitate at the sound of that familiar voice, turning and wrapping her arms around his neck. Finally she released the breath she'd been holding, letting her head fall against Edwin's chest as he held her tight.

"Sorry I scared you, child. Is everything alright?"

"It's ok Edwin. I thought somebody was following me. I'm sure it was just my imagination," she replied in a shaky voice, continuing to hold onto him, soaking up his warmth and familiar touch, when she noticed he wasn't alone. Behind him stood the very man she had hoped not to see, staring back at her with those mesmerizing azure eyes. He was even more handsome in the light.

She remembered her reflection in the mirror and cringed.

Why did he have to see her like this? As if she hadn't made a big enough fool of herself already.

"Do you still feel it?" Edwin asked, placing her feet back on the floor and searching the space behind her.

"What?"

"You said it felt as though somebody was following you."

"Oh. No. I don't think so." No, all she could feel now was this stranger's eyes roaming over her body, fighting away the chill of the breeze. That urgent nagging inside still told her to run, but she no longer feared it was because of somebody watching her. The person she should now be running from stood just behind Edwin.

"You seem a little jumpy. Are you sure you're alright?"

"I'm fine. Thank you. I just need to relax and clean up."

Soaking in a hot tub had never sounded so appealing. She thought the run would calm her shaken nerves, but instead this strange feeling made her stress levels rocket.

It was like her peculiar dream all over again.

*The feeling of being watched washed over her in a wave, startling her awake.*

*She looked around her dimly lit room, but she couldn't see any eyes staring back at her.*

*Relieved, she lay her head back on her pillow and rolled to her side, curling her knees up to her chest and hugging them tight for comfort.*

*The feeling grew stronger, forcing her out of bed to glance out of her window. She unlocked the glass doors and took a peek outside.*

*The crisp breeze blew across her face, forcing the air from her lungs.*

*Blowing onto her hands, trying to warm her frozen body, she leant out further, peering down at the ground below.*

*Her heart calmed when nothing jumped out at her.*

*She searched the vast land behind the house, looking for anything that seemed out of place. Nothing hid in the large park, only flickers of metal shining in the moonlight that broke through the heavy clouds. Beyond that, a dense wood spanning as far as the eye could see. Only, in the shade of those trees, she spotted two glowing orbs staring back at her, drawing her in.*

*There was something eerily familiar about those eyes, as though she had seen them a thousand times before.*

*She studied them, watching as they drew closer and closer, until he came into view. A wolf. Huge and black. Watching her every move as he paced back and forth in front of the trees. The urge to go to him was strong, willing her to surrender to the beast, but her feet remained frozen to the spot, fear overpowering her other senses.*

*She watched him as he moved closer, his pelt shimmering in the broken moonlight.*

*He looked beautiful; his coat almost strokable.*

*A low rumble escaped his throat as he stopped below her, the sound causing her skin to erupt into goosebumps.*

*He sat staring up at her, those big swirling blue depths beckoning her forwards, to touch, to pet and learn. His eyes seemed to glow brighter, lighting up the night sky as bright as the moon above them.*

*She leaned over the edge further, rocking on the windowsill, all fears of falling or being in danger forgotten.*

*He growled again, much deeper and louder, peeling his lips back over his fangs in a nasty snarl. Was he warning her to stay where she was?*

*Suddenly a noise sounded behind her, that same uneasiness that had woken her coursing through her body. The wolf hadn't been the danger. Something else was here.*

*Her door swung open and crashed into the wall making her jump back and turn around trembling. Nothing but a strong breeze greeted her.*

*When she peered back to the wolf below, he was on all fours, his hackles raised and his teeth bared in a vicious snarl.*

*As she stared down at him, he seemed to calm, cocking his to the side as he looked her in the eye.*

*She turned to check over her shoulder, the door still swinging on its hinges in the gentle breeze she could feel blowing against her back, but nothing came rushing through like she feared.*

*When she turned back to the wolf a second time, he was gone. She scanned the treeline and saw him running, darting between the trees until he disappeared from sight. So fast and agile, graceful like a cat, his body sleek and full of lean muscle beneath all that fur.*

"Anya," a faint voice called. "Anya!"

"Sorry," she muttered, blushing a bright pink when she noticed Edwin, and the man she still didn't know the name of staring at her.

"I have some business to attend to right now, my dear. I'll come by later if you still want me to. It will give you a chance to freshen up."

She looked down at herself horrified to once again be reminded that she looked a mess. Why was it that she kept making a fool of herself in front of this stranger?

She dared a glance over Edwin's shoulder, but the man was no longer there. Shrugging, she turned back to Edwin. He raised an eyebrow at her and smiled a knowing smile.

The next time she saw him, she swore she would look good. There was no way she was going to make an idiot of herself or appear weak and helpless to him; not again. She would be dressed to kill. He may not respond to her much and may seem uncaring and rude, but she could see the desire in his eyes when he looked at her and she had every intention of making him want her as much as she wanted him. Maybe then he might kiss her again and this ridiculous infatuation with him might vanish.

How could it be that she was attracted to someone who intimidated her? Someone who didn't even seem to like her?

Suddenly she felt breathing on her neck as somebody came to a stop behind her. She spun around fast, almost losing her balance. He caught her, correcting her on her feet before letting go quickly as though she'd burnt him. His eyes flashed a dark blue making her breath hitch as she inched away from him.

His eyes grew darker as he watched her retreat until eventually, he smiled. Only it wasn't pleasant. He seemed pleased that he'd scared her, which only frightened her more; annoyed her even.

She got a hold of herself and took a step back toward him, causing him to raise a brow.

"It's rude to sneak up on people, especially when it's obvious they've had a bad morning."

"Your night wasn't going so smoothly either. You seem plagued by bad luck."

Instead of turning around embarrassed and ashamed by her misfortune like she normally would, something inside of her snapped. She took several more steps forward, coming to a stop close enough that she had to crane her neck up to look into his face. His eyes dimmed back to their usual ocean blue. This time, she smiled. He wasn't expecting her to stand up for herself, or to overcome her fear of him. He obviously didn't know her.

"Firstly, none of this started until I bumped into you; which by the way, was your fault," she insisted, getting closer and poking his solid chest with her index finger. "And then you act rude."

His eyes flashed an icy blue as he leaned in close to her face, smiling when she flinched. "You do have a backbone. Good. I like that.

# Chapter 5

Thane couldn't understand why Edwin chose a pub for their meeting, not until the rich scent of her drifted to his nose. The sweetest honeysuckle filled his nostrils, making him close his eyes in ecstasy. It was like someone had taken a hold of his heart and squeezed it tight.

He tried not to watch her when she entered, but he couldn't avert his eyes as she walked across the room. She looked even more beautiful than he remembered. Those low-hung, tight black jeans hugged her heart-shaped rear, drawing his attention with its gentle sway. Her baggy top dipped low at the back flashing him a huge portion of her creamy skin making his mouth water and his hands itch to touch. Then she turned and he could see her profile. Her top stretched across her generous bust, flowing down into a V between her thighs.

He heard a rumble coming from his own chest as he watched her, his jeans becoming unbearably tight when she smiled at the group she joined.

How was it possible that he could find a human so stunning? For weeks he'd been watching her, hoping to find out more about her, figuring Edwin would let something slip eventually. Nothing. All he knew was her name and the disturbing fact that he couldn't get enough of her. Her scent enticed him, her beauty fascinated him. Heck, she'd even stood up to him. A bold and risky move for anyone, but with her, he smiled, full of admiration and desire. What on earth was he thinking? This girl was trouble; an enigma he couldn't figure out.

Forcing his attention away from her and back to the two men he sat with, Thane noticed that Edwin watched her too.

"She's why we're here, isn't she?" he accused, his frustration flaring to life inside of him. "You planned to come here knowing she'd be here?"

"I don't know what you're talking about."

"Don't give me that shit. You haven't stopped staring at her since she entered."

"Thane's right, you haven't," Duncan, the other man with them chimed in, turning toward her with a smirk. "Why else would you pick to meet here? It's not exactly private."

"You know as well as I do that this place is owned by Oleander. We're quite safe to talk here."

Thane huffed. A vampire.

He didn't hate the vampires, they were much more preferable to humans after all, but he didn't like them either. They were leeches and they disgusted him, but they did come in handy within the Guard. The only way to kill one, thanks to their incredibly quick regeneration, was to remove their head, or cut them into hundreds of small pieces; good luck with that. Vampires were known for their lightning reflexes.

As if on cue, Oleander joined them at their table, slouching in the chair with his long arm draped over the back. "What can I do for you, Edwin? I'm a busy man."

"Did you get the information I asked for?"

"Yes, but it was tricky, especially when you insisted that she wouldn't notice me there."

Thane growled, causing Oleander to flinch and push back into his chair.

Was he the one Anya had felt watching her? The one he'd sensed in her room? Impossible. The presence surrounding her didn't smell like a vampire. In fact, it had no scent at all, confusing and disturbing him both.

He turned back to Oleander and scowled, clenching his fists to stop himself from breaking something. He may be one of their allies, but Thane still wasn't sure where Oleander's loyalties lie, and he certainly didn't trust him around women, especially this one.

Anya was beautiful, he couldn't deny that. He found her irresistible and unbelievably tempting. But Oleander had a weakness for human females, everyone knew it.

"Calm down, wolfman. I haven't touched her."

Why was he defending himself? She was nothing to Thane. All he wanted to know was why Edwin had asked the vampire to watch her and gain information on her. What could he possibly need to find out that he couldn't just ask her?

As the others continued to talk, Thane's attention drifted back across to where she stood. She was smiling and laughing with her friends, the sound making his heart skip a beat, yet she seemed distant and uninvolved, holding back as she just went through the motions. He couldn't help but wonder why.

His ears pricked up trying to listen in as one of the men moved toward her and whispered in her ear. *"You look beautiful."*

Thane had to agree, but as the boy slid his hand lower down her back, he saw red.

How dare he touch what's not his?

There goes the wolf again, playing tricks with his mind,

claiming her for his own. She couldn't be his. How could she be? She was human, the only creatures Thane considered to be monsters. Except, part of him knew she was different. That she wasn't cruel and judgmental like the rest of her kind. Perhaps it was because she hadn't run screaming from him when she'd seen him as a wolf the other night. She'd looked upon him with curiosity and wonder, making his body tingle with the urge to go to her.

No. He couldn't let her get close to him. But neither could he look away. He tried to force his attention elsewhere, telling himself not to become involved, but with each passing second, it seemed impossible, especially when the fool stroked his hand over her body like he owned it.

Before he knew what he was doing, Thane jumped out of his seat and headed toward her, his heavy boots stomping on the wooden floor.

Quickly locking the beast away behind a well-enforced cage, he switched his direction toward the bar, making sure he knocked the boy as he passed.

The boy stumbled, cursing under his breath as he turned and watched Thane walk away, but he didn't say a word. Thane knew he wouldn't. The only person brave enough, besides the other Guards, was Anya. Maybe she was tougher than he gave her credit for. He shook his head, dislodging the thought before he clung to it. He couldn't afford to think of her like that. He needed to remind himself that she was just a scared little human girl. Someone who needed to be protected and couldn't fight for herself. Someone who came from a race of monsters. Someone he could never have.

Thane sighed and ordered a strong drink, hoping to calm the building rage. If he didn't gain control soon, something or someone was going to meet the wrong side of his claws.

A strong tap on his shoulder had him spinning around, ready to snap until he saw her, hands on hips glaring up at him. "What do you think you're doing?" she demanded, tapping her foot on the floor as she scowled up at him.

"Ordering a drink. What's it look like?"

"You did that on purpose."

"I don't know what you're talking about," he replied, turning his back on her.

She grabbed a hold of his arm and pulled him back around. "Yes, you do. You pushed into him on purpose. Why?"

The girl's backbone was growing into steel. This was not good.

He leaned down close to her face, hoping she would back down and run like she should have; but not her. She continued to glare, holding his gaze. Impressive.

"Accident," he shrugged, hoping his voice didn't give away his burning desire.

"Bullshit," she snapped, her eyes flashing a brilliant green.

He was the one who stumbled back, confused by what he thought he saw.

"Why did you push him?" she asked again, more calmly as though finally noticing who she was staring down.

"You looked uncomfortable."

Anya turned around, taking in the room, smiling when Edwin caught her eye.

"Why?" she whispered when she turned back to him. "Why were you watching me?"

"Edwin is fond of you. I was curious what he saw in you."

It wasn't a lie. Edwin seemed to care more about her than anyone else in his life. He was determined to keep her safe. He'd even asked the vampire to keep an eye on her and find out some information. She didn't need to know that he was jealous of the boy touching her, or that he was fighting to control the wolf that was howling inside, begging to claim her before anyone else could.

Anya blinked up at him several times, relaxing her stance,

buying into the half-truth he told her.

"Edwin's the closest thing I've ever had to a family," she paused, looking over to where he sat, smiling wistfully toward him. "He thinks I need protecting from something, though he won't tell me what he's afraid of."

"Maybe you do," Thane replied, more to himself than to her.

"What's your name? I still don't know what to call you."

"Thane."

"Thane," she repeated, making his heart stop. The way his name sounded on her lips was like a punch to his soul. "You may scare me, Thane, but something tells me you're a good guy."

"Don't be so sure," he mumbled.

She moved closer, the warmth of her body making his skin burn.

Hesitantly, she reached her hand out, stroking a finger over his rough jaw and the scar that marked it. He closed his eyes and clenched his jaw tight to stop himself from moaning and grabbing hold of her.

"There's something gentle inside of you, no matter how hard you try to hide it. Why else would you have helped me?"

Her cheeks flushed red as she removed her hand, letting it fall limp by her side.

The first thing he noticed was her eyes as they glazed over, making her look lifeless and scared. Her breathing slowed, her heartbeat now weak to his ears.

"What's wrong?" he demanded, placing a hand on her shoulder to keep her steady.

Slowly she turned to his hand, before locking her eyes back on his. Her eyes now so bright it pained him to look at them.

Had she drunk too much? It would explain her sudden courage, but nothing could explain those eyes.

"Anya?" Edwin appeared by his side the next instant,

concerned and looking over his shoulder at the group she had been spending time with.

"Get her out of here, Thane. Nobody can see her eyes like that!"

Thane nodded, trying to usher her out of the building, but she wouldn't budge. Frustrated, he lifted her over his shoulder in a fireman's lift and headed toward the door.

He expected her to struggle and fight against him, but she felt limp and lifeless in his arms. Her skin was cool against his. Too cool; like ice.

"What do you think you're doing?" the boy demanded after breaking away from the group, moving in Thane's way when he tried to step around him.

Instead of answering, Thane pushed the boy aside and raised a brow, daring him to make a move again.

"W—where are you taking her?" he stammered, cringing at himself, and making Thane smile. "You can't just take her like that."

The boy stood taller this time, trying to square his shoulders, but he still came up short compared to Thane's towering height.

"Hugh, I asked him to take her home. Miss Shaw has had a little too much to drink."

"Then I'll take her home."

"I don't think that would be wise, do you?" Edwin countered in a non-too-polite tone. "You've had a little too much to drink yourself, and you're not known for your restraint."

Hugh's face turned scarlet, frowning at Thane before turning back to Edwin scowling like a spoiled child, exactly like Thane thought he was.

"What makes you think he's more trustworthy?" he asked, staring pointedly at Thane as he crossed his arms.

Thane didn't care to listen to the boy any longer. He

pushed him aside once more and barged his way out of the pub. He needed to get her home and away from the eyes of strangers. There had to be a reason her eyes were glowing like that and he intended to find out.

# Chapter 6

Anya sat on the edge of her bed, teasing a comb through her wet and unruly hair when she heard a hammering knock at the front door. The suddenness of it took her breath away, causing her to drop the comb to the floor.

With a sigh, she made her way down the steps, the pounding knock grew louder and louder in her head.

"Hang on," she growled, fastening her hair behind her as she went to cross the small hall, only to freeze, staring blankly at the distorted shape through the frosted glass oval in her door.

That was not like her at all. She may have been stressed, waking up with no memory of the night before; or how she'd made it home only to find herself draped in somebody's leather jacket, but she didn't normally snap or shout.

Perhaps she'd come back too early, but she missed everyone here.

For months Keri had begged her to come home, insisting

she needed to meet her new friends. Though honestly, Anya didn't see what the big deal was. Chase, Keri's boyfriend, seemed like a jerk, with his wandering eyes and massive ego. And Hugh; she wasn't sure how she felt about him. He was a nice, compassionate guy, but she got the feeling he was hiding something. Not to mention his frightening father. No. The less she saw of them, the better.

The person she missed the most, the one who'd never wanted her to go in the first place, was Edwin. He was family. Not once making her feel unwelcome or like an outsider as he brought her up alone. For as long as she could remember, he'd been there. Her rock. Only now he seemed to be lying to her as well.

The knock grew louder, bringing her sharply back to reality.

"Sorry, I—" Anya began, pausing mid-sentence when she saw Keri standing in front of her. "Keri?" She wasn't sure who she'd expected to find banging at her door, but it certainly wasn't her.

"Hey chick. You look rough," Keri commented, looking her up and down with a scowl. "That guy didn't touch you, did he?"

"Which guy?"

"The same one who took you home after the party."

No. Not him again.

She hated to appear weak in front of anybody, but with him, she got the feeling he would enjoy it. She couldn't give him that satisfaction.

"Hugh argued of course. He's a gentleman like that," Keri winked, nudging Anya with her shoulder. "but the guy wouldn't listen. I was worried he'd done something to you. Maybe he was the reason you had to rush home in the first place."

"What do you mean?"

Her memories were still foggy. Little snippets of the evening breaking through the haze. The loud music, and bright lights. The colourful, alcoholic drinks Keri had passed her not long after she'd gotten there. The sweet flavour still lingered on her tongue. Only now it mixed with something bitter and metallic.

"Well, you didn't have much to drink. Then you went to talk to him, and next thing I knew you passed out, being carried by him."

Could he really be responsible? She didn't know him, and she certainly wasn't sure she should trust him. But he'd saved her from falling when she'd only just met him. Carried her home and waited for her to wake before leaving. He'd even draped his coat over her last night to keep her warm. Those weren't the actions of a man who meant her harm. Besides, he knew Edwin. He wouldn't trust just anybody with her safety, that she knew for certain.

No, Keri had to be wrong.

"Who is he?"

"He's a friend of Edwin's."

*Thane.*

That's right. She knew his name. Some of what Keri was telling her must be the truth, but then she always had exaggerated.

"Doesn't mean he didn't spike your drink or something just to take you home for a second time," Keri sneered, her eyes seeming to sparkle briefly as she turned to glance back over her shoulder.

Maybe Anya should find Edwin and speak with him. She just couldn't believe he'd entrust her safety to someone who was dangerous. Someone who was capable of tampering with her drink.

"Are you busy?" Keri asked, quickly changing the subject when she turned back to face her.

"I was just on my way to work."

"Oh yeah, I forgot you worked weekends at the bookshop. Only, I've got something important to talk to you about. Can you swing by Hugh's when you're done?"

"Erm—" The last place Anya wanted to go was back to Hugh's, risking bumping into his father. But Keri was squeezing her hand painfully tight leaving her with little choice. "I guess so."

ᚠ ᚩ ᚦ ᚹ ᛁ ᚾ

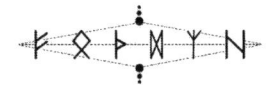

The sun was already beginning to set when Anya found herself outside Grosvenor hall, Hugh's mansion. Her heart was in her throat, staring up at the building that towered above her.

There was something intimidating about how the gargoyles scattered on the rooftops loomed over her, watching as she drew closer. She hadn't noticed them the last time she was here. The light spilling from the open doorway and windows had obscured her view in the darkness. Now that it was daytime, she could see everything about the oppressive building that terrified her.

A small voice inside told her to run, never step foot inside, but she shook her head and trudged forward. It couldn't be that bad. She'd been here once before.

Gulping, she climbed the steps to the huge oak doors and raised her hand to knock.

The doors swung open before her hand made contact with the wood. It was like something out of a horror movie. The voice inside now screamed in protest as she crossed the threshold.

No turning back now, she told herself taking in her surroundings and turning back to the entrance, expecting to see Keri holding the door open. Instead, a short, plump, and balding older man stood in her place. He looked quite friendly, at first, until he smiled. His big grin reminded her of a rodent. All teeth and squinty eyes, making her take an instinctive step back.

"Follow me, Miss Shaw," he called in a monotonous voice as he began to lead her through the corridors. Everywhere looked the same to her. All whites and creams, reminding her of a hospital.

Trudging along behind the small man, Anya glanced from side to side, hoping to see something interesting, but nothing caught her eye; not until she spotted a flash of colour to her side. A thick, blood-red curtain hung in front of an unusual wooden door. Dark mahogany etched with strange symbols and carvings. The closer they stepped, the more her intrigue grew, even as her heart pounded in her chest. She studied the etchings, noticing what appeared to be men holding a variety of weapons, surrounded by intricate symbols and writing carved in a language that made her head throb as she tried to remember where she'd seen them.

One by one the older man began to unlock a series of bolts and chains securing the door. Each click and groan of metal made her squeeze tighter around her middle.

What could possibly be so important that they had to take such measures to keep it hidden?

Her heart raced faster, the voice springing back to life inside her head, telling her once again to run as the door before her swung open. She stepped inside and looked around another endless and plain corridor, just like all the rest. This wasn't what she expected. Not at all.

Suddenly, the door clicked shut behind her, the man locking it just as tightly as it had been on the other side.

*What have I done?*

Frozen to the spot, her head spun, forcing her to hold her stomach and calm the nausea building. Sweat beaded on her forehead as she struggled to catch her breath. She didn't like this; she never had.

"Are you alright, Miss?"

She couldn't respond. Just leaned back against the cool wall, her throat closing up as she gasped for air.

"It's alright, James," a familiar voice called, breaking through some of the panic consuming her. "I'll take her from here."

Keri.

Anya closed her eyes, relieved she was no longer alone with a stranger. Listening as the man muttered something obscene under his breath before he stomped away.

"Don't worry, Anya," Keri whispered, placing a firm hand on her shoulder, and squeezing gently. "Let me show you around."

Breathing deeply, and counting backwards, Anya's heartbeat slowed to a less erratic pace. Her vision cleared to reveal Keri's smiling face. She was right. There was nothing to worry about. All they had to do was unlock the door and she'd be free. She wasn't trapped.

"Thanks."

Keri took Anya's hand, pulling her down the corridor, pointing to various rooms along the way describing what was inside each one. A whole other house locked away from just anybody to see. But why?

Anya was rapidly losing interest, her anger simmering just beneath the surface as she wondered why she'd been asked to come when she spotted another door that looked unusual in its surroundings. Except, this one was not wooden or etched, but stone. Strong and heavy. Seeming to glow with runes and inscriptions, reminding her of those decorating the inside of the ring that hung around her neck. Neither of which she knew the meaning of. An unknown feeling deep in her chest urged her toward it.

"I knew you'd be drawn to that one," Keri whispered, following her gaze before resting her hand across Anya's back, urging her further down the hall. "We'll explain later."

Anya couldn't help but wonder what was behind that door, especially when Keri refused to tell her. What could it be? And why was it glowing like that?

"Hello again, Miss Shaw," Hugh's father greeted from his seat at the head of a large oval table.

She'd been so consumed in her thoughts about that door that she hadn't been paying attention to her surroundings, not noticing that they'd entered a room.

"This is Hugh's…friend. Be polite gentlemen."

The way he spoke the word 'friend' made her flinch as

several heads turned her way with sneers and smirks. Each of them rose from their seats to stare, causing the hairs on her arms and neck to stand on end.

One by one they approached, taking her hand and placing a kiss on the back as they introduced themselves. Lost for words, her body trembling at the look on their faces, she forced herself to smile until they'd finished. The look on Hugh's father's face taking pleasure in her discomfort chilled her to the bone throughout the whole ordeal.

"Come with me," Hugh groaned as he took her hand none too gently, dragging her along behind him.

Anya wanted to argue and demand he release her, but more than that, she wanted to get away from the stares of those other men, and more importantly, Hugh's father, Richard. There was something in his menacing grin that terrified her. His cold stare made her skin crawl as his lifeless eyes followed her every move.

She shuddered and wrapped her free arm around her middle, just waiting for the right time to break away from Hugh's hold.

"What are you doing here, Anya?" he growled, glaring over his shoulder.

"Keri insisted I come."

She hadn't wanted to. She'd even considered making up an excuse to text Keri, but she'd come up blank. Only, her fears that it was really Hugh that wanted to see her turned out to be false. So why was she here?

"You should have just stayed away."

# Chapter 7

"Let go of me," Anya finally snapped, snatching her hand from Hugh's grasp when they were far enough from that room full of people.

Why did I even come? she asked herself, eyes roaming around the cold, dull hallways. What did Keri want with her? Without a word, she'd abandoned her in that room full of unfamiliar faces. She'd told her not to worry, but how was she supposed to do that when all she could see was Richard's leering grin as he watched her? The smug look on his face as he introduced her to all those men. And Hugh; he'd looked angry to see her, even telling her she should've stayed away.

"I'm going home. I shouldn't have come in the first place."

"It's too late now," Hugh's defeated voice sighed as he turned toward her, avoiding eye contact and biting his already stubby nails.

Anya opened her mouth to ask what he meant by that when he shoved a book in her arms. It wasn't an ordinary book, more of a journal, filled with loose handwriting and various sketches, all of which were amazing.

"Keep going."

"But this is just a storybook?"

The pages were filled with frightful images of monsters and creatures from stories and movies. All things that didn't exist. *Vampire. Witch. Siren. Demon. Muse....* The list went on. Why show her this? Suddenly her hand stopped moving. The bold letters reading '*Shifter'* seeming to jump from the page. The detailed eyes stared back at her.

Anya frowned, studying the drawing of what appeared to be nothing more than a bear. Except for those eyes. Shaded in such a way, they seemed to glow. She leaned closer, swallowing the lump in her throat, reading some of the text that surrounded the drawing;

*'Shifters are extraordinary creatures with the ability to change their form from human to animal; and back again.*

*One of the hardest of the Lore to identify, seeming no different from their animal or human counterpart.*

*Their biggest indicator is their eyes, glowing wildly when emotions are high.*
*Anger a shifter and they will expose themselves.'*

Anya leaned in close, tracing a finger across the image as she remembered the wolf from her dream. It had seemed more human than animal, but that was just a dream.

She continued to stare down at the picture, haunted by the familiarity of those glowing eyes.

*'Shifters have lightning reflexes making them difficult to*

*keep up with, and even harder to catch, but be careful, they're also extremely strong. It's believed that different species of shifter have different strengths and weaknesses, making it difficult to pinpoint the best method to kill. Various poisons seem effective, as does piercing their heart with silver.'*

"Why show me this?" she whispered, lifting her eyes to Hugh, expecting to see him smiling or curious why she'd been quiet for so long, but he wasn't even looking her way.

"This is part of what Keri and Richard wanted me to show you," he paused, glancing briefly over his shoulder toward the door, before turning to her, still avoiding eye contact. "The rest is downstairs."

"You expect me to follow you when that's all you're going to tell me?"

Hugh sighed, leaning his back against the wall as he stared up at the ceiling, his body tense as he clenched his teeth shut. "There is a man I'd like you to meet. A man from the book I just showed you."

Before Anya had a chance to ask any more questions, Hugh grabbed firmly around her wrist, dragging her through the halls. Her arm ached from the pressure of his hold. She knew he didn't want her here, he'd told her so himself, but why was he being so rough?

"Hugh, you're hurting me."

"Sorry," he muttered, loosening his grip slightly, allowing the circulation to return to her fingers. "I don't like going down there."

He sighed, releasing her wrist to grab hold of her hand instead. His hand was cold and clammy against hers, sending a chill through her entire body, heart pounding when she saw where they were headed.

The glowing of the door intensified with each step they made toward it.

She gripped tightly on her necklace, pulling the ring from side to side.

"They're just runes on the door," Hugh explained, smiling over his shoulder to her, except it didn't reach his eyes. That normal twinkle and charm nowhere to be seen.

"They won't hurt you though, at least—" His words trailed off, too quiet to hear. Not that she was paying much attention to him. Not when the glow of the door seemed to be moving in a slow circle around it as Hugh pulled out a massive key from his pocket.

Her heart froze. The door slowly crept open with a loud groan, revealing a stone stairwell leading into darkness.

Anya bit down on her lip, still gripping tightly onto her chain whilst Hugh struggled to light a wooden torch beside her, cursing as he burnt through several matches.

A gust of wind blew through the open doorway, taking her breath away as it whipped her hair across her face.

What was that noise? It sounded like a growl, but that wasn't possible. It had to be the wind groaning through the tight stairwell.

With the torch finally lit, Hugh took her hand once more and pulled her over the threshold despite her attempts to dig her heels in.

A tingling sensation coursed through her body. Her skin felt like it was on fire, burning deep through the layers of tissue. Her throat closed, making it impossible to swallow.

Steadying herself on the wall, her hand landed in something thick and sticky, but she didn't look. She didn't dare; fearful what it could be.

"Keri mentioned your fear of small, dark spaces, but I never thought it was this bad," Hugh said with a frown, rummaging through his pockets. "Here. It'll help if you know you can leave whenever you want."

Hugh passed her the huge key he'd used to unlock the door, mistaking her reaction for her phobia. She couldn't tell him that she didn't think that was the problem. That this was something she didn't understand. The only time she'd felt anything vaguely similar was just before she'd fainted at the party.

The key in her hand did seem to help, allowing her to cling to reality rather than drifting into darkness.

Controlling her breathing, Anya snatched her hand away again, ready to turn away and escape from this horrid place, when she heard her name whispered from below.

Part of her still wanted to leave, not wishing to find out what horrors awaited her below, but something about that voice sounded familiar, calling her closer. Every logical part of her body rebelled, demanding she turn and run, but her heart got the better of her, needing to know who could be down there. If it was someone she knew, she had to help them.

Steeling her nerves, Anya took a step forward, descending deeper into the darkness. The smell of rotten flesh and blood assaulted her nose, turning her stomach. She plastered a hand over her mouth to stop herself from spilling the contents of her stomach over the floor.

The odour grew stronger and stronger the further they went, forcing her to stop every few steps to catch her breath.

*What on earth is down here?*

Finally they reached the bottom, but she hesitated to take the last step, dreading what she could be standing in.

Slowly, she released her nose, taking in some much-needed oxygen, no longer caring about the stench. To her surprise, the smell wasn't so strong. The odour must have drifted out the small open window if you could call it that; it was really more of a slit in the wall. Obscured by thick metal bars that surrounded the middle of a circular room. Some broken and jagged, others still intact, flickering in the light of the torch as they stepped closer.

A prison. She gasped, placing a hand across her mouth before she could let out another noise.

Anya took another step toward that sliver of freedom when she was stopped by two glowing green eyes shining brightly in the darkness.

She was mesmerized, walking closer and closer to the bars, until Hugh gripped her shoulder, pulling her back.

"Be careful."

That's when she heard a deep, throaty growl much like the wolf in her dream. Except this was louder, echoing around the room.

She watched, frozen in awe as those small orbs of light drew closer until she saw a man's face appear. He was almost beautiful beneath all that grime and dirt covering his angular face, his green eyes shining like a gem through the mats of unruly hair restricting her view. There was no doubt this man had broken many hearts with his handsome looks before he was locked away here, left to starve. His face now gaunt, causing his high cheekbones to stand out sharp.

The man moved closer still, knitting his eyebrows between his eyes as he watched her with the same amount of curiosity as she watched him.

Instead of moving away from the man like she knew she should, Anya found herself creeping forward, drawn to him by the sorrow in his eyes.

Did she know this man? There was something vaguely familiar about the way he looked at her.

How long had he been down here, trapped like some kind of beast? Everything about him showed the tolls of being kept a prisoner for years. All except his eyes. Still young and vibrant, full of fight and determination.

He cocked his head to the side and sniffed at the air, frozen as he watched her, tears pooling in the corners of his eyes.

She had to look away from that mournful expression, focusing instead on his hands, shackled with shiny manacles that restricted his movements. Yet he strained against them, reaching a hand toward her.

She flinched instinctively, immediately regretting it when he dropped his hand with a whimper and turned away from her.

After several deep breaths, Anya stepped toward him once more. He turned straight away, fear and pain shining in those stunning emerald green eyes that doubled in size.

He was afraid. Shouldn't she be the one scared of him; so why wasn't she?

Even though she trembled inside, her heart insisted she trust him; that there was a connection between them.

As she continued to watch him pace inside his cell, her vision blurred and her hands shook by her sides. She bit down on her quivering lip to stop the sob escaping her throat as she saw a tear roll down his cheek.

Hugh moved between her and the bars, making the man spin toward him with a growl. The sound loud and predatory, causing her to flinch and hold herself close.

"He's the reason you're here, Anya," Hugh muttered, wrapping his fingers around the bars, his knuckles turning white from the pressure. "The man Richard wanted me to show you."

With a sigh, he kicked what looked like a chocolate bar toward the man.

Anya watched him glance down at the offered food, scrunching his nose up before he turned away. Not that she could blame him. She doubted she'd accept the pathetic offering either; not from someone keeping her prisoner. But why was he here? She saw nothing dangerous about this man. Yes, he was large, muscles still visible on his lean frame. Scars and welts patterned his skin showing his struggle. But his eyes held nothing but gentleness and warmth.

"Why does Richard have this man locked away like an

animal?" Anya fumed, hands clenched into fists by her sides. This wasn't normal.

"He's dangerous. Richard imprisoned him to keep others safe."

"If that's true, and I doubt it is, he should be in prison, not locked in your basement," Anya snapped, patting down her pockets, searching for her phone to call someone, anyone.

"You don't understand," Hugh pleaded, snatching the phone from her hands before he reached a hand toward her face.

Anya stepped back quickly at the same time the man behind let out a deep growl, lunging at the bars, making her yelp and cling to Hugh's sleeve before she'd realised what she'd done.

"If you just stay here a minute, I will get Richard to explain, he's much better at this than me."

Before she had a chance to say a word, Hugh had dashed up the stairs, leaving her alone with the man she wasn't sure whether she should fear, or not.

The sound of the door slamming at the top of the stairs made her flinch and hold herself tight. Her heart raced as she searched the room, the darkness swallowing her whole as the walls seemed to move toward her. Her head spun violently, her breathing erratic. Vision blurring as panic consumed her.

No. Not now.

"Do I scare you?" the man asked his hoarse voice strained from lack of use.

Anya shook her head, unable to speak as her throat constricted tighter.

"Come closer, child. I will not harm you."

Anya turned to him then. Those words spoken reminded her of Edwin. Perhaps that was how she recognised him. A friend of Edwin's who had come to the house when she was younger.

She took a tentative step toward him, as he did the same on the other side of the bars. He reached his hand through and waited for her to take it.

Hesitating, she held her hands close to her chest, before squeezing her eyes shut and brushing her fingers over his palm. There wasn't time to second guess her actions; he pulled her sharply into the bars, catching her head before it met with metal. His large hand held her head against his solid chest. The coolness of his skin stung her cheek.

"Listen to my heart, nothing else. It will anchor you and bring rhythm back to your breathing."

A little nervous, but calmed by his soothing words and touch, Anya closed her eyes and counted with the steady beat of his heart. She leaned in further, pressing her face against him. Embracing the touch he offered her as he began to pet her hair. His actions were comforting, reminding her of a distant memory she could barely grasp.

"Thank you," she whispered, opening her eyes and taking a step back. A little more relaxed in her surroundings.

"I learnt a few tricks from the healers before I was captured."

"They want you to join them, don't they?" the man asked when silence fell between them. That haunted look back in his eyes.

"What do you mean? What are they?"

"Hunters," he growled, springing to his feet to resume his pacing. "They search out anyone and anything different. Capturing and killing them."

"Like you?"

"Others like me. Only Richard has another use for me."

Richard. She knew there was something about him that unnerved her, but to think he was a killer. Then there was Hugh and Keri. What was their role in all of this? The Keri she knew would never go along with murder.

"They're monsters," she whispered, narrowing her eyes as she stared hard at the ground.

"You're so much like your mother, in body and spirit."

"You—you knew my mum?" she choked, trying not to let her tears fall.

How was it possible for this man to know her mother when she could barely remember her? Whenever she tried, all she could see was an image that looked so much like herself, she doubted it was even real.

"Yes. She was a remarkable woman." Unshed tears gathered in his eyes, a faint whimper escaping his throat as he hurried to look away. When he looked back to her, he smiled, eyes twinkling, taking her breath away. "You've inherited your father's eyes though, along with the name he chose for you."

Anya gasped, unable to contain the tears that left hot streaks down her face.

He knew them both. She never had a chance to know them. All she remembered was being taken from her mother as a child, by strange men whose faces still haunted her dreams.

The man opened his mouth to speak, only to be interrupted by the loud groan of the stone door at the top of the stairs, the sounds of voices echoing all around the room.

Anya jumped back, swiping at her eyes, hoping the limited light would be enough to conceal her blotchy face. Who knew what these, *hunters,* would do to either of them.

"Move back to where the boy left you," the man instructed, his face etched with concern as he pointed to a worn spot on the ground. "Richard will punish us both if he sees you close to me."

# Chapter 8

"Wait!"

Richard turned to her, eyebrows raised in query when she stepped in front of him and Hugh, halting their advance on the man behind bars.

She spotted Richard pulling a dagger from his jacket pocket the moment he'd taken the last step into the room.

"What are you doing?" she demanded, holding her hands out in front of her.

Richard may terrify her, but she couldn't just stand there and let him attack this man for no reason.

"He refuses to make this easier on himself. This is for persuasion," Richard sneered, spinning the dagger between his thumb and forefinger. "Besides, these beasts heal fast, it's what makes them so difficult to kill. It won't even scar unless I cut deep enough."

She wanted to argue, only she was powerless to stop him.

"Maybe she could reason with him?" Hugh suggested,

giving her a faint grin when she looked up at the sound of his voice. "You wanted to test her too, did you not?"

Richard looked at him and snarled, concealing the small blade back inside his jacket, huffing as he stomped to the back of the dark room and leaned against the grimy wall.

"Ask him to prove what he is," Hugh advised her, lowering his voice to a whisper as he stepped beside her, "Just don't get too close. Richard's begging for an excuse to use that knife."

"Thank you," she whispered back, holding her head high. She turned toward the bars. Richard wouldn't have the satisfaction of knowing she was afraid.

The man, whom both Hugh and Richard had called Lucas came closer on the other side, mirroring her every move.

"I don't understand what it is they want you to show me, but I do know that I can't stand here and let them hurt you."

"I'm a little rusty, and you may not like what you see. The change, it's not always pleasant to watch. Especially like this."

Without a word, Anya took a step back and waited for whatever was about to happen; except nothing could prepare her for this.

Lucas sat back on the filthy floor and closed his eyes. His broad chest rose and fell quickly as his body began to contort and bend. His bones and muscles rearranged themselves under his skin.

Anya gasped, holding a hand over her mouth watching on in disbelief. Unable to tear her eyes away even when he roared in pain. The bones in his arms and legs moved against the shackles still confining him, cutting into skin that rapidly sprouted a beautiful caramel fur, his ragged clothes disintegrating into pieces around him.

In a matter of minutes, there was no longer a man sitting before her, but a large wolf that looked exactly like the one from her dream all those weeks ago; just as big, and powerful.

Watching him in silence, she could feel tears well in her eyes, and her throat turn dry. She'd never seen anything like it. How was it possible for such creatures to exist?

Yet, even though she felt intimidated by the large beast in front of her, nothing terrified her more than the menacing grin that stretched across Richard's face.

This man was no monster, despite what they were telling her. Yes he was different, his ability to change into such a large and fearsome animal unnerving, but she knew from her time alone with him how gentle and caring he was. The only monsters here were those standing behind her. They'd captured and trapped this man, torturing him for years.

"Why are you here?" she mumbled to herself, rubbing her hands up and down the tops of her arms.

"Other than being inhuman and taking a human mate, nothing."

Anya stumbled backwards, catching herself before she fell.

She'd never expected an answer from him. Nor did she think she'd be able to understand him. Especially when neither Hugh nor Richard seemed to respond to the words Lucas spoke.

"Impressive," Richard commented, pushing away from his leaning space, that same wicked smile on his face making her blood run cold. "A little too impressive actually. In fact, if I didn't know better I'd say you knew about these beasts already. Maybe even in league with them."

"Of course, she doesn't," Hugh argued, pulling her toward him with a gentle tug on her shoulder. "You saw her face when she saw him change. That wasn't the look of someone who'd seen it before."

She may have never seen someone change in front of her the way Lucas had, but she had to wonder whether the wolf from her dream was linked in some way. It seemed like too much of a coincidence to have such a vivid dream after what she'd just seen.

"Then bring her upstairs so we can begin."

"What, so you can brainwash me?" Anya snapped, shrugging out of Hugh's hold and backing away from him, appalled that he'd been touching her.

Hunters. Just how many people had they killed or captured? How many innocent lives were lost due to their ridiculous belief?

"This man is no monster. You are."

Without warning Richard sped toward her, taking hold of her shoulder and squeezing down hard enough that she felt it pop. She winced, biting down on her lip as he dug his fingers deep into the muscle and leaned in close to her ear, his hot breath fanning over her face.

"I'll show you monsters," he smirked, that same evil grin contorting his features.

Lucas jumped to his feet, roaring loudly as he lunged at the bars, biting down on heavy metal with his powerful jaws. The noise sickening as he rushed to protect her.

Her heart clenched, helpless to do anything to make it stop.

Richard huffed and turned to watch Lucas pace inside the cell. His thin lips curved up at the sides. A wicked gleam in his deathly stare when he turned to her before he stomped from the room, leaving her alone with Hugh and the wolf once more.

Anya turned to Lucas and made a silent promise to herself. She would not give up. There had to be a way to free him.

# Chapter 9

Anya couldn't sleep. Whenever she closed her eyes, Lucas's face was there; his green eyes glowing like orbs in the darkness.

The moment she'd stepped foot out of that place, she'd gone to the police and told them what had happened, and despite them insisting they'd look into it, nobody moved a muscle. For several hours she'd waited outside the station, but not one cop had emerged.

What was wrong with them? Didn't they care?

Kicking her legs over the side of her bed Anya groaned in frustration. It seemed like the only time she got a decent night's sleep anymore was when she fainted.

Sighing, she threw on some clothes and headed outside. Maybe a run might tire her enough to sleep peacefully.

Once outside, the crisp night air hit her, forcing the air from her lungs as her breath misted in front of her. The windows surrounding her fogged with condensation. The grass crunched under her feet as she stood on freshly settled frost. Shivering, she rubbed her hands up and down her arms, attempting to warm her skin beneath her thin shirt, but nothing seemed to fight the chill.

Anya increased her pace, walking briskly she pulled her music player from her trouser pocket, tucking the buds in her ears. She needed something to take her mind off of Lucas, and those eyes that held so much emotion.

Jogging now, Anya stepped onto the field behind her home, the run beginning to warm her frozen skin and stretch her over energised muscles. It wouldn't be long until she grew tired; or so she hoped.

In the middle of the empty field, that unmistakable feeling of being watched crept over her, rooting her feet to the ground.

She spun around looking for signs of movement, hoping whatever it was meant her no harm.

Removing the buds from her ears, she listened carefully. A loud growl sounded to her left, drawing her attention. Those same blue orbs greeted her from what she assumed had been a dream.

Anya continued to stare at the wolf in the distance, waiting to see what he would do.

She didn't have to wait long. He moved toward her, his black coat shimmering black-blue in the moonlight.
"I wasn't dreaming the first time I saw you was I? What do you want from me?"

Sniffing at the air, he continued to pad toward her, closer and closer, making her heart race, but she didn't move, didn't run or scream. She was too curious to leave now.

His chest rose and fell quickly as he panted, stopping close enough that she could touch if she just stretched her hand toward him. But she was afraid. What if he didn't want her to touch him?

Last time she'd seen this wolf, he'd growled a warning at her. Why would this time be any different? Only, she couldn't help herself. She had to know what he felt like.

The wolf darted his head toward her, peeling his lips back, he stared at her, a low grumble sounding from his chest.

Anya dropped her hand immediately, but stood her ground, refusing to back down to the beast, knowing it would be pointless to run.

Each passing second he watched her seemed like a lifetime, just waiting for him to attack, or flee. To her surprise, the wolf moved closer, nudging at her hand with his strong muzzle, sliding it up over his head. She gasped and smiled wide. Her fingers glided through his thick fur.

"It's so soft," she breathed, continuing to pet him.

The wolf closed his eyes as her hand skimmed over his back, intensifying her smile.

She'd never been this close to such a large animal, even if this one was more human than she had first thought.

Since the first moment she'd seen this wolf, she'd wanted to touch him, her love for animals overpowering her fear. She also wanted to touch Lucas when he changed, curious how that beautiful caramel fur would feel beneath her fingers. Would they feel the same?

The wolf's chest rumbled beneath her fingers, an unmistakable sound of pleasure.

She inched closer, her leg brushing against his.

His eyes snapped open, glowing a shocking sapphire blue, locking with her own. They were beautiful, taking her breath away with their intensity. She tilted her head studying them closer, noticing the faintest speckles of green when he licked her face, making her gasp before she giggled and wrapped her arms around his neck unable to stop herself.

He paused and stiffened, before hesitantly laying his large

head on her shoulder, accepting her affections.

"Why am I so comfortable around you? Logically I should be terrified, but I'm not. This feels, right."

She lifted her head and studied his face, her brows knitted in confusion. Why wasn't he responding to her like Lucas? Had she imagined it all like she feared, or was this wolf not like him? One day, she hoped she would find out.

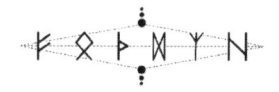

---

They sat under the twinkling stars for what felt like hours. Her arms wrapped around him tightly, her head resting on his shoulders. It was like holding a large teddy bear, just as warm and comforting. She could feel her eyelids growing heavy and her limbs loosening, her lack of sleep finally getting the better of her. That's when that eerie feeling crept over her skin for a second time that night, meaning it hadn't been just the wolf watching her, but something else.

Anya darted up, looking around them, noticing the wolf did the same.

"You feel it too?" she whispered, cuddling up closer to him for protection.

"Shh," he snapped, startling her. She hadn't expected to hear him talk, and he clearly hadn't expected her to hear him by the way he watched her, tilting his head from one side to the other.

Shaking it off, he continued to look around them, searching and sniffing at the air. Maybe he was like Lucas after all.

His head snapped to the right, staring toward the trees. He jumped to his feet and growled loudly, the hackles across his back rising in warning at whatever threat came closer to them.

"Run," he demanded, not daring to take his eyes off

whatever he had spotted in the distance.

Anya didn't hesitate, pushing to her feet and sprinting back toward her house. Her legs and chest protested with each step, burning from her earlier run, but she knew she couldn't stop, couldn't look back.

Suddenly the wolf was beside her, still glancing over his shoulder to see if whatever was behind them gave chase. Obviously not pleased with whatever he saw, he jumped in front of her, making her skid to a halt before she collided with him.

"Get on," he commanded, crouching down low to the ground to assist her.

"What?"

"There's no time," he growled, flashing her his sharp canines. "Get on. Now!"

She rushed, her hands trembling and fumbling as she straddled his powerful back. He didn't wait before he started moving again, running much faster than she could ever have dreamed of, forcing her to hold on tight. Happy with her strong hold, he ran faster still.

Everything around them blurred as they zoomed past.

Incredible. The rush she felt. The wind blew through her hair. She felt alive and exhilarated. It didn't seem possible that anything could move this quickly and still be so agile. She wanted to enjoy the feel of this powerful creature beneath her, enjoy the adrenaline coursing through her veins, but how could she when she feared what was behind them. What if whoever it was caught up with them? What if it was one of the hunters? Surely they wouldn't be able to catch up, would they?

She couldn't let them take or kill him, but what could she possibly do to stop them? The police wouldn't help her, and she was weak. Pathetic really. Scared of the hunters, worrying what they could do. She'd left Lucas alone when she should have fought harder for him.

All of a sudden, the wolf below her jumped, causing her to slip and pull at his fur. He roared loudly but didn't say a word as he slowed, allowing her to get a better grip. She ducked her head low, wrapping her arms tightly around his neck, rubbing her face against his thick fur. He didn't seem to mind, just increased his pace once more.

She couldn't understand why he was protecting her, possibly even risking his own life in the process. Lucas had done the same when Hugh or Richard got too close, but why?

Slowly the wolf below her came to a stop, his heartbeat racing against her ear.

"Has it gone?" she whispered, lifting her head so she could peek behind her. "What was it?"

He looked over his shoulder as he slowly padded around, searching and sniffing the air to see if they were alone.

"I'm not sure," he replied at last, taking one last glance over his shoulder before lowering himself to the ground.

A mixture of different emotions flowed through her when she noticed they were back outside her house. Relief, fear, happiness, disappointment and confusion.

She didn't want to climb off of him, didn't want to be alone again. She wanted to know who this incredible creature was and why he was here. What could these shifters possibly want from her? Could they know about her past? Maybe even Edwin knew who they were.

She'd seen so many different people when she was living with Edwin. Some friendly. Some not so much.

Glimpses of glowing eyes and long canines flashed before her eyes. She grew nauseated and her head pounded trying to focus on the images, pulling her memories forward. Why had she repressed these memories? Had something bad happened?

She shook her head. Edwin couldn't know about this. He would never keep something this huge a secret. Maybe she was just trying to make everything fit; letting her imagination run away with her. But she wasn't imagining the creatures she'd seen recently. Nothing could explain them.

"You should be safe, for now," the wolf whispered, bringing her back to reality. The fact she could still hear him disorientating her.

She sighed and climbed down, getting the hint.

Her legs felt a little wobbly, but the wolf stood, supporting her with his strong head, his blue eyes shining wildly in the moonlight as he watched her. Something about them so familiar.

# Chapter 10

    Thane told himself he'd only come this way to check on Anya before making his way to Edwin's, but he knew it was a lie. His heart had softened the other night when she'd held and pet him. She was braver than he'd given her credit for. Most people wouldn't dare touch him. Some didn't dare to come near him, even members of the Guard he worked with all the time, but Anya was different. No matter how much of a jerk he was to her, she still came back, still spoke to him and even stood up for herself. Then, surprising him even more, she had touched him as a wolf.

    This was dangerous. He couldn't let her get close to him, couldn't let her into his heart.

    He sighed, glancing at her house, trying to hurry past it before she noticed him. He couldn't speak to her now, not when he didn't know what he was doing.

    It was too late. He caught her scent on the breeze, guiding his feet toward the large park in front of her home. The smell intoxicating, luring him into a garden full of flowers and bushes. The rich aroma of magnolia, with a faint undertone of roses and lilies hit him as he stepped onto the grass, but nothing dulled the alluring scent of her as he drew closer.

He saw her and froze, admiring the view of her laying on her stomach in front of him, her feet swinging in the air as she hummed a tune he didn't recognise. Her rear drawing his attention, tightly clad in some low hung jeans. The barest amount of flesh exposed on her back where her jumper had ridden up from excessive movement. Her skin so smooth and creamy. His mouth watered to taste it.

Remembering how he'd licked her face the other night, he instantly grew hard. If only he were in his human form so he could have kissed her properly. She'd been delighted with the lick, but for him it wasn't enough, and he feared it never would be. He could feel himself becoming addicted to the taste of her, so sweet and delicious against his mouth.

Moving closer, he spotted headphones in her ears, which explained the catchy song she hummed and her lack of response whilst she sketched in a journal laid out before her.

Thane knew he shouldn't look over her shoulder, knew it was rude of him to pry, but something on the page caught his eye.

She was drawing him. Well, his wolf form; and it was magnificent. He'd never seen a drawing of himself before, and hers was spot on. Every detail. Every shade. He caught himself smiling again. Something that seemed to come naturally when he was near her.

He circled around in front of her and crouched down on his haunches.

Her head snapped up, her eyes wide with shock.

"T—Thane?" she stuttered, pulling the buds from her ears and pushing herself up into a seated position.

"You should be more careful. Anyone could sneak up on

you when you're lost in your own world like that," he teased, smirking when she frowned up at him.

He realised he liked playing with her. Liked when she smiled and reacted to him. But he was also afraid for her safety. Whilst she was detached from her surroundings, she was completely vulnerable. The creature he'd sensed before had been the same one he'd felt in her room all those weeks ago. The same dark and unusual presence that made him shudder. Never had he come across anything like it. It's lack of scent was disturbing, it's presence menacing. Whatever it was, she needed to be more careful. He couldn't always be there to protect her.

"If people didn't sneak around, I wouldn't have a problem, would I?" Anya bit back, making him smile yet again.

"I'm glad you haven't lost that backbone you so recently acquired."

"I never needed one before," she huffed, studying his face with curiosity.

He couldn't help but wonder what she saw when she looked at him. Did she see the resemblance in his eyes?

Her eyes skimmed lower down his body, over his stretched thighs, warming him from head to toe. She blushed and licked her lips, not attempting to avert her gaze.

Thane watched on, mesmerized as her pink tongue slowly traced her top lip, before she bit down, gently nibbling the bottom.

He had to snap himself out of it. Fast.

"Your drawing is impressive," he commented in a husky voice, still very much aroused and fighting the urge to push her back to the ground, pinning her with his weight.

"Thank you," she whispered, playing a loose strand of her hair between her fingers as it fell over her shoulder.

"I know it was rude of me to look, but I couldn't help myself."

"It's alright. Usually I don't show people my work, but it's nice to know it's appreciated," she smiled, brushing graphite dust off the page.

"Why don't you show anyone? It's good."

"My drawings are more like a diary of my thoughts and feelings. They're personal."

He was intrigued what she could be thinking about him, but he didn't dare ask.

"Mind if I take a closer look?"

She nodded and handed him the sketchbook without hesitation.

He was surprised she trusted him with something so precious after how he'd treated her. Would she still be so trusting knowing the truth about him?

Thane sat down beside her and traced his finger by the drawing, careful not to touch the lines. He didn't want to smudge it and destroy the trust she had offered him.

"This is amazing. There's so much detail."

She smiled at him, her cheeks turning pink as she twiddled her thumbs.

"What's this you've started to draw behind?"

"Me—"

"Riding on his back," Thane finished for her.

He knew from her huge smile and sparkling eyes that she'd enjoyed running with him, but he never would've guessed how much. Perhaps she wouldn't treat him any differently after all.

No. What was he saying. Of course she'd think of him differently, they all did.

"How did you know?"

He ignored her question, allowing her to think what she wanted. He stood ready to walk away, needing to move away from her before he lost himself to his desires. She was still just a human, and the wolf needed to remember that.

"Oh. I almost forgot. Edwin was looking for you," he said,

looking back over his shoulder as she sat looking up at him with her hands clasped on her lap. "He wanted to talk to you about the other night at the pub."

"I guess he saw me with Hugh then."

"What?" he asked, pausing at the sound of the boy's name.

"Is that not why he wanted to talk to me?"

"I don't know. Why would you assume it was?"

"He warned me to keep away from him, that he was bad news," she paused, turning away from him to fiddle with the hem of her top. "I didn't believe him until I found out what he was," she muttered to herself, obviously finding out something she didn't like.

Thane knew he didn't like Hugh, but he'd assumed it was jealousy that the boy was touching something the wolf considered his own. Was there more to it than that? Maybe the wolf had picked up on something else he didn't like.

"You're muttering," he interrupted, smiling when she blushed.

"Sorry. Maybe I should go see what he wants."

Thane nodded and started to walk away, until Anya jumped up and grabbed hold of his arm, halting him in his tracks to stare down at her hands.

"Sorry. I didn't think—" she blushed once again, dropping her hand from his arm and plastering it to her side.

"It's fine," he reassured her, wanting her to place her hands back on his skin. Needing the contact.

Now he really was in trouble.

She loosened her stiff stance and looked back up at him. "Where is he?"

"Edwin? I'm headed there now."

She turned from him and bent to grab her things from the floor, stuffing them in a small canvas bag before joining him on the edge of the grass.

What could she have meant when she spoke about Hugh? What was he? Thane just couldn't forget her words no matter how hard he tried. She'd been happy enough to spend time with him at the pub, laughing and joking with the others, even if he could sense her discomfort when the boy leaned in close. Why the sudden change in opinion of him? What could he have done?

Really it was none of his business, but what kind of man would he be if he let the boy get away with hurting her.

"What did he do?"

If he'd touched her, hurt her even, Thane doubted he'd be able to control himself. The boy wouldn't see him coming.

"Pardon?"

"You said until you found out what he was. What did you mean?"

"He's cruel, and malicious, and barbaric, and I want nothing more to do with him."

"Did he hurt you?"

"No," she replied, shaking her head with a sigh. "That would have made things a whole lot easier," she whispered, pausing to stare up at him through her thick lashes, blinking at him several times before scowling. "Why do you care?"

He didn't know how to respond. He couldn't tell her that he cared more about her than he wanted to; that her safety meant more to him than anyone else's. If he said the words aloud, it would mean admitting the truth to himself. He would have to continue the lie, make her think he was the rude bastard she no doubt already thought he was.

"Edwin wouldn't be pleased if I stood by and let anything happen to you."

She stopped dead, staring into his face, her eyes watering and her cheeks draining of colour.

He'd upset her? That wasn't the response he had been expecting, but it was too late to take it back now. She wouldn't believe him if he tried.

"Tell Edwin I'll be there later. I'd rather not walk with someone who was only speaking with me to get in his good books."

"That's not what I meant—"

"Then what did you mean, Thane? Enlighten me."

"I—Never mind."

He walked off, leaving her alone. It was one of the hardest things he'd ever done, but he supposed it was for the best. He needed to push her away. Needed her to hate him enough that she would keep her distance. It was better that she walked away now than to get tied up in a world she had no escape from. The hunters would never leave her alone once they found out she knew the truth. How long could she possibly outrun them for? He had to spare her a life of constantly looking over her shoulder, dreading the day they caught up with her. Just like Amelia.

# Chapter 11

Just when Anya was beginning to see Thane's softer side, he had to go and ruin it, telling her the only reason he cared was because of Edwin. Why it upset her, she didn't know. He'd been telling her stuff like that since she'd met him. Everything he'd done for her; catching her when she fell. Carrying her home and waiting for her to wake. Even taking her home that night she fainted at the pub. All of it was Edwin's doing.

What a fool she was.

Deep down she knew she had feelings for him. She had since the moment she met him. Nobody enthralled her as he did. He was her drug, craving the next time she was near him. It was hopeless to try and get close to him. She should just move on and forget about that kiss they shared. Everything about him screamed trouble, yet she couldn't help herself. She needed more of him.

After waiting for almost an hour, sitting on Edwin's

doorstep, Anya finally decided to call it a night. If he wanted to speak to her that badly, he would have to come to her. She was done waiting.

"Maybe it's a good thing Edwin wasn't home," she muttered to herself, glancing back over her shoulder toward Edwin's front door. She was in a foul mood and would likely make an idiot of herself, or lose her temper. If Thane was there, it was guaranteed. Nobody managed to get under her skin the way he did.

Anya kicked a can on the curb and groaned. Why did she let him bother her?

She wanted to ask Edwin about him. Why he acted the way he did, or how they knew each other, but the man was never around when she needed him lately. All she wanted was her old, simple life back. The one where she didn't have to worry about things like hunters, shifters, and Thane. Heck, even Keri seemed different somehow. The only thing that never changed was Edwin, and where was he?

She had one last look over her shoulder, back toward Edwin's, wondering whether she should turn around and wait a while longer when the dreaded fear that someone was watching washed over her. An unforgettable feeling. Only this time, it felt different from all the others. Less intense. Less chilling.

Maybe this time it wasn't the mysterious dark figure that kept following her. Perhaps it was the wolf.

Suddenly a loud thud sounded to her left, causing her to spin around quickly to see what was there. She stumbled and missed her footing on the edge of the curb, twisting her ankle and landing in a heap on the floor; half on the path, half on the road.

Cursing she tried to push to her feet, but couldn't. Her ankle was sore, already swollen and throbbing with pain that made her eyes water when she tried to put weight on it.

"Damn it," she cried, searching the open space around her for anything that could be causing this unnerving feeling.

Another loud noise sounded in front of her, drawing her attention forward, but she couldn't see a thing. For the first time she had met him, she hoped it would be Thane that came around the bend.

When nothing happened, she began to calm down, figuring it was just her imagination. There was no imagining the pain that shot through her ankle however as she attempted to stand once more.

A deep throaty growl sounded to her left, then her right. Whatever it was, it seemed to be circling her; like prey.

Was it the wolf? Had he scared something else away like before?

She heard a grunt from behind. Hesitantly she turned, to see bright amber eyes staring back at her from the shadows.

Her heart stopped.

"Oh god. Please don't hurt me," she begged as something leapt from the shadows toward her.

She closed her eyes and waited for the impact, but nothing happened. Instead she heard a loud cry of anger and a sickening thud.

Anya peeked between the fingers she'd plastered over her eyes and gasped with terror. Thane was there wrestling with a full-grown jaguar.

"Run!" Thane shouted over his shoulder. The similarity in his tone froze her to the spot. "Anya. Move. Now."

"I—I can't," she stuttered, clutching at her ankle as she continued to stare at him. "My leg."

Thane growled, shoulder-barging the jaguar in the side as it jumped for her once again. His strength was unbelievable. He shouldn't be able to fight off a powerful animal like that.

Thane stepped toward her and swore under his breath, turning back to the jaguar that quickly rose to his feet. The big cat roared, its amber eyes glowing fiercely staring at her.

81

"It's her fault" it snapped, taking another step toward her.

Thane didn't give the creature another chance to speak or attack before he grabbed her in his arms and began to run, the jaguar close on their heels.

Tears fell freely down her cheeks as she looked over Thane's shoulder.

Why was he so angry? What could she have done?

She looked up at Thane, struggling to see past her tears. He didn't look afraid, didn't even show any signs of being out of breath, but his eyes were glowing just as brightly as the jaguars. Was Thane one of them?

Not daring to ask questions, she snuggled into his chest, savouring the heat and the protection he offered. She may not understand him or his motives, but she was grateful to him for everything he'd done for her since she'd met him, whether he'd chosen to do them himself, or not.

"Thank you," she whispered against his chest.

He squeezed her tighter, holding her close like she was precious.

Her heart broke. She knew then that he did care whether he wanted to admit it or not. She could sense it, could hear the unsteady rhythm of his heart as he held onto her. So why did he keep fighting it?

Anya expected Thane to take her home, leaving her alone with more questions, but instead, he brought her to a small and cosy-looking house not too far from her own.

A faint light shone from the front room, showing off the minimalist decor inside. It was his.

"You'll be safe here. He probably already knows where you live."

"I don't understand what I've done," she sniffed, brushing

the back of her hand across her puffy eyes.

"I'm sure you did nothing to provoke that."

Perhaps he was right. Maybe the jaguar had mistaken her for someone else, or he'd seen her exiting the hunter's home and assumed she was one of them. It didn't make sense. She'd been feeling someone watching her for weeks. Why would he only attack her now if it was him?

"How did you find me?" she asked, trying to fill the silence while he rummaged in his pocket for his keys.

"I was on my way to Edwin's when I spotted you. Then I noticed him."

"Thane!"

Thane spun around with her still in his arms as the jaguar roared his name from the alley behind them.

He stalked out of the shadows, saliva dripping from his canines, the hairs on his back raised. "Why are you helping her? She did this to me. I can't change back."

Thane responded in a language she didn't understand, his eyes changing from their usual blue to a frightening navy. He looked furious, stepping down off the porch toward the cat with her still cradled against him.

She clutched onto him, heart racing the closer they got to one another, fearful the jaguar would attack her once more. Thane squeezed her tighter, possessively in front of the jaguar before crouching down, taking her with him.

Anya closed her eyes and held on tight, expecting the worst, but all she felt was the warm breath of the cat in front of them blowing over her skin. When she opened her eyes, she saw the jaguar's head bowed in submission.

What could Thane have said to him to make him cower?

Slowly the jaguar turned, exposing his side and the arrow embedded deep in his leg, causing him to limp.

"We need to get that out," Thane said, this time in English

so she could understand, sucking a breath through his teeth.

"Wait," Anya interrupted as Thane placed her on the ground and went to grab the arrow. The jaguar snapped his head around, roaring in her face once more. Thane growled louder, shoving the jaguar back a step, going nose to nose against him, speaking yet again in that foreign language. Amazingly, the jaguar backed away, pacing side to side.

"You can't just pull it out," she explained, remembering some of the things Edwin had taught her over the years, only now did they begin to make sense. "You'll leave the arrowhead embedded in his leg. They're designed for easy penetration, but impossible to pull out that way."

"What do you suggest I do? I can't leave it there."

"I know how to get it out, but you'll have to help me," she paused, turning to the jaguar, "and he'll have to promise not to try and attack me again. It wasn't my fault he got shot."

"It was," he cried, rushing toward her.

"How was it my fault?" she snapped, soon realising what she had done.

She shouldn't have shown them she could understand them. She didn't trust this jaguar and she wasn't sure what Thane would make of it.

The jaguar looked at her, stunned, turning back to Thane with what she assumed was confusion. When Thane smirked, she felt her heart leap. He really was handsome when he smiled, even among all this chaos.

How did Thane know she could understand? She'd only found out herself when Lucas had spoken to her; the wolf confirming she wasn't imagining it.

Before she had a chance to figure things out, Thane was standing, taking her with him, heading back toward his front door

"Follow me, Ty. We'll get that arrow out, then you can explain what happened and why you were following her."

The jaguar huffed, following Thane into the house, limping on his back leg.

"Thane. Are..?"

"Not now, Anya," he interrupted, turning to her with still glowing eyes. "You can ask me questions later. First, we need to get that arrow out from Tynan's leg before it does any more damage. No doubt that thing is tipped with silver which will poison him if left too long."

Anya nodded, hoping that this Tynan would keep his word and not attack her after she'd helped him.

She didn't understand why he blamed her for what had happened, or why he was following her, but this man seemed to know Thane. He must have had a reason, and she wanted to find out what.

All questions pushed aside, Anya sat on the living room floor, stretching her injured ankle to the side of her.

"Ty, lay in front of her. "

The jaguar glared at Thane and roared, displeased with his suggestion.

"I'm happy to leave the arrow in your leg if you'd prefer, after all you did attack me," she bit back, finally losing her patience with him. She didn't mean to snap, knowing this must be difficult for him if he believed it was her fault, but she couldn't reassure him any other way than proving she was only trying to help.

He huffed, sprawling out in front of her, stretching and moving much like a real jaguar. If it wasn't for the size difference, the glowing eyes and the fact she could hear him speak, she never would have guessed he was part human.

Before Lucas, she never realised these beautiful creatures existed. Now she had met three. She couldn't believe how stunning they were, how animalistic they acted, even if they were a little frightening.

"This might hurt a little," she said, placing her hand on his leg, praying that he could take the pain without the drugs usually used for this kind of procedure.

His fur felt smooth and warm against her skin, causing her hand to tingle with electricity, much like when she had touched Thane for the first time.

Taking the small blade Thane offered her, Anya cut small incisions either side of the arrowhead, hoping it would help ease it loose as she asked Thane to help tug it out.

The arrow was embedded deep, no doubt injuring important tissue, but if Hugh and Richard were correct about shifters healing fast, he would recover quickly, but could she trust the word of a hunter? Richard had only said that to justify what he was about to do. It was likely that he was lying to her.

She shook away the thoughts distracting her from the task and began to clean the wound with the supplies Thane had found in the first aid kit under his sink. It wasn't the best she'd seen, only consisting of the basics, but it was better than nothing.

She flushed the wound with clean water and swiped an antiseptic wipe around the opening, hoping it would be enough to keep it from becoming infected.

To her surprise, the wound had already begun to heal. The skin slowly knitting itself together on the edges of the incisions. Perhaps Richard hadn't lied after all.

To help him heal faster and to minimize the chance of a scar, Anya stitched the gaping hole closed using some light brown thread, hoping it would blend with his skin.

When she'd finished, Thane grabbed her arm and gently pulled her to her feet.

"Go clean up. I'll finish here."

Anya assumed that the jaguar had passed out from the procedure due to his lack of movement and response, but then she heard Thane telling him to shift, insisting he would heal faster.

Edwin had to know about the shifters. He knew Thane

after all, and there was no longer any doubt he was one of them.

Her chest ached. How could Edwin have kept something like this a secret?

Footsteps in the hallway broke her free of her thoughts, bringing her crashing back to reality. What if the jaguar was already awake and come to finish what he'd started?

Her heart raced as she spun to watch the door, ready to flee if he came near her.

To her relief, it was Thane who entered the room carrying the arrowhead. The sight of the blood still dripping made her stomach queasy.

In the heat of the moment, all had been well, but now everything was calm, the sight and smell of the blood surrounding her turned her stomach. She needed to get away from it all.

# Chapter 12

Thane could feel Anya's eyes on him as he passed by in the kitchen.

He turned to look at her, sensing her discomfort. Her hands visibly shaking, her face pale and clammy.

He placed the arrow out of sight, hoping it would settle her if she could no longer see the blood, and took a step toward her. She flinched staring up into his face, not backing down when he returned her gaze.

He studied her in amazement for a few moments, shocked by how well she was coping with everything.

There weren't many things that could prepare someone for an attack from a raging jaguar, but here she was standing still and silent whilst that jaguar remained in the other room. She was either incredibly brave or extremely foolish.

"Are you alright?" Thane asked, taking another step toward her.

He got his answer when she moved toward the table, still limping and grimacing.

"Sit," he commanded.

When she looked at him puzzled, he pointed to her ankle. She glanced down and nodded, taking a seat on the chair just behind her.

Thane crouched down in front and slowly lifted her ankle onto his lap, careful not to grip it too tight as he pushed up her jeans, taking a closer look.

"It's bruised quite badly. You'll have to stay off it for a while."

"Easier said than done, especially when people have habits of following me lately," she replied in a snarky tone.

"Sorry about that," Ty called, joining them in the kitchen, still fastening the jeans Thane had thrown at him earlier.

Anya flinched again at the sound of his voice, pulling on her leg and causing herself more pain.

"Shh. Keep still. He won't hurt you," Thane said, rubbing his palm up and down her calf in an attempt to calm her.

"Pass me an ice pack from the freezer, Ty."

"Seriously? I'm injured too you know."

"It's your fault she is, so do as you're told," Thane bit back through clenched teeth.

"It's her fault I was shot in the first place," Ty snapped back, rushing toward them.

Thane quickly placed her foot on the floor, gentle not to knock it before he darted to his feet, standing between them once more.

"Back off or that wound will be the least of your worries," he growled, flashing his elongated canines. If Anya hadn't guessed who he was already, she would surely know now.

"Why are you defending her when she's a hunter?"

"I'm not a hunter," Anya cried, climbing out of her seat,

scrambling to hide behind Thane, her small, delicate hands resting on his waist, causing him to shudder.

"Then why were there hunters with you? Hunters that shot me I might add."

Was it the hunters that kept following her? Surely not.

That thing he had felt watching them wasn't human. That he was certain of. Tynan had to be wrong.

Thane looked over his shoulder. Her hands still trembled, her knuckles blanching white as she tightened her grip on his shirt.

"I don't understand," she whispered, shaking her head. "Why would the hunters be following me?"

"So, you're not denying you know who the hunters are? Bit suspicious if you ask me," Tynan replied, crossing his arms over his chest, taking another step toward Anya.

"I told you to back off," Thane growled, shoving him back forcefully.

He would not stand there and let anybody threaten her. This girl meant something to him. Seeing Tynan lunge for her had provoked feelings in him that he could no longer deny.

"They asked me to join them, but I refused, calling the police instead, but they wouldn't do a thing."

"Of course not. The hunters are the police in most towns, or they're paid off."

"I can't believe I thought they'd help me free him."

"Him? What are you talking about?" Thane asked never taking his eyes off Tynan, keeping him at a distance.

Was the boy, Hugh, a hunter? Could that be what she had meant when she said she'd found out his true colours earlier today? It would explain her reaction. It could also explain why she was running alone so late at night when he'd found and watched her.

He had wanted to ask questions then, but he didn't think she'd be able to understand him. Only now did he know differently. Everything was pointing to one outcome. She wasn't entirely human.

But how could that be? She certainly smelt human, even if her scent had somehow become stronger, more potent to him.

"Lucas," she muttered, snapping Thane from his thoughts with a name he thought he'd never hear again. "They took me to him and forced him to change. They wanted to scare me, brainwash me into joining them."

How was it possible she had seen him?

"Lucas?" Tynan asked when Thane's voice abandoned him. "You're sure?"

"That's what they called him."

All these years Thane had insisted Lucas wasn't dead. Now Anya was telling them she had been shown a man in a cell who called himself Lucas. A large wolf with dazzling green eyes; as she put it.

He continued to watch her, looking into her eyes, eyes that now he thought about it were just the same as Lucas's. That couldn't be possible.

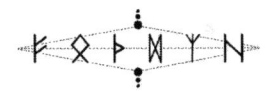

---

Thane sent Anya upstairs to shower and change from her blood-soaked clothes. She put up a fight, refusing to leave his side, not that he blamed her. She had to be afraid of Tynan. The way she hid behind him and held on for protection. Yet she refused to run like most would have. Not that it would help her. Tynan would have no issue catching up with her, especially with her injury.

Even now he was still fuming, making Thane regret his decision to leave her by herself, but he could tell the sight and smell of all the blood was getting to her. She needed to relax, and he didn't want her around while he cleaned up.

Thane placed some clothes on his bed, hoping they would fit her small frame, and returned downstairs to talk with Tynan.

He still couldn't believe that after all these years they might have finally found him.

When Lucas had first gone missing, Thane refused to believe he was dead. He'd continued searching for him for years, never giving up. The only reason he wasn't actively searching these past few months was because he'd promised to help Edwin. He'd also made a promise to himself to find out more about her. A girl who played havoc with his emotions and left him confused and hungry.

"I can't believe she found Lucas. We thought he was dead," Tynan said as soon as Thane re-entered the kitchen. "Why would the hunters keep him alive so long? Richard hates him."

"Richard was jealous of him and claimed he stole Amelia away. He must want vengeance of some kind."

"Surely killing him would have been easier."

"But then he would never find her again."

Not long before Lucas had gone missing, they had discovered that the hunters were onto them. Amelia was sent away with their newborn child to hide whilst Lucas remained, drawing the hunter's attention.

Thane had been with Lucas when they fought a group of hunters in the woods before they got separated. Even now he could still hear the gunshots in the distance. He'd sprinted toward it, hoping they'd missed. But when he got there, he couldn't see a thing. The clearing was empty. Footprints in the dirt and an empty shotgun shell were the only signs of anyone ever being there.

For years they'd searched, ransacking hunters' homes and headquarters in search of him, but never found him. All they ever found were corpses of prisoners left to rot.

How had Edwin not known he was under his nose this whole time?

Thane growled and scratched his nape as he stared up at

the ceiling.

Ever since he'd met Anya, he knew there was something more to her. She could hear them speaking when they were transformed. Her eyes had glowed that night in the pub, bright enough to stun him. Perhaps the change in her scent was just him picking up on these changes. Or perhaps she wasn't human like he'd first believed.

Thane closed his eyes and leaned back against the cool kitchen wall, trying to make sense of everything.

How was it possible for her to hide what she is unless she doesn't know herself? Then there was Edwin. He'd not said a thing when Thane told him about her hearing him speak. He'd even seen her eyes glow, yet nothing. The only emotion he displayed was concern. What was the old man hiding?

"What if it's all a trap and the hunters are using her as bait?" Tynan asked, interrupting Thane's thoughts as he scoffed down a sandwich he'd helped himself to.

Thane contemplated that for a second. She certainly was tempting, but he just couldn't see her being a pawn to the hunters. Anya was too kind and compassionate, her gentle nature reminding him of the little sister he'd lost all those years ago.

For months Thane had been trying to convince himself she was untrustworthy and a danger to them, but he knew it was all a lie. If anyone was in danger, it was Anya. The hunters were clearly interested in her, and an unknown creature was following her around.

"She's not one of them," Thane finally replied, following his instincts.

"How do you know?"

"She's just not."

"Your judgement with humans isn't exactly known for its accuracy, Thane."

Thane moved across the room in a blur, pinning Tynan to the wall by his throat, his feet dangling a foot above the floor. He struggled to pry Thane's hands away, kicking and flailing as Thane lost control of his temper.

"I'm. Sorry," Tynan gasped, his face paling.

Thane loosened his grip and turned away, rolling his shoulders, and cracking his neck.

"I'm sorry, Thane. That was a low blow."

"No. You're right. My judgement was impaired back then and it could be now, but not Edwin's. He wouldn't be so easily fooled."

"Depends. The old man has his weaknesses. Maybe she's one of them. They could have gotten to her before we had a chance. Why else would hunters be following her like they were tonight?"

"I don't know. But I intend to find out."

# Chapter 13

Anya didn't know what to do. The change of clothes Thane had laid out for her were huge. She couldn't go down and ask for something else while wearing just a towel, but she couldn't wear these either.

Standing in front of a small mirror she studied the reflection staring back at her. The top kept sliding down her arms. The trousers had to be held or they'd pool around her ankles.

Sighing, she looked around the room for her old clothes seeing no alternative, but they were gone. Thane must have taken them when he brought her the clean ones.

Anya plonked on the bed behind her and wrapped her arms around her waist, the top sliding down both her arms and almost exposing her chest.

"This is no good," she grumbled, searching the room for something she could wrap around herself.

She knew showering here was a bad idea, and now she

was stuck like this.

Thane would come and check on her if she didn't come down soon, and he couldn't see her like this.

In the corner, she spotted a chair with some clothes piled on top of it. Rummaging through the heap, she found a shirt large enough to cover her. Picking it up, she held it against her, gauging its size.

Thane's rich aroma drifted to her nose making her inhale deeply, holding the soft cotton against her cheek.

She never thought a simple scent would relax and comfort her like this. Why did she have to desire him? He shouldn't be the type of man she was attracted to, but it didn't matter how much she told herself she hated him, she knew she was lying. She craved his touch and his gentleness, hoping that each time she saw him, she would witness the softer side of himself that he tried so desperately to hide.

Suddenly footsteps sounded in the hall outside, coming in her direction. With no other choice, she threw the shirt on.

As she suspected, it was massive, hanging halfway down her thighs, the sleeves burying her hands under the fabric. But, at least it stayed up around her shoulders.

A knock sounded at the door behind her, drawing her attention away from the mirror, gasping when whoever was behind the door didn't wait for her to call them in.

"T—Tynan?" she faltered, spinning to face him and backing away toward the bathroom so she could lock the door between them if needed; even if she doubted it would hold against him for long.

"I wanted to apologize for how I acted before. I shouldn't have jumped to conclusions, but in my defence, it's kind of hard to think when you're being shot at."

"It's fine. Really," she replied, taking another step away from him as he walked further into the room.

Now that Thane wasn't here to protect her, she felt vulnerable, her body already shaking and tensing.

"I'm not going to hurt you, Anya," he sighed, running his hand through his golden hair. "I understand if you're scared of me, but you don't need to be. Hell, you trust Thane and he's worse than me."

"You attacked me, then tried several more times, even after you promised not to. Thane has always helped me."

He raised a brow, seeming shocked by what she was telling him but shrugged it off before she could ask questions.

"I'm sorry. I just wasn't thinking clearly," he replied with a heavy sigh, plonking down on the edge of the bed and staring at his feet.

"Why were the hunters following you?"

"I don't know. Maybe Lucas was right when he said that they wouldn't let me walk away so easily after showing me what they had."

"What do you mean? What did they show you?"

"They took me to Lucas. Richard, he was going to use a dagger to force him to change, but they let me ask him instead of using violence," she paused, taking a tentative step toward him. "I didn't think he would change for me, but he did."

"I don't understand. Why would they let you intervene? Why would they keep him alive all this time?"

Anya knew they were rhetorical questions, but she couldn't help but wonder how long Lucas had been missing. It was clear Thane knew who he was too.

"When was he taken?"

"Over twenty years ago."

Anya's heart broke. How could they be so cruel, keeping him in that prison for all those years?

"He must have been just a boy when they took him," she thought aloud.

Tynan laughed. His eyes shone a yellowy green as he looked up and smiled widely at her, his cheeks dimpled on either side of his mouth.

"Lucas is well into his eighties, love."

Impossible. Lucas couldn't have been older than his mid-thirties. No wrinkles or grey hairs. Nothing to show his age.

She turned to Tynan and stared. What about him, and Thane? Neither of them looked much older than her. Possibly even the same age. But how old were they really?

"We don't age the same as humans. We have to mature much faster," he sighed, stroking fingers through his hair once again as his eyes seemed to water. "But as we become adults, our ageing process slows."

Lucas's, Tynan's, and even Thane's eyes held so much emotion, so much pain. Anya couldn't help but wonder what traumatic things had happened in their past, and why they seemed to hate humans. She suspected the hunters were to blame.

"You know, it's funny. I'm not usually this awkward around women," Tynan joked in an attempt to break the ice. "Then, I guess I don't make a habit of attacking them either. I really am sorry."

Anya watched him as he sat in silence, sensing he was uncomfortable with the way things were between them. She now understood why he'd attacked her, maybe she would have done the same, but she wasn't sure she could trust him.

"I don't blame you," she muttered, taking another hesitant step toward him.

"I shouldn't have been so careless. If I was paying attention and concentrating as Thane had taught me, I would have known that you weren't with them. I might have even worked out why they were following you."

"Thane taught you?"

"Yeah. He's a great mentor, one of the best in fact. He

won't accept any praise though."

"Lucas taught him, you know," he added as an afterthought, frowning as he watched her shift her weight from her injured ankle.

"Thane is one of you, isn't he?" she asked, hoping to distract him from her weakness. If he did intend to attack her again, she couldn't let him know she was still hurting.

Tynan stared at her, his eyes swirling with different emotions, flickering from their normal light brown to the glowing greenish amber she'd seen before.

"I thought you knew."

"I had my suspicions, but he's never told me."

He cursed under his breath, springing from the bed and headed for the door.

"It's best you talk to him. I've said too much already."

"Wait," she called, wincing as she reached out and grabbed hold of his arm before he managed to disappear out the door.

When he looked down at her hands, she let go quickly, remembering who she was holding on to.

"I met a wolf recently, is it him?"

Tynan turned around and leaned forward, closing his eyes and inhaling deeply by her neck. She couldn't help but shiver as his warm breath tickled her sensitive skin. When he reopened his eyes, they were glowing brightly, taking her breath away.

"Like I said, darling," he smiled wide, resting his large hand on her shoulder. "Talk to Thane."

Damn. She had hoped that Tynan would slip up and tell her what she wanted to know, but he was smarter than she gave him credit for. But why was he smiling at her like that?

"What?"

"I can't believe I didn't notice it before. Again, I'm sorry I scared you and hurt your leg. It will never happen again. You have my loyalty now, and forever."

He kissed her forehead and winked, making his way down the hall.

"Wait," she called, limping after him.

She couldn't let him leave. Not yet. She needed to know more about Thane before she lost the chance.

"I don't understand."

"I'm sorry, but there's not much more I can tell you. Not yet."

It went without saying that he didn't trust her. Understandable considering how they met, but she couldn't help but feel disappointed. All she wanted was to understand Thane. To know what had happened in his past to make him the way he was.

She turned to walk away as Tynan fled down the stairs, but something caught her eye behind her, forcing her to turn back.

At the bottom of the stairs was Thane, his eyes almost white as he stared up at her.

She pulled down on the shirt, trying to conceal herself, fearful what he would make of her wearing his shirt. Slowly he walked toward her, staring at her as though she were prey to some hungry beast. Anya knew she shouldn't flee and anger him more, but she didn't know what else to do. Before she'd realised it, he had ushered her back into his room, his eyes still burning on her skin.

"I'm sorry," she blurted out, worried he was angry with her. "The clothes you left me were too big, so I grabbed something quickly before Tynan came in."

Thane continued to stride toward her, letting the door swing closed behind him. His hungry eyes wandered over her body, warming her from head to toe.

"Thane?" she gasped, breathless.

He didn't stop, not until his body was inches from her own, her back pressed firmly against the frame of his bed, his body heat seeping into her own. A hardness pressed into her abdomen. He wasn't angry at all.

He placed a hand by her shoulder, against the bed frame, while the other played the collar of the shirt between his thumb and fingers.

"Do I scare you?" he whispered in a deep, husky voice that sent shivers down her spine. All she could manage was to shake her head, her heart pounding like a drum in her chest.

"Then why are you trembling?" he said softly, bending his head toward her neck and inhaling deeply. His hand skimmed lightly over her chest and ribs.

Suddenly his eyes flicked back up to hers glowing painfully bright like they had at the bottom of the stairs, yet she couldn't look away from their swirling depths.

"You're not wearing anything beneath?" his voice cracked.

Again, she shook her head, unable to speak.

He rested his hand on her hip, caressing her side with his thumb as he pulled her closer, making her mind go numb and her knees turn to jelly.

She'd been craving his touch for so long. She never imagined it would feel this good.

He snatched his hand away, his eyes still burning white. His chest rising and falling quickly, his forehead glistening with sweat.

Why did he stop? She wouldn't let him. Not now that she'd felt his hands on her body.

She pushed up on her tiptoes and pressed her lips against his, tangling her hand in his hair when he didn't push her away.

A loud moan escaped his lips as he took hold of her waist once more, pulling her even closer to return her kiss.

Anya pressed her body against his, craving his warmth against her skin, losing herself to her desires. She couldn't get enough of him.

For a long time, she'd convinced herself that if she could

just let go and kiss him again, this mad desire she felt for him might vanish. But kissing him and having his body pressed up so close to her now, she knew she was a fool.

Thane deepened the kiss, pushing her against the bedpost, pressing into her with his firm body. Slowly, trailing a line of kisses from her mouth down her jaw, nibbling at the sensitive spot between her ear and her collarbone. She moaned and clenched her thighs tight as goosebumps erupted over her body.

Never had a kiss felt this good.

Following her instincts, she dug her nails into his back, causing him to growl against her neck, bringing her to all new levels of pleasure as he bit down harder. Mixed feelings of pain and pleasure confused her senses.

He placed one of his hands on her bare thigh, stroking his way up frustratingly slow, making her shiver as he pressed in closer to her. The friction of his trousers against her core making her dig her nails in deeper.

Suddenly, his eyes flickered open, but they were no longer the eyes of a man looking at her. She could see the wolf she now knew he was, staring back at her, claiming control.

He turned his face away from her as his canines grew into long sharp points. His eyes were full of sadness, slowly dimming to their usual shade of blue.

He removed his hand from her skin and roared so loudly into the air, she could feel his chest rumble from the force of it.

"I'm sorry," he whispered, his voice gravelly and raw.

By the time she'd regained her composure, he was gone, his footsteps already pounding on the stairs.

Anya leaned back against the wooden frame, stunned and confused.

Why did he stop?

It may have surprised her a little to see the wolf take over. Nervous what would happen when she spotted the fangs protruding from his mouth, but she hadn't wanted him to stop. Not once did she feel threatened, or have the urge to run.

Anya plonked on the bed behind her, glancing at the spot they'd been kissing, and gasped. The frame of the bed had four deep gashes carved into the wood, near where her head rested.

She walked over to the post and ran her fingers along the grooves.

"Is this why you stopped?" she muttered to herself, resting her head against the marks.

# Chapter 14

    Thane longed to climb the stairs and go back to Anya, craving her touch and warmth against his skin, but how could he lose himself with her? Even if she wasn't human like he'd first thought, she spelt trouble for him. She drove the wolf insane and messed with his better judgement. His control was on the brink of snapping, yet still she pushed harder, forcing him to flee before he did something terrible.

    How could she be so foolish? How could he?

    He rested the back of his head against the wooden door and sighed.

    He couldn't deny that he cared about her. She'd somehow enticed feelings from him since day one, something not many others were capable of. His need to protect her overwhelmed his other instincts, despite what he may or may not believe she is.

    What was Edwin playing at?

    Thane suspected the old man knew more about this girl.

Who she was, and why her eyes glowed. Hell, he even seemed to think she could be in trouble with the hunters no matter how much he denied it. He watched her constantly, arranging his meetings around her.

Was the old man planning on Thane's reaction to her? Was it why Edwin kept secrets from him? Somehow, he was determined to find out, but not before he dealt with the trouble at hand.

Two people were in his house, both of which he'd prefer not to be there.

Tynan, someone Thane actually trusted and considered a friend, even if at times he annoyed him, like tonight. It was his lack of judgement and incompetence that meant Anya was here in the first place. He needed to keep his distance from her, not be stuck in the same house with her upstairs, wearing nothing but his shirt to cover her curvaceous body.

When she'd kissed him, pressing her warmth against him, he couldn't help but respond.

This beautiful, brave, and foolish girl was going to be the death of him.

He paced side to side in the kitchen, rubbing at his temples, trying to rein the beast back in, but with her scent clinging to his every fibre, he knew it was futile.

He growled loud and deep, releasing his claws, destroying the furniture around him. Fur bristling beneath his skin, itching, the wolf fighting to be free.

He wanted to escape and run off some of the tension, but how could he leave Tynan alone with her? Anya was still wary of him, not that he could blame her. A huge jaguar springing at you from the darkness had to be terrifying for anybody to endure. He'd even tried to attack her several times since, despite Thane's warnings. No, he couldn't leave her alone and let Tynan hurt her.

As though sensing he was being thought of, Tynan peeked around the door, letting out a low whistle when he saw the carnage

Thane had created.

"Damn. I didn't realise it was this bad, Thane."

"I don't know how much longer I can keep this up. I was this close to losing control and taking her," Thane roared, gesturing with his hands.

"Have you ever thought she could be your mate?"

"Don't be ridiculous."

"Come on, Thane. It all makes sense. Your reaction and uncontrollable desires. Her need to be near you despite her fear."

Thane knew she didn't fear him. She never had, despite him clearly intimidating her. She always moved closer, always felt the need to touch. But there was no way she could be his mate.

"Impossible," Thane growled, letting his claws loose on the surface beside him.

"I can't believe I didn't notice it before," Tynan muttered, ignoring Thane's reaction as he shook his head and sat on the only remaining chair Thane hadn't destroyed in his rage.

"Your scent is all over her."

"That can't be."

"Why do you think the wolf's losing it?" he asked, motioning to the chaos around him. "The beast always knows when they've found their mate, and whether you believe it or not, deep in her skin is your scent."

Thane had convinced himself for so long that it was just his imagination, that he was just hungry for the contact he'd been starving himself of.

He'd fallen for his own lies.

"I can smell her in yours too, Thane. Why do you bother trying to resist it? You know you can't for long."

"Look at me Ty. Do you really think she can handle me, especially like this?"

Tynan glanced around the room again and shrugged his shoulders, "She's tougher than you give her credit for. Most people would run screaming. Hell, you terrify me sometimes. But her. She trusts you, she even sticks her ground. That's impressive."

"She's not seen what I'm capable of. All she sees is someone strong enough to protect her."

"Perhaps she's not the weak human you thought she was."

"I may care about her safety, but to think she could be my mate?"

"Are you really willing to risk losing your mate because of her being human? Lucas wasn't as quick to judge."

"I don't know if she is human. Not anymore. But that's not the problem."

"Then what is?"

Thane didn't know how to respond. No matter how hard he tried to deny it, Anya meant something to him. Whether it was his need to protect, or whether she was indeed something more. But could she really be his?

The irrational behaviour, her scent on his skin. Even his uncontrollable lust for her all told him she could be his. But could he let her in?

His trust in others had been destroyed a long time ago when everyone he cared for was taken from him. How would he begin to trust an outsider, someone who knew nothing about them, or him?

It didn't matter to him what she was, it hadn't for a long time. But would she still have faith in him when she discovered his bloody past; or would she run, tipping him over the edge?

"You're a coward if you give up before you even try," Tynan scoffed, turning to leave him alone, a wise move after he dared to insult a superior for a second time, but before he left he added, "You bit her you know. The mark is already showing brightly and still she hasn't fled. Don't keep being a fool by pushing her away. The hunters might take the chance from you."

Thane stared at the door for a long time, letting everything

Tynan said sink in.

He'd bit her, marked her as his. That must have hurt, yet she remained under his roof? This girl doesn't know what she's let herself in for.

Sighing, he perched himself on the worktop, clenching and unclenching his fists.

Tynan was right. He was a coward. Constantly pushing people away so he wouldn't have to face losing or hurting them. He'd seen the hurt in her eyes when he looked down at her before he left, and it had nothing to do with him biting her.

She wanted him as much as he wanted her. Only, he was weak. Unable to rein the beast back and keep control.

Even now the wolf was howling to break free, to run back and finish what they'd started, taking her to all new levels of pleasure. But could she handle the beast when it overtook him entirely?

# Chapter 15

*Thane and Lucas exited the gym, their eyes still glowing wildly with exhilaration. Both covered in sweat and each other's blood.*

*They spotted Amelia in the distance waiting for them, standing and joking with Edwin. Lucas's smile was wide and full of joy, Thane couldn't help but feel a pang of jealousy. He'd been searching for his mate for a while, but nobody was suitable. He didn't want a submissive female, but very few people dared to put him in his place.*

*Thane sighed, but smiled and waved along with Lucas.*

*"She's beautiful, isn't she?" Lucas asked as they headed toward her.*

*"She's alright for a human," Thane joked, receiving a jab to the ribs. "You're a very lucky man, Lucas."*

*"I know. But you'll know the joy yourself someday."*

*"I don't think I'll ever find a female who's willing to go*

*head to head with me."*

*"I have something to tell you, Thane. I wanted you to be the first to know."*

*Thane turned to him with curiosity. What could Lucas possible want to tell him?*

*He knew that he and Amelia were trying for a child, had been for the past year. Shifter babies were rare. When one was conceived, everyone gathered to celebrate it. Surely they hadn't succeeded, had they?*

*"Amelia's pregnant," Lucas informed him with the biggest smile painted across his face, his eyes shining a brilliant emerald. "I think it's a girl, but don't tell Amelia. She doesn't want to know. She's told the healers not to say anything either."*

*Lucas's grin grew wider, his whole face lighting up with overwhelming joy. Thane smiled back at him, wrapping his arms around him in a tight embrace.*

*"Then you are indeed a lucky man, Lucas. She'll no doubt be beautiful like her mother. It would be such a shame if she ended up with your ugly mug," Thane laughed, receiving yet another jab as Lucas laughed with him.*

*"You want me to kick your ass again, boy?"*

*"That was weeks ago old man. You're getting slow. I'm pretty sure I won that last match."*

Thane stirred in his sleep, remembering the look on Lucas's face when he told him about his child. He'd never seen Lucas as happy as he had that day and the months that followed.

Amelia may have been human, but she was one of the few that had earnt Thane's trust, despite his resentment toward her in the beginning.

How foolish they'd all been to trust her family with their location and the truth about who they were. They'd handed all the information over to the hunters, disowning their daughter and despising Lucas for being different, never giving their grandchild a second thought

*Lucas wrapped his arms tightly around Amelia, holding her close as she wept. His face was torn, but he knew what must be done. They all knew the hunters were coming for them. They just didn't know when.*

*Lucas and Thane had assembled a team of men and women to accompany Amelia and her unborn baby to safety whilst they stayed back, luring the hunters away.*

*A miracle baby they had all been waiting for. The first wolf shifter in over ten years.*

*"You must go, Amelia. Protect our child. I'll find you once it's safe."*

*Amelia couldn't speak past her sobs as she was pulled along by some of the healers leaving with her.*

*Lucas turned away as they dragged her into the car waiting for them, the sight unbearable to witness.*

*Thane wished he could spare them both this fate, but they needed to send her away to safety. If she remained here, their baby would die. Richard knew the child would soon be born and had sworn to make Lucas pay for taking Amelia from him.*

*They couldn't let that happen. He couldn't be allowed near the child.*

*Amelia's screams cut through Thane like a knife, reminding him of his past, but he couldn't turn away. The sight of Amelia holding onto her round tummy draped in a blanket covered in protective runes.*

*The door to the car slammed shut, yet Thane could still hear her cries as she fought to be free, a shifter now sitting on either side of her.*

*She was in safe hands. Richard wouldn't find her.*

*The sound of the engine echoed in the space around them, all remaining sounds of hurt and anguish disguised by the roar of the car. Lucas glanced over his shoulder, a single tear sliding down his cheek as he closed his eyes and howled to the moon above them.*

*Thane fought the urge to howl along with him. He had to be strong. Had to save him and the family he had created. He wouldn't let anything happen to them. Not his pack. Not the only people he had left.*

*"Thane!" Lucas shouted from behind. "Up top."*

*Thane spun around, aiming his pistol into the sky just in time to shoot another hunter who had taken to the trees like a cat. If he hadn't known better, he'd have sworn the man wasn't human.*

*The man's large body fell to the floor with a thud as another five men rushed them from the bushes.*

*"It's no good," Lucas whispered, defeated. A gaping wound on his side, blood soaking through his thick jumper. Thane's leg sliced to the tendons making each step agony. But he wouldn't give in. He couldn't allow Lucas to give up. He had a mate, and a child. He had to keep fighting, if not for himself, for them.*

*"Run, Lucas. I'll hold them off for as long as I can," Thane insisted, pushing Lucas toward the trees before he transformed, his eyes shining wildly in the low light around them.*

*Lucas went to argue, but knew he'd be wasting his breath. nodding, he held onto his side and hobbled away, transforming as he went. Both of them knew they had the best chance of survival if they were in their wolf form. Their hearing and sight was far superior to the humans surrounding them.*

*Lucas ran toward the shadow of the trees, his caramel coat flickering in the moonlight, his voice a whisper on the breeze. "Gratias tibi."*

*Thane knew he wouldn't survive five versus one, but he would buy Lucas enough time to find shelter or help. He would risk his life for his pack.*

*One of the hunters circled around him, hoping to bypass Thane and follow Lucas.*

*Thane couldn't allow it. He leapt through the air, pinning the man to the floor by his shoulders. The man's eyes were white as he stared up at the dripping canines above him. Like Thane had first thought, this man didn't smell human. But what was he? His scent was like nothing he'd smelt before.*

*Thane looked down at the man beneath him and growled. He didn't have time to think or question what was going on, he needed to end this man before anymore tried to make it past him. He needed to stall them for as long as possible.*

*Thane sunk his teeth into the man's chest, piercing his heart as he heard a shot behind him.*

*He spun around fast, jumping up off of the corpse beneath him. A woman stood several feet away with a shotgun pointed in his direction. She was human, and from the looks of the tattoo around her bicep, she was a hunter.*

*Thane had learnt his lesson by hesitating to kill a woman, he would not make the same mistake today. He lunged toward her, springing up from the ground to grab hold of her throat, but he was too late. As he moved through the air in what felt like slow motion, he felt a piercing pain shoot through his side.*

*The bullet missed his heart and lungs but shattered several ribs. They would heal with time, but the pain was excruciating.*

*He landed on top of her, slicing his claws across her face as he fell, determined to kill her before she killed him and went for Lucas. His mouth found her neck, her screams gurgling on blood as he bit down hard.*

"Thane." He heard someone shout his name, and felt a

tight grip on his shoulders. "Thane. Wake up."

He opened up his eyes and froze. "Amelia?" he asked, leaning forward.

She cocked her head to the side and frowned.

She looked so beautiful and so young in front of him. He wanted to kiss her, but why? She was Lucas's mate. He had never had those feelings toward her before.

"Thane, it's alright. You were having a bad dream."

Thane pushed her away, holding her at arm's length, staring into her face.

This wasn't Amelia. Those eyes weren't hers. Those were the eyes of Lucas staring back at him.

"Anya? "

She nodded, her face etched with concern as she slowly lifted her hand back to his face.

Without hesitation he pulled her back toward him and clutched onto her, savouring the feel of her as he reminded himself what was real and what wasn't.

She didn't fight him, didn't push him away or ask questions, just let him hold her.

"Are you OK? " she finally asked once he let go.

"I haven't had that dream in a long time."

"Whose Amelia?"

"My friend's mate," Thane replied, unsure what else to tell her.

How had he not noticed the similarities in their looks before? She was the spitting image of Amelia, except for her eyes. They were definitely Lucas's. And her scent, why didn't she smell like them?

"What happened to her?" Anya asked, wrapping her hand around her necklace, something she did for comfort Thane noticed.

"I don't know. She was sent away a long time ago. Nobody has seen her or the baby she carried since."

Thane watched her for any reaction as she fiddled with the ring around her chain, again something he had never truly paid attention to before now. The ring was Lucas's. No doubt a gift he'd given Amelia before she was born. How could he have been such a fool?

"That's terrible. I hope they're both alright."

"I don't think Amelia survived the trip," he replied, his voice shaking as he said her name and continued to stare at Anya in disbelief, "but I have a feeling her child did."

He needed to speak with Edwin and tell him what had happened.

Either he was losing his mind, his dream giving him false hope; or the girl before him was indeed their child.

"Why are you up so early?" Thane asked. Anything to break his mind free from the dream and the possibility of who she was.

"I had a bad dream too. One I used to always have when I was little."

"Oh?" he asked now very intrigued. It seemed unusual that both of them would have an old dream at the same time.

"It's silly really. I never see anything. I'm just locked away in the dark and all I hear is my own breathing and my thoughts."

"You fear the dark?"

Anya gave a quick nod, her cheeks turning pink.

Was she ashamed of her fear? Foolish child.

"It's OK," he reassured her, holding her to him. "It was only a dream. You're safe here."


"I wasn't expecting you so early," Edwin commented as Thane burst through the doors, filling the dimly lit room with sunlight.

"I want to know more about Anya," Thane demanded,

plonking down on the chair opposite him. "I thought you didn't care. She's just a human, remember?"

"Don't get cocky with me, Edwin," Thane growled, digging his nails deep into the wood of the desk, his teeth sharpening into razor-fine points as he peeled his lips back, not caring about reining the beast back in. "You know more about her than you're letting on."

"What do you mean?"

"Explain to me why she looks the spitting image of Amelia. Why her eyes glowed that night at the pub? She's not human is she?"

Edwin continued to stare at him, the colour draining from his face as he pulled out an old photograph from his top drawer, running his fingers gently across the border.

"As she grew older, of course I began to wonder. From the moment she came to me, I believed she was more than human, always doing my best to keep her away from the hunters."

"Then why didn't you tell me that in the first place?" Thane spat, punching the desk with clenched fists.

All this time he'd been pushing her away because of his hatred for humankind, never realizing how much danger he was putting her in.

He'd sworn to protect her before she was born, and now, he may well have damned her, letting her get close to that hunter boy.

"I was never certain, not until Oleander confirmed it for me. I couldn't give you false hope, Thane. Nor did you seem to notice those similarities until recently."

Edwin slid the photograph across the desk toward him, holding a hand to his face as he spun around in his chair, facing the wall behind him.

Thane stared down at the three people smiling back up at him and sagged back in his chair.

Edwin was right of course. Damn him, he always was.

He hadn't seen anything but a beautiful human stranger when he'd first met her, her emerald eyes nothing but a colour.

He'd felt something for her in that instant. A hunger he'd never felt before, nor understood. But he'd refused to see past her human facade, judging her before he knew her.

What a fool he was. If only he'd looked harder, trusted the wolf's instincts.

"How did you find her?"

"When she was just a child she was left on my doorstep, battered and bloody with a small note tucked in her pocket," Edwin muttered, sliding yet another photograph toward him, paper clipped to a worn-out piece of paper.

"That was her sixth birthday. We spent the day playing in the garden with some of the other cubs and pups in the area. Nobody ever made her feel unwelcome, they all loved her as much as I did."

Carefully Thane unwrapped the note and studied the faded writing.

*Edwin,*
*This is Anya. I found her caged like an animal in a small hut whilst on a hunt.*
*I don't know much about her, and she refuses to speak to me, cowering whenever I look at her.*
*I hope you have better luck than I did.*
*Please take care of her. I've grown attached to this little dot in the two weeks she was with me.*
*Erebus.*

"Erebus later told me what he'd seen in the hut, sending me a file listing the girl's details. We assumed the place was owned by hunters, using it as a base to carry out experiments on people of all ages and backgrounds."

"She wasn't alone when he found her?"

"No. They were healed as much as possible and freed. The girl, Anya, was only four."

Thane felt his fur bristle beneath his skin, the wolf fighting to break free and cause some damage.

How could they cage such a small child? Children were everything to shifters. Their one true weakness.

He continued to stare down at the photograph, mesmerized by Anya's beautiful eyes. So much passion and emotion in such a small child.

She'd been through hell at such a young age, yet here she was, smiling up at a man who clearly loved her with all his heart after such a short time together.

"Why didn't you ever tell me about her?"

"I wasn't sure what she was, Thane. I didn't know how you'd feel about me taking in a child who could possibly be human. It's no secret how much you despise them."

It's true he resented every human he'd ever met, treating them as badly as he would a hunter. But she was just a child. He could never have blamed her for being what she was. It was only as they grew that a human's mind was turned against them. Brainwashed by the hunters.

"But she's not human is she, Edwin. She's half shifter."

It explained her eyes glowing the way they had at the pub, and how she could understand them whilst in their animal forms. It also explained Thane's overwhelming need to protect her just like he'd promised Lucas he would the moment he'd found out Amelia was pregnant. The only wolf pup to be born in over thirty years, and she doesn't even know what she is.

Thane slouched back in his chair and held a hand to his throbbing head.

When did his life become so complicated?

"If I'd have known. I would have told her sooner."

"Excuses, Edwin," Thane growled, glaring at him below his hand. "You should have told her about us. About what you are, rather than bringing her up ignorant to it all."

"How would that have helped?"

"She wouldn't have gone near the hunters. Hunters you let her befriend."

Edwin was at a loss for words, something that rarely happened. Still Thane didn't feel better. He knew what Edwin had done was to try and keep the girl safe, sparing her from their world of constantly running or hiding from those that would rather see them dead. But in doing so he'd left her unprepared and unprotected. Luckily for them, and herself, she had chosen to side with them, despising the hunters for what they did. But things could easily have ended differently.

# Chapter 16

Anya had been putting off going to Edwin's, afraid what he might tell her.

She wasn't sure whether she was ready to learn the truth yet, but she couldn't hide from it forever.

Anya strolled up to Edwin's front door, hesitant to enter for the first time in her life.

She loved Edwin like the father he had always been to her. Could she handle finding out how much he'd lied? She'd always believed that there was more to Edwin. He acted like a man who had seen the world change, always staying so calm and collected no matter the situation.

Was he a shifter like Thane and Tynan? If not, what was he? How did he know about them?

Anya slotted her key into the lock and sighed as she pushed open the heavy front door.

Thane's voice boomed from down the hallway. There was

no mistaking that gravelly tone. But why did he sound so furious? She couldn't understand what they were arguing about, the words sounding foreign as she stepped over the threshold, unsure whether she should turn and leave.

Biting her lip, Anya steeled her nerves and slammed the door behind her, hoping someone would hear. She didn't want them to think she was eavesdropping on their conversation.

"Anya?" Edwin called from down the hall. "Come in child."

Anya walked into Edwin's study, both men staring at her, making her feel uncomfortable. She fidgeted, pulling down on the hem of her tank top as she glanced from one to the other.

Thane's eyes were dark and dangerous, all hints of his usual blue shade vanished, leaving those dark navy pits behind. His expression was hard and menacing just like it had been the other night when he'd awoken from his nightmare.

What had happened between them to make Thane look this angry?

She turned to Edwin, curious to see if he too showed signs of rage.

Nothing. He looked just as calm and unfazed as he always did, no doubt annoying Thane further.

"Sorry I interrupted," she whispered, suddenly feeling very out of place and awkward. Perhaps she should have left and came back later, allowing them to continue their heated discussion.

"Nonsense. Thane and I were just done," Edwin shrugged, leaning back in his chair, clasping his slender fingers in front of him.

Thane turned and glared at Edwin, anger pouring off of him in waves, but he didn't argue, just stormed from the room without another word, nodding his head in the slightest gesture as he passed her.

"Sorry about that my dear. Thane was just expressing his distaste with some of my choices," Edwin sighed. "If he finally accepted his position, he'd be able to make the difficult decisions for himself."

"What position?"

"He is to succeed me as leader of the Guard."

"What's that?" she found herself asking, not expecting an answer from him without working hard for it.

Edwin sighed and picked up his glass. A concoction of apple and cinnamon, a drink and scent she always associated with him, making her feel at home.

"The Guardians are an alliance that was formed centuries ago by several different factions of Lore. Each race involved sent forward their strongest warriors to become Guardians, fighters for the alliance." Edwin explained, never taking his eyes off of her as he spoke, draining the contents of his glass between sentences.

"As a Guardian, our job is to protect the alliance and the humans. We keep the hunters in check and stop leaks about our kind spreading, causing panic and mass hysteria. No matter what, we protect what we are and those around us, even if that means putting down our own men and women when they lose control or turn rogue."

Anya grabbed hold of the ring secured to her necklace and dragged it back and forth along the chain. She knew he was hiding something from her all these years, but she never expected it to be something so big. He wasn't human, like them.

Her chest tightened as her world unravelled around her. Everything she knew had been a lie.

She understood why Thane hadn't told her he was the wolf she had met. He was doing his job after all, protecting his secret and being cautious with hunters around, but Edwin, he was supposed to have been her guardian. Her father figure. He should have trusted her.

"What, are you?"

"Like Thane, and Tynan, I am a shifter. A lion shifter to be precise."

Her heart continued to pound painfully against her ribs, making her gasp for breath and cling even tighter to her necklace.

Just what else had he been hiding from her all these years?

"I'm sorry I didn't tell you what I was sooner," he sighed swishing the remnants of his drink in the bottom of his glass as he lowered his gaze from her.

"I thought it was best to keep you in the dark about it. I had hoped you would grow up and feel safe at last, but I fear I've made matters worse. I hope you'll forgive me."

"How could you have made things worse? What aren't you telling me Edwin?" she demanded, pushing to the edge of her seat, waiting for the bombshell he was about to drop.

"I lied to Thane, claiming I wanted his help with the hunters, when in fact I wanted him to protect you. He's my successor and the only person I trust with your safety."

"Well, he clearly wasn't happy with the task you gave him."

"He never knew," Edwin sighed, rubbing his hand across his nape, his eyes now returning to their usual pale yellow shade. "I don't know how much of your past you remember my dear, but I told Thane how you ended up in my care. How you came to be so important to me."

Anya furrowed her brows. She didn't remember much before the age of five. That was when she remembered playing with some of the other children that dropped by, and when she used to sneak into some of the meetings to sit on Edwin's lap whilst he did his work. She never realised what it was he did, but he hadn't once told her to leave.

So many faces had come and gone over the years, but Edwin's remained. The only constant thing in her life.

"I don't remember," she replied quietly.

"You were found caged inside one of the hunter's hideouts, along with several others," Edwin told her, stepping round the desk to crouch down beside her, taking her trembling hand in his.

Suddenly a face with glowing eyes of fire flashed before her. Could it be a memory of the one who found her; or one of the men who'd taken her?

"None of us knew who or what you were, but our biggest weakness is children and nobody argued when I told them I was keeping you with me. Everyone was just appalled and sickened that they could be so vile to a child."

Anya's heart began to pound against her ribs, her breathing quickening as the floods of memories she'd tried so hard to suppress filled her mind.

*Locked away in the darkness. All she could see were the shiny bars that held her captive, glistening in the sliver of light that flickered in the distance. A small candle placed in the corner of the room, lighting up a blank face that haunted her dreams. A man with a vicious and weasel-like smile, always smirking, even when he hurt her. Bile rose in her throat as his hands had bent and prodded at her body.*

"Shh. Anya, don't force yourself to remember this. You don't need to remember," Edwin spoke, trying to soothe her with his gentle voice and warm touch, but it wasn't working. Darkness overwhelmed her mind, filling her vision with nothing but that smile.

How could she have forgotten what those men did to her? To her mum.

A loud sob escaped her throat, tears falling freely down her face.

She could see her mother's face. Those beautiful light blue eyes stared down at her as she held her in her arms, holding her tightly to her chest. Her long, wavy, burgundy hair blew in the wind under the sun. Then the memory changed. She could see her mother tied to a bed with men looming over her, knives and other instruments in their hands.

She could hear her mother screaming, telling her to hide, but it was too late, they'd already spotted her.

All she could hear was her mother's sobs as two of the men plunged a dagger into her chest whilst another held Anya, kicking and screaming, crying for her mum.

"They—" Anya tried to speak around the lump in her throat, tears burning their way down her cheeks. "They killed her in front of me."

Edwin jumped to his feet and pulled her into a tight embrace, holding her head to his chest as the tears fell silently. Her body trembled as she hiccuped, trying to hold back the tears.

"I'm so sorry. I should never have asked you to remember such things," he cooed. "Maybe if I had asked you what had happened sooner, none of this would have happened. I just couldn't bring myself to question you when you appeared so broken. It took you two years to even begin speaking."

"This is why Thane and I were arguing earlier," Edwin sighed, pinching the bridge of his nose between his thumb and fingers. "We all thought Lucas was dead. All of us, except Thane. He was the only one insisting we keep searching and not give up. The rest of us thought it was a fool's mission. Turns out, we were the fools."

"What are you talking about?" Anya asked around her sobs, grabbing hold of Edwin's arm to regain his attention.

"The man you saw in the hunter's basement, Lucas. He's your father."

Anya froze.

Her heart felt like it stopped beating as she clenched her hands into fists, her knuckles blanching of colour.

For years she'd believed she had no family left. Now Edwin was telling her that Lucas, the man she'd met, was her father.

How was that possible?

"I know it's hard to believe my dear, but Lucas is your father."

"How do you know? How could you possibly?"

"Your mother's name was Amelia."

"I don't know my mother's name!" she insisted, her hands now shaking through anger and grief.

"No. But you know her face," Edwin replied, pulling an old photograph from his pocket, holding it out for her to take.

Anya glanced down at the three people she could see in the photo, all of them smiling happily.

Not daring to touch it, she stared down at those familiar faces.

Her mother smiled with a man's arm draped around her shoulders. A man who looked so much like Lucas. His green eyes were like looking into a mirror. And behind them, Thane. He looked so young, his face matching those around him with a genuine smile.

The sob she had been trying to hold in broke free.

"I never thought he was still alive. I would never have given up on him if I had any idea."

"Why didn't you tell me when you found out?"

"I haven't seen you since," Edwin replied with a frown, pulling on his shirt cuffs.

"You could have come and told me. Don't use my absence as an excuse, Edwin. I had a right to know," she replied, knocking his hand away so he'd look at her.

"If I hadn't found out about all of this from the hunters, would you have told me?"

"I can't answer that."

"Would you have told me?" she demanded, raising her voice, hands balled tightly by her sides.

"I don't know," he admitted, hanging his head in shame.

"Since the moment you were brought to me I've wondered whether you were human or not, but I never knew who you were. Somehow your scent had changed."

Her whole life with Edwin had been a lie. He'd brought her up ignorant to the world she was living in, even when he doubted she was human.

"It was Thane who figured it all out. If you hadn't found out about Lucas from the hunters, it may never have triggered his memory."

"You should have told me when he figured it out."

"I'm sorry. I was a coward," Edwin replied, glancing up at her, his eyes full of pain and sorrow.

Anya felt numb as she thought about all he was telling her. All the times he told her she was imagining things when she asked about someone who seemed different, confiding in him when something scared her.

She clenched her hands tighter until her nails dug into the palm of her hand.

"I may not be human and you lied to me," she shouted, slamming her hand down hard on the table. "All those times I told you I'd seen something strange. You told me I had a vivid imagination."

"I should have told you sooner. I'm sorry."

"Even when I spoke to you months ago, scared that I was going crazy. You still said nothing, knowing what you did."

"I didn't know who your parents were at that point."

"You still lied," she shouted, running from the room as fast as her legs could take her.

She could hear Edwin shouting behind her, asking her to stop and listen, but how could she? She couldn't sit there and listen to the one man she'd trusted all her life. A man who'd been lying to her for the past sixteen years.

Silent tears fell, streaming across her face as she continued to run, her body shuddering, fighting the sobs that coursed through her. Her chest heaved, fighting for every breath.

Anya slowed when she realised she could no longer hear Edwin chasing after her. No longer hear his lies as he insisted it was for her own good.

She couldn't face what he was telling her, couldn't bring herself to consider that he might be right, that she was half shifter. There would have been signs she was different.

She stopped, catching her breath, leaning over with her hands on her knees.

Nausea overwhelmed her. She pictured Lucas's face behind those bars, remembering how connected she'd felt to him. His long, tangled hair matted around his thin and tired face. His body battered and bloody.

Had he known who she was; is that why he fought to protect her when Hugh and Richard came close?

Edwin had given up on him, the man meant to be his successor. He'd told everyone he was dead instead of continuing to search for him.

Fresh tears cascaded down her cheeks, burning red hot against her fevered skin. How could he give up on someone he claimed to care so much about?

A noise sounded from behind her, forcing her to start running once more. She didn't want to stand there and listen to Edwin plead for forgiveness. Not when all she could picture was the haunted look in Lucas's eyes as he stared at her in disbelief.

She cried harder, making it impossible to breathe, forcing her to stop.

She remembered talking with Thane the night she found out what he was. He'd told her that mates were connected, that they felt each other's pain, knowing when the other was in danger. That they would know when the other had died.

Lucas must have gone crazy not being able to reach her mum as she fought for her life and that of her child.

How had he continued to fight knowing everything he loved had been taken from him?

"Anya?" she heard a male voice calling her in the distance.

She didn't stop to listen and find out who it was, or what they wanted. Didn't want to talk to any of them, not now. Her emotions were too raw.

Fighting the exhaustion from her body and the fire in her lungs, she continued to run hoping they gave up before she did. Only, whoever was running behind wasn't giving up. In fact, they were gaining on her, quickly. She should have known she would never outrun one of them. She'd seen for herself how fast they could move.

There was no alternative. She would have to hide instead and hope they were unable to track her. The woods to her right gave her the best chance.

Just as she was about to enter a small gap in the trees big enough for her to crawl through, a strong hand grabbed her shoulder.

She spun around, flailing her arms wildly, trying to hit him, but he was too quick, catching both her arms in mid-air, holding them still above her head.

"Calm down," he commanded, holding her in a vice-like grip.

Her face snapped up to meet those stunning azure eyes and she cracked, bursting into tears once again.

Thane let go of her wrists and wrapped his big arms around her, holding her tight while she continued to fight against him, pummelling his solid chest.

"Shh," he soothed, leaning his head on top of hers, stroking his hand over her hair.

Anya gave in, leaning her head against him, sobbing into his chest.

"How could he—" she hiccuped, her voice hoarse. Her throat sore and dry. "Why didn't he tell me?"

"I can't speak for Edwin. He's the only one who can answer why he kept it from you for so long," Thane replied, continuing to pet the back of her head, comforting her, "but I know Edwin does what he thinks is right. He probably thought he was protecting you."

"He should have told me when he found out. When he had the first inkling I was something more."

"Yes, he should have."

"He used you too you know. Lied to you."

"I know, Anya. I am angry with him as well. But he didn't lie about everything. He honestly thought Lucas was dead. We all did," Thane replied, holding her at arm's length, his blue eyes flickering a darker shade.

"You didn't."

"No," he sighed, looking away from her gaze.

"Why?"

"I refused to give up on him. He was my mentor and my friend. I couldn't believe someone like him, someone so strong, could die."

"But everyone dies."

Though it broke her heart to admit it, she knew it to be true.

It didn't matter how strong or powerful, rich or poor, eventually everybody died. Her family had, at least that's what she had believed.

"I know. I just refused to believe it. Everybody told me I was losing it, but my heart refused to let go. It destroyed me," he admitted, hanging his head in shame. He slumped to the floor, pulling her down onto his lap, wrapping his arms around her waist from behind.

"I know what it's like to lose everyone you care about, Anya. I know how hard it is to cope and how easy it is to give in, but Lucas saved me from becoming a monster," he whispered in her ear, his warm breath sending shivers down her spine as it tickled her sensitive skin, "You should never give up on those around you. Edwin cares deeply about you. He just wanted to save you from a life of always looking over your shoulder."

She didn't want to think about Edwin now. He may have thought he was protecting her, but he'd only made things worse.

"Why did you follow me?" she asked, trying to change the subject.

She knew someone would come for her when she ran, but she hadn't expected it to be Thane.

Ever since she'd met him he'd been determined to push her away even though she could see his hunger for her.

He may have helped her when she fainted and when Tynan attacked her believing she was a hunter, but he never let her in. Even when she thought he'd warmed to her, he pushed her away leaving her wanting more. "Did Edwin make you come?"

He sighed, resting his head in the crook of her neck.

"When I let your family down, I shut myself off from everyone, searching for Lucas despite everyone's protests," he sighed, squeezing his arms tighter around her waist. "It was easier to push you away than to admit I cared about a human, a race that took everything from me."

"Thane, I—"

"I'm sorry," he whispered, interrupting her, nuzzling at her neck. "I was a coward and I was weak, using Edwin as an excuse when I couldn't cope with my emotions."

# Chapter 17

Anya wasn't happy about being back at the hunter's mansion, but if she wanted to see Lucas again, she had to endure it.

Edwin would be furious, scared that she'd be caught, but that didn't matter right now. Lucas needed her. Needed to know that she now knew who he was and that she wouldn't rest until he was free. That the Guard now knew where to find him.

So here she was, walking through the endlessly plain corridors surrounded by hunters, none of which made her feel at ease. Not even the girl who she used to call her best friend.

How could she stand there listening to the rubbish spewing from Richard's mouth?

Anya couldn't understand what had made Keri turn to the hunters in her absence. The girl she used to know would never agree to kill innocent creatures.

With a heavy sigh, Anya trudged along behind, waiting for the perfect opportunity to slip away undetected. Except, with this many people around, it was proving impossible.

"What are you doing here?" a furious whisper growled in her ear. A large hand encircled her forearm, squeezing tight.

"You're hurting me," she bit back, tugging on her arm in a vain attempt to break free of Hugh's hold as he pulled her aside from the group.

"You shouldn't have come back."

She couldn't argue. She knew she shouldn't be here either, but how could she stay away knowing her father was locked in their cellar?

"I thought you wanted me to join," she asked in a snarky tone, finally snatching her arm out of his grasp, glaring as he tried to reach for her again.

Anya didn't want him touching her. In fact, she didn't want him anywhere near her.

His gentlemanly facade made her skin crawl now she knew the truth of what he was.

"Richard is testing all the new recruits today. You'll be humiliated for refusing him before. You need to come with me. Please."

Her eyes darted from Hugh to his father at the head of the group slowly walking away, torn.

Richard terrified her. Had since the moment she met him. Only now did she understand her fear. A subconscious need to steer clear of him and his kind. Yet, she never feared Hugh. He always seemed to be hiding something from her, but she never felt threatened. Perhaps he would be the lesser of two evils. It would certainly be easier to sneak away from him alone than it would a whole group.

"Won't your dad notice me missing?" she whispered, taking a hesitant step toward him.

"I have an idea to get rid of Richard, but you'll have to follow my lead."

Suddenly being alone with Hugh didn't sound like such a good idea as they fell into step at the back of the crowd.

More and more rooms passed them by as they made their way through the corridors. Anya's heart beat quicker with each step toward the large open doors in front of them. Her mind racing with the possibilities of what could be behind that blinding light shining through.

Without a word, Hugh grabbed her hand and pulled her aside, pushing her against the wall.

At first Anya was at a loss for words, confused by Hugh's actions until he pressed in close.

She fought against him. Kicking and lashing out with her arms, only to be pinned by his large hands. His face moved in close to hers.

"Keep still," he whispered, pressing his cool lips firmly against hers.

Using all of her weight, she tried to push him away, but he leaned in closer, entwining his legs around hers to stop her movements, her back pressing painfully against the wall.

With little alternative, Anya bit down hard on his lip. A rush of metallic liquid hit her tongue as she held on tight.

Hugh groaned loudly against her mouth, but still he refused to move away until they both heard someone clearing their throat just behind him.

"I'll leave her in your care then, Hugh," Richard smirked, a rare twinkle in his eye, making Anya's skin crawl. Keri's smiling face peeked around his shoulder.

Hugh nodded, keeping himself firmly pressed against her until Richard and Keri moved away with the rest of the group.

"What the hell, Anya," Hugh groaned, padding his fingers lightly over his lip. His fingers coming away stained with blood."I told you to follow my lead."

"You expect me to stand there whilst you force yourself on

me?" Anya snapped, wiping the back of her hand across her mouth. The taste of coffee on her lips was turning her stomach. "I should have bit you harder."

"I'm sorry, Anya, but I'm trying to help. You don't seem to realise the danger you're in."

She knew perfectly well how risky it was to come here, but she didn't understand how Hugh knew.

Anya bit her tongue before she asked what he meant and gave herself away.

Hugh couldn't possibly know what she was, she'd only found out herself a few days ago. He had to be meaning something else. Perhaps the humiliation he spoke of earlier. Richard certainly seemed like the kind to punish someone for telling him no.

"I care about you Anya, even though I know you don't return my feelings," Hugh sighed, running a hand through his short hair, staring up at the ceiling to avoid eye contact. "I just hope he's worth it."

Anya was at a loss for words.

Surely he hadn't picked up on her feelings for Thane? If he had, just what else did he know?

Her heart pounded loudly in her chest. The walls seemed to shrink around her as she took several steps back, ready to flee. Sweat beaded on her skin. Slowly he lowered his eyes to hers.

"There's something I want to give you. Something that might just help keep you safe," he muttered, reaching out his hand, palm side up, waiting for her to take it.

Anya hesitated, staring down at his outstretched hand when she knew she should be running, just like that little voice in her head demanded. Only, she found herself stepping toward him full of curiosity.

She just hoped she didn't regret it as she slowly lowered her hand on top of his.

ᚠ ᛟ ᚦ ᛗ ᛧ ᚾ

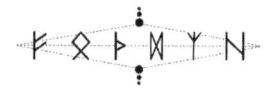

"Wait here," Hugh instructed her as they stepped inside the library, the door swinging behind them, making her jump as it closed with a bang.

Anya watched him cross the room to an old bookcase covered in dust and filled with thick, leather-bound tomes. His finger slowly ran along the spine of each book, until he paused at one, lifting it free from its spot with two hands.

She tilted her head to one side, trying to read the title before he dumped the book on a nearby table, returning to the spot it had come from. A soft click in his direction regained her attention.

Little by little, the wall behind the bookcase began to move back, revealing a small, dark space just big enough for someone to squeeze through.

With a grunt, Hugh moved to one side and pushed on the casing, until it began to slide on its own.

Cold sweats broke out over her body, that dark space seeming to pull her forward, surrounding her in darkness. Her heart raced in her chest as she scrambled backwards.

"Don't be frightened, Anya," Hugh gasped, grabbing hold of her hand before she darted out the door.

"I hid something inside a long time ago. A journal that might help you."

Frozen to the spot, Anya watched Hugh disappear behind the bookcase, returning with a small diary that looked handmade.

"Here," he said, placing the book in her hands before he led her by the shoulders to a nearby chair.

Anya stared down at the book, trying to focus on the worn-out words carved into the leather.

"It's written in Latin," Hugh informed her, untying the

straps before he began to flick through the pages.

"Keri told me that you like challenges, so I'm sure you'll figure out how to read it. She also told me you're an incredible artist."

Hugh paused at one of the pages, holding it open for her to see the intricate writing and detailed sketches.

"Amazing," she gasped, bringing the book closer to take a better look, "but why are you giving it to me?"

"I was told there were lots of hidden secrets inside. It's an old journal from a hunter who switched sides," Hugh informed her, watching her face for a reaction.

"Maybe there is something in there that's helpful to you."

He opened his mouth to say something more, resting a hand on top of hers, when they both heard his name bellowed in the hallway. Hugh snatched the diary from her hands, closing it forcefully and shoving it down the side of her chair, completely hidden from view.

"Hugh," a large, balding man called, barging into the room, glancing toward her with a wink and a smirk.

"What is it, Carl?" Hugh snapped, taking a step to one side, blocking her from the man's view. The harshness of his voice made Anya flinch and sink deeper into the cushions of her chair. She'd never heard him raise his voice before.

"Keri and Leigh are fighting again down at training."

"What do you want me to do about it? You know what those two are like."

"Keri has already got a shiner, and Leigh's looking a bit bloody. Nobody can break them apart, and Richard's busy with the new recruits."

"Can't you see that I'm busy as well?" Hugh groaned, gesturing to her, "Let them sort it out between themselves. Maybe one of them might learn something."

"It's ok, Hugh," Anya insisted, "I can wait here while

you're gone."

She hoped that Hugh fell for her offer. She needed a break from being around him and all the other hunters. But more importantly, she needed a chance to find her way back to Lucas. With Hugh stuck to her, she'd never find her escape.

"You know Leigh always has a concealed weapon. It's only a matter of time before he pulls it out and someone really gets hurt."

Hugh made a sound of frustration before turning back toward her, placing his cool hand firmly on her knees, leaning in close to whisper in her ear, "I'll be as quick as I can. Just don't do anything stupid."

# Chapter 18

Anya peeked around the library door, searching for any signs of Hugh or another hunter heading her way.

Happy the coast was clear, she quickly ran back inside and stuffed the diary inside her jacket pocket, hoping that nobody would spot it if she got caught.

She crept through the halls, her back kept firmly against the wall, flinching and jumping at every little noise she heard. Constantly, she checked over her shoulder as she made her way to the next bend.

Peering around the corner, Anya cursed under her breath. There were three different hallways that looked identical to the one she had just crossed. An eternal maze she would never find her way free from.

Tears burned behind her eyes, her heart pounding in her chest. She couldn't get lost in here. What would happen if she was found alone roaming the halls?

She squeezed her eyes shut and slid down the wall, slumping over her knees, crouching on the floor. "Get a grip," she muttered, running her hands through her hair.

She took a deep breath, filling her lungs, releasing it slowly before she reopened her eyes. There was no point panicking. It wouldn't get her anywhere. She needed to remain calm and think. There had to be a way to navigate these halls. A mark on the wall. An unusual aroma in the air. Or maybe a painting that she would recognise.

"I can do this."

Before there had been a crude depiction of a wolf shifter fighting on its hind legs. If she could find that painting among the tons hung on the walls, she may be able to navigate her way through this place. But what direction should she try first?

Anya glanced down each corridor for a second time, looking for any other clue that might help her decide.

Footsteps sounded to her left, gradually getting louder. Someone was headed her way.

With no time to think, she darted straight across and hoped whoever was coming didn't see her cross the hall.

She pressed her back up close to the wall behind her, praying that the small alcove would be large enough to conceal her. Her heart pounded with each loud footstep headed her way.

Anya covered her nose and mouth with her hands, fearful that whoever approached would hear her loud breathing. Their huge shadow darkened the wall beside her when they stepped in front of one of the lamps nearby.

Had they spotted her run across the hall? What if they had gone to fetch her from the library only to find her missing?

Anya peered out, only to see a man standing at the crossing of the hallways, glancing down each of them, a confused and deathly expression on his scarred face.

"Russell?" a deep, female voice called, "hurry up. We

haven't got all day."

Anya continued to hold her breath waiting for him to move from his spot.

"Coming," he replied at last, his shadow retreating from the wall beside her.

She let out a long, slow breath and sunk to the floor.

That was close. Too close. She needed to be faster. It was unlikely she'd be able to avoid someone a second time.

Anya climbed up from the floor and headed down the hall, picking up her pace. Perhaps if she looked like she belonged there, nobody would question it.

Countless, easily forgotten corridors later, Anya found the painting she'd been searching for, and traced her fingers across the frame, turning to look left, and then right. Both the corridors on either side of her looked the same, but there had to be something.

There, to the left was another painting of an animal. A large bear, similar to the one she'd seen in the book Hugh had first shown her. She followed it, hoping it would lead her in the right direction.

Several paintings later and a few dead ends, she finally found what she was searching for.

The door appeared to be glowing brighter than before, it's colour now a violent red rather than the icy blue that reminded her of Thane's eyes.

She stepped closer and reached a hesitant hand toward the doorknob, gulping when her fingers brushed the metal.

Anya now knew what the runes were and what they were supposed to do. Was it possible her reaction before could have been something to do with her being half human?

She breathed in and out deeply, closing her hand around the metal.

Nausea she'd felt the first time was nothing compared to the overwhelming agony coursing through her body now.

Tears filled her eyes as she tried to push past the pain, determined not to let it stop her from going to him. But the door wouldn't open. It wouldn't even budge.

"No," she cried, her hand dropping from the doorknob, throbbing with pain. She leaned back against the wall for support.

How could she help Lucas if she couldn't even get in to see him? What was she going to do now?

Maybe if she returned to the library, one of the books would have a section on inscriptions and how she could bypass them.

Anya continued to study the door, frowning as the glowing light seemed to move in a circular pattern across it until she heard a noise. Footsteps stomped down the hall toward her, causing her hands to tremble, and her heart to race.

She couldn't be found here. What would they say?

She looked around frantically, hoping for a place to hide, but this was a dead end, the only door the one she couldn't pass through.

There was no alternative, she would have to pretend she was lost, wandering around aimlessly.

Anya made herself look upset, which wasn't difficult considering her whole mission had backfired.

Not a moment too soon, she stumbled out of the dead-end corridor and looked around, coming face to face with Keri.

"Anya? What are you doing back here?" Keri asked, peering down the corridor she'd come from, raising an eyebrow.

The man before hadn't been exaggerating when he said Keri had a shiner showing. Her eye was black and puffy, watering as she padded her fingers on her cheeks, conscious of Anya's staring.

"Does it hurt?" Anya asked.

She may be angry with her friend for turning to such people, but she couldn't help feeling somewhat to blame for her ending up here. She was the one who abandoned her with her drunk mother after all.

"A little," Keri replied, wincing when she hit a tender spot with her fingers. "Leigh is such an arsehole. He thinks he's special because he's strong, but he's slow. I hope he chokes on his lunch."

"Perhaps we should go find you some ice?" Anya suggested.

"Yeah, why not," Keri shrugged, linking her arm through Anya's and leading her away.

Anya risked a glance over her shoulder and sighed. At least now she knew a way to navigate the halls.

"Oh," Keri exclaimed, coming to a halt, pulling Anya back. "I forgot to mention. I saw that guy you've been seeing a lot of recently."

"Here?" Anya asked, her eyes bulging as she tried to comprehend what Keri was saying. What was Thane doing here? Surely he hadn't come for her. More importantly, how did Keri know that she'd been seeing a lot more of Thane?

"Well, yeah. Richard's testing all the new recruits so he can determine which section they would work best in. You should have been there too, but then I guess Hugh's giving you special treatment," Keri winked, nudging Anya's shoulder with her own.

Anya wasn't interested in Hugh and he knew it. The only interest she had in being here was to find a way to help Lucas. To help her father.

She looked at Keri and wondered what her role was and whether she was happy here. It was her choice after all, but the Keri she knew wouldn't have come to them willingly.

"Anya?"

"Sorry, I was just curious whether you ever competed, after all, you're dating a member."

"Yeah, I was more than happy to prove myself," Keri laughed, giving her a quick wink, "turns out I make a good hunter. I may never have been as fast as you, but I'm excellent at traps."

# Chapter 19

Anya trudged along behind Keri, glancing from side to side in hopes of learning her way around, but it was pointless. The interior of the house was confusing enough. Out here, it was a literal maze. The tall hedges created an intimidating labyrinth that had her quickening her pace to keep up.

Her hands twitched by her sides as the sounds of metal on metal clashed together in the distance. Roars and cheers echoed all around them. What if she was walking into a trap; what if Thane had to?

There was no way Edwin had agreed to him coming here. What was he thinking? It was bad enough that she'd risked her own safety coming back. Fearful Richard would discover her past, or find out about her new acquaintances. But at least they thought she was human. She didn't feel anything but human.

Thane. He was a shifter. If they found out, he'd be killed; or captured like Lucas. She'd never see him again.

"What are you doing?" Anya mumbled, hugging herself tightly. Unable to bear the thought of anything happening to him.

Ever since that first meeting with him, there'd been a spark. An uncontrollable lust that forced her to act and kiss him. Only he'd pushed her away, hiding behind his tough exterior. Now she knew the truth. That he really cared about her. He'd proven it the day he came running after her. Holding her close in the woods and letting her lash out, giving her a glimpse of his past.

Anya sighed and looked up at the clear blue sky.

Who was she kidding? It would be foolish to fall for him. She was still half human, a race that Thane despised. His feelings for her were nothing more than a need to protect and keep her safe. Whether it was for Edwin, Lucas, or himself, it didn't matter.

"Keep up slow coach," Keri called from in front, linking her arm through Anya's the moment she caught up, dragging her toward the towering stone arena ahead.

With each step they took, the shouts and grunts grew louder. The roar they'd heard from a distance was now deafeningly loud. There had to be a lot of people inside. A lot of people that could discover what Thane was. What she was.

"What have I done?" Anya muttered to herself, biting down on her lip and gripping her necklace tight. The stone structure loomed over her.

"There you are. It's about time," Chase groaned, already pulling Keri through the gates after glaring in her direction. Leaving her alone with Hugh.

"Let's go."

Hugh held out his hand, waiting for her to take it. She knew she should. He needed to believe she trusted him so he didn't grow suspicious, but she didn't want to touch him.

Taking a deep breath, Anya closed her eyes and reach her hand toward his. Before she had a chance to change her mind, Hugh grabbed it and pulled her toward him, almost protecting her. She glanced up at his face and frowned.

This close, she could see the strain around his eyes, and smell the strong liquor and coffee overpowering his cologne. He hadn't smelt like that earlier. Nor had his eyes appeared dead and lifeless like they did now.

Shaking off her concern, Anya tried to pry her hand from his as he pulled her through the gates, but his grip was too tight, threatening to cut off the circulation to her fingers. His pace was gruelling as he dragged her up the steps to their seats. An announcer called out a long list of names, none of which she recognised until she heard his.

"Thane. Speed and endurance."

The list continued with Anya's heart in her throat.

He may be alright at the moment, but he was still in danger of being caught. How could he possibly think to survive should any of them grow suspicious of him?

The crowd surrounding them cheered, waving their arms in the air as the long list of competitors stepped into the clearing. But she didn't see Thane.

Chewing her lip, Anya searched the growing crowd frantically. All of her fears vanished when she spotted him among a large group of people standing toward the back.

She let out a long breath and leaned back in her seat, thankful she was sitting down, her whole body trembled.

Thane was safe, but for how long?

Slowly, some of the competitors made their way to the track, but Anya's eyes were glued to Thane. Especially when she noticed a tall, curvy woman with golden blonde hair and far too little clothing step toward him, pressing her body into his.

Anya's blood boiled. What did that woman think she was doing? Only, the woman didn't stop. She took hold of his arm, pulling it between her overly large breasts and tip-toed to whisper in his ear.

How desperate and needy. It was pathetic really.

Hugh nudged at her arm, trying to gain her attention as he passed her something cool, but she was too engrossed in what the woman was doing to acknowledge him. All she wanted to do was march down there and slap that pretty little grin off her face.

A prickling sensation erupted in her fingertips, finally managing to draw her attention away from the scene before her. At first she thought it was the cool drink Hugh had placed in her hands, but when she heard a low growl escape her own throat, she knew it was something more.

"Oh god," she muttered, wrapping her arms around her middle.

When had she become so jealous and possessive? That wasn't like her at all.

"What's wrong?" Hugh asked, turning toward her with a raised brow.

"Nothing. It's just really hot out here," she lied, shrugging out of her jacket.

She rubbed at her temples, trying to dislodge the jealous thoughts of clawing at the blonde's face, but when she began entwining her fingers around his and brushed her lips against his cheek, Anya saw red, bracing herself on the edge of her seat, but Thane looked down and snatched his arm away, scowling and rolling his shoulders.

Anya couldn't help but smile.

"Something wrong?" an all too familiar voice whispered in her ear, making her skin crawl and her fists clench tight.

"The show's about to start. Enjoy it pup," Richard snickered, placing a hand on her shoulder, his grip a little too tight and demanding.

Anya didn't dare turn to him, fearful what he'd see when he looked at her. Just hoping she'd misheard him. Surely he couldn't know; how could he?

147

She turned to Hugh whose eyes were glued to the ground below him.

Did he know? Was the journal, and him leaving her alone all just a trap to find out what she was? Maybe she was the one in trouble here, not Thane.

How was she going to escape when she was surrounded by strong and powerful hunters?

"Next competitors, step up to your positions," the balding guy from the library bellowed through a microphone making her ears ring.

It was too late. There would be no chance of her making it to Thane now.

She may have been able to use the distraction to get herself away if it wasn't for Hugh watching her every few seconds, and Richard's arm never moving from the back of her chair. If she tried to move, one of them was bound to notice.

Slumping down in her seat defeated, Anya looked down to Thane who was now making his way to the track

Three tall, lean men joined him, walking with a swagger that made her wrinkle her nose. Each of them looked at Thane and another well-built man, snickering and nudging one another.

Anya scoffed at their arrogance. Thane may be large which would slow down most men, but he wasn't like them. She'd seen how fast he could run. Felt his power as she rode his back. His solid muscle gliding beneath his fur with each long stride, every step light and accurate, graceful even.

Thane looked sideways at the men and shrugged, turning to the other large man, saying something she couldn't quite hear.

Bang!

The starting pistol fired, causing her to jump a mile high.

Hugh rested his hand on her knee to comfort her, but all she was interested in was the race before her.

Thane was holding back, running at a leisurely pace

toward the front of the group.

"He's quick, but he won't beat Sean," Chase mocked, crossing his bare arms over his chest.

Was he purposely holding back to stop them from growing suspicious?

"I don't know. He's gaining on Luke." Hugh replied, pointing down toward them.

Thane ended up finishing in third place, beating one of the three men who decided to mock him before they'd started. He smiled, looking at each of them, walking past to drain the contents of his water bottle.

Richard appeared beside him the next instant, clapping and patting his back. Anya hadn't seen him move. Hadn't even heard him get up from his seat. How could he move so quickly and quietly?

Anya watched him suspiciously, amazed he'd managed something she would have believed impossible, especially when she was so aware of his presence beside her.

She turned to Hugh, curious to see what his expression would show. But his face was like stone, just like Thane's as Richard continued to talk to him. The occasional nod was the only indication he was listening.

Only, Thane wasn't as calm and emotionless as he appeared. Blood dripped from his hand when Richard stepped away. The glass bottle he'd been holding crushed in his palm.

"Next event. The spar," the announcer called.

Thane stepped forward, brushing his bloody hand against his black sweats, at the same time a huge guy pushed his way through a gathering crowd.

This guy matched Thane in height and width, the veins in his arms bulging. His muscles straining against a top that looked two sizes too small. His upper body was massive, but his lower seemed to belong to another man. Thane on the other hand was perfectly proportioned. His whole body muscled and truly magnificent to look at.

Both men entered the sand pit, staring at one another.

The man raised an eyebrow, clearly doubting Thane's abilities. If she was honest, she wasn't sure he could beat this guy either. He was massive, like a bulldozer, making Thane look small.

This guy was no new recruit, he was clearly there to test Thane.

The crowds went silent, waiting in anticipation.

"This the best you've got, Richard?" the tank of a man scoffed, turning to face Richard on the sidelines. "I was expecting a challenge. This guy's smaller than the last one you brought me."

"Don't worry little man. I'll make this quick," he mocked, turning back to Thane, taunting him loudly for the crowd.

"I'd like to see you try and hit me first."

The man roared loudly, aiming his first punch high, toward Thane's face. He ducked and punched him in the gut, making him spit blood.

Anya turned to look at Richard, hoping he wasn't suspicious, but when she looked at him, ice coursed through her veins. His face contorted in the most unpleasant smile she had ever seen, his dead eyes sparkling with excitement.

"Lucky shot," the man grunted, wiping the blood from his lips before taking another swing.

Thane ducked and weaved each shot, sweat gleaming over him. His tight T-shirt stuck to his body like a second skin.

He was incredible. So fast and agile, connecting blows the other guy couldn't dream of dodging.

She watched the battle in awe, gasping when the man managed to connect a punch to Thane's face. His lip burst open, blood spraying across his chin. Anya held her breath, but Thane continued unfazed by the blow.

The fight lasted almost fifteen minutes before the large man collapsed to the floor exhausted, his chest rising and falling rapidly with each laboured breath.

Thane stood over him, his face covered by shadow making it impossible to see his expression.

Slowly he crouched down and offered the man a hand up, but he brushed it away and turned to his side to cough up more blood, spitting and spluttering all over the floor.

"What a sore loser," Anya mumbled under her breath, knowing how hard that must have been for Thane. The man was disgusting and rude.

"Don't worry, Anya, the fights not won yet," Chase sneered, leaning around Hugh with a lopsided grin.

"What do you mean?"

"Your friend there has to fight until he loses, or until he's beat every opponent. Which of course won't happen."

Anya turned back to Thane, ignoring the snickering Chase, her heart pounding in her chest. How was he supposed to continue fighting after that? Surely they couldn't expect him to fight until he dropped?

She didn't have to wait long before Richard sent in two more men, confirming what Chase had just told her.

Thane threw another water bottle to the floor with a crash, ducking the first blow with a slide. Dodging and dancing around them. Missing almost every blow that came his way. Landing several of his own in the process.

Anya studied his face looking for any signs of fatigue or injury, but other than his bloodied lip and the odd red mark, he looked fine. His golden skin glistened in the sun as sweat clung to him, his breathing normal. His reactions were just as fast and flexible as when he'd started.

She didn't truly understand what it meant to be a Guardian, what the role entailed, but his training had to be intense for him to have so much stamina.

She watched speechless as he defeated three more men.

Each of them collapsed to the floor with fatigue.

How much longer did Thane have to fight?

Despite his steady footing and relaxed face, she'd already noticed signs of him slowing. More and more blows connected with his body. His chest was now rising and falling rapidly as he wiped the back of his hand across his brow.

It had to be over.

Yet another man stepped toward him with a crooked smile. Something large and shining glinting behind his back.

Anya sat up straight in her chair, gripping the seat in front of her to stop her hands from shaking uncontrollably. Her chest tightened so much she could barely breathe.

No. They couldn't hurt him. He couldn't have given himself away.

Richard stepped out on the opposite side of the ring and raised his arm, halting the man in his tracks.

"Enough. Thane has proven himself."

Anya sagged back in her chair, her arms hanging limp by her sides as she let out a long breath. She never expected to be grateful to see him, but right now, she couldn't be happier with his timing.

"You did well. Follow me," Richard insisted when Thane joined him by the ringside.

Richard turned to her then and smirked that same nasty, cruel smile he always did making her skin crawl.

"I'll take you home," Hugh interrupted beside her. Resting his hand on her shoulder he leaned in close to her ear."It'll give you chance to study what I told you."

The journal.

Anya wasn't sure she wanted to look through it. What if it was a trap like she feared? A magic spell placed upon it that would tell them the moment she opened it. Were such things possible? She didn't know anymore.

# Chapter 20

Anya couldn't stop fidgeting and searching the room around her.

Once again she found herself surrounded by hundreds of people, only this time they were all hunters.

For weeks she'd been studying books and scrolling through web pages trying to find anything she could on inscriptions, hoping to find a way of breaking the ones stopping her from entering the basement. Nothing. It was like the hunters had removed all traces of such a thing. She found the odd mention of runes and old religions that used such things. But whenever she thought she was on the right track, the information seemed to stop, or alter. It was fast becoming apparent that her task was impossible. The only thing forcing her to continue, determined there had to be a way, was knowing that Lucas waited at the bottom for her.

If only she could swallow her pride and forgive Edwin for his deceit, he might know of a way to help her. Or perhaps he already was.

She still didn't know Thane's plan for being here, or if Edwin was aware of it.

Since Thane was always busy surrounded by hunters; or worse, Richard, Tynan had been dropping by her house almost daily.

He claimed he was protecting her from the hunters like Thane had been, but Anya got the impression he was just lonely. Unfortunately, he hadn't known how to help either.

Defeated, Anya slouched against the white panelled wall behind her, staring at nothing in particular. Just glad to be alone at last.

If it wasn't Tynan letting himself in her house and making himself at home, it was the hunters following her every move.

Tynan she didn't mind, most of the time. At least now she felt safer around him.

How could she possibly stay mad at him? Every day for weeks he'd sent her flowers. Notes apologising again and again hidden among the leaves. Just the thought of it brought a smile to her lips.

The hunters on the other hand made her feel anything but safe, and not just because of what she was.

Hugh, she tolerated. At least he was friendly. She just wished he'd stop trying to get close to her knowing she would never return his affection. Yet, she preferred him to Chase. In fact, she kind of felt sorry for Keri. Not only had she abandoned and left her to befriend the hunters, she'd also let her end up with a pig of a boyfriend like him. A guy who thought he was god's gift to women, chatting up any girl he saw. Flirting, kissing, and who knows what else behind her back.

Maybe there was still hope for Keri, despite her claims of being a good hunter. Perhaps they hadn't completely brainwashed her yet.

Then there was Richard. She would prefer to be in a room

full of hunters, like now, than be anywhere alone with him. Relaxing was completely out of the question whenever he was nearby. His cold eyes never left her. Even now, surrounded by a mass of hunters from all over, she could feel his eyes on her as he lurked among them, the strength of his gaze chilling her to the bone.

Anya looked around the busy room, searching for a means to escape this torture when she spotted Thane standing near the back of the room, alone and staring right back at her.

"I didn't think you would come," she commented making her way toward him.

"It would've looked suspicious if I refused, especially when this whole thing is meant for the new recruits," he muttered, continuing to stare at her making her blush. "New dress?"

"How did you know?"

"It looks good on you," he replied, ignoring her question.

Never had she expected him to compliment her like that. Usually he only said something nice when she was upset, or when she stood up to him. Maybe he was softening toward her more than she realised.

Perhaps there was hope after all.

She glanced back at him and saw his eyes had not left her, making her stomach flutter and her heart race.

"Careful," he smirked, leaning forward and whispering in her ear. His warm breath tickled her sensitive skin. "You need to learn to control your emotions before they give you away."

"Sorry."

"It takes years of practice, but you'll get there. Just don't let your guard down around these people."

What was he doing to her?

"Have you begun your training?" he asked filling the silence between them.

Anya shook her head and stared down at her feet.

She knew she should go to Edwin and find out more

information about what she was capable of, but she wasn't sure she was ready.

Perhaps if someone else offered to train her. Someone she trusted; like Thane. Maybe then she would consider it.

"I know it's hard to accept, Anya. But you really shouldn't wait too long. The longer you leave it, the more danger you'll be in."

"I've managed all these years. What're a few more months?" she snapped, cringing as the words left her mouth.

It wasn't fair of her to blame Thane for Edwin's mistake, but it was true. She'd survived this long on her own, never letting anything get under her skin. That was, until she bumped into Thane. Ever since she'd met him, she couldn't control her emotions.

If he was really that worried about her safety, why hadn't he offered to train her?

"I guess you're right. Just be careful who you let see your true colours."


After almost fifteen minutes of agonising silence, she finally summed up the nerve to ask him the one question she'd been wondering the past two weeks.

"Have you seen Lucas yet?"

"No."

"Why hasn't he taken you to him? I thought they took all the new recruits to him to show them what they're up against. What if something's happened?"

"I'm sure they're just being careful who they take to him. Why would they do anything now when he's been their prisoner for so long?"

"I guess."

But what if Thane was wrong? What if they no longer needed him?

Maybe he did something after seeing her that caused them

to hurt, or kill him.

Thane told her about the bonds that mates shared with one another. How strong and powerful they could be. But she never had the chance to ask him whether family were connected the same way.

Would she know if something had happened to him? Would she feel it?

There were still so many questions she had about all of this, about what they were.

She'd tried asking Tynan some of her questions, but he hadn't known how to answer them, and others he didn't appear to want to tell her.

She wished Thane wasn't so busy. It seemed that he was the only one who told her the truth, holding nothing back.

Anya sighed, leaning against the wall beside him, and looked up at the glass ceiling above them.

The stars were shining brightly, filling her with a longing to be outside with friends rather than here, surrounded by people she despised.

"I thought you planned to sneak in there while nobody was looking."

The sound of Thane's deep voice spoken so closely to her ear made her jump, almost spilling her drink down her dress. He had a habit of knowing what she was thinking. She couldn't help but wonder whether he could read her thoughts.

"I did, but I couldn't get past the door."

"Why?"

"There's some kind of glowing runes etched into the door."

"I see," he muttered, standing back up straight. "You didn't ask anybody about them, did you?"

"No, I'm not a complete idiot," she fumed, irritated that he thought so little of her, even after his compliment. "Even before I found out about everything, I knew not to ask, or mention the glow.

Of course I wouldn't ask now. Even if it's changed."

"How do you mean?"

"Before they were glowing a faint blue colour, like y— like ice," she stuttered, catching the words before she embarrassed herself. "Now, they seem more aggressive. Stronger even, and they're red."

"You tried to get through? What happened?"

As if she could forget the intense and agonising pain she felt as her hand wrapped around that handle. It was like a thousand small knives slicing against her skin, burning as they pressed in deep. Her mind screamed, begging her to stop as she swayed on her feet.

Even now just remembering the pain, she could feel the knives pressing into her flesh, making her head light and her legs feel like rubber.

"No need to answer. I can already guess from your expression."

# Chapter 21

"Anya!" Hugh called. "I'm glad you made it."

Thane watched in silence as Hugh wrapped his arms around Anya's neck, kissing her cheek before he took a step back.

He fought the urge to growl and rip the boy to shreds as the wolf demanded.

He couldn't lose control and blow his cover.

"Keri and I were about to pop outside with a few others. We've got a fire in one of the gardens if you want to join us. It will get you away from certain people in here."

Did the boy mean him? Perhaps he wasn't as stupid as he looked. He was right to feel threatened by him, but could he allow her to go with him? He had to. He had to protect her.

"I—Erm."

"Well she seems bored by my company, so don't let me stop you," Thane commented.

Anya turned and looked at him, her expression somewhere

between upset and deathly.

He knew she wouldn't be happy, he wasn't himself, but he'd started to hear talk about Richard closing in on Lucas's '*long lost daughter*'. What better way to avert their attention from Anya than to have her appear friendly with his son?

He'd also noticed several of the guests watching them tonight, gossiping. He couldn't let them think anything was happening, not when he was here to cause problems and free Lucas. She'd be blamed too.

No, she needed to keep her distance when around the hunters, even if it pained him to send her away. Especially with the boy.

"No, there's nothing keeping me here at all," she spat, staring at him while she said the words, "I'd rather be with you and Keri."

Hugh smiled wide, obviously pleased that she'd chosen to follow rather than stay with him.

Thane instantly felt pain as he watched her leave, hoping he'd done the right thing.

"Thane?" an all too familiar voice called from behind.

Thane continued to watch her exit the room, feeling stupid and agitated.

She was going to be pissed at him, but there was nothing he could do. Her safety had to come before anything else.

Once out of view, Thane turned to the voice calling him. "Yes, Richard? "

"I have a special surprise for you. I've been promising to show you for weeks, but I think you're ready."

Thane knew he was talking about Lucas. Richard had told him about '*the man downstairs*' many times, explaining that he couldn't go until he was ready, until the man was healed. He hadn't told Anya because he knew she'd worry, but even he was concerned.

Usually they healed much faster than humans. A deep cut

only took a couple of days or so to heal. What could possibly have kept Lucas out for this long?

"I'll need to find Miss Shaw first. She will come in handy. Have you seen her? "

"Last I saw, she was headed outside with Hugh."

Thane couldn't help but wonder whether he'd just sent her into a trap when Richard snickered, obviously pleased with his son.

What was Thane thinking? The boy could be lying, wanting to get her alone so he could make a move.

Thane closed his eyes briefly to contain the light as he fought the urge to run after her. The wolf's hunger for the boy's blood was harder to ignore.

"Let's go interrupt them, shall we?" Richard suggested, walking toward the patio doors which Anya had not long exited through.

Thane was more than happy to oblige, though, after his dismissal, he doubted she would be pleased to see him.

He followed behind Richard in silence, curious why they needed Anya.

Did Richard already know what she was? Was he hoping that she wouldn't pass through the door like she'd described only moments before? Would he be able to pass through either? His whole cover would be blown before he had chance to execute his plans.


As soon as they stepped outside, the fresh air soothed him, allowing him to think clearly for the first time all night.

He'd never been a fan of large parties, even among his own kind. There were too many different scents. Too much noise. All of which handicapped him when on duty.

Outside where there were fewer people, he felt at ease, recognising each scent drifting to his nose, and although he couldn't hear her yet, nothing dulled the lure of her intoxicating odour. It alone was enough to have his body hum and make the wolf restless with the need to be close.

It didn't take long to spot the fire Hugh had mentioned. The flickering orange hues lit up the trees and bushes surrounding them.

Thane was relieved to see that Hugh had not been lying, there were other people with them. But that didn't stop the look of unease on her face.

Once again he'd forced her to do something she didn't wish to do. He felt like the monster everybody made him out to be. He should be protecting her, making sure she was comfortable and happy, not sending her away into the arms of another man.

Hugh moved close to her, placing his hands on her waist. He pulled her back toward his lap. She resisted, leaning forward to grab a drink in order to escape his hold. Until she spotted him.

She turned away, looking at the warm fire and leaned herself back into Hugh's arms. Thane only just managed to stop the growl escaping his throat, making it sound more like a grunt. Richard didn't seem to notice as he continued to move toward them, that same reptilian look in his eyes, and that sly grin curving his thin lips at the sides.

Nothing would bring Thane greater pleasure than wiping that hideous smile off his face. But not now. He needed to bide his time. Luring him into the trap he had already begun to place.

"Anya. I need you to come with me."

Anya flinched at the sound of Richard's gravelly voice. She clearly hadn't seen him. Thane could tell by watching her that she was afraid of him, wary what he needed her for, but still, she stood and asked, "What for?"

Never had he guessed someone's character as wrong as he had with her.

"I need your help with Lucas. He seemed to like you, changing for you without the use of violence. I was hoping you would ask the same of him now. "

"Why not just make him change by force?" Thane asked, needing to know why Richard was sparing him the fate he knew he endured daily.

Anya looked past Richard, a murderous gaze in her eyes.

Good. It was better that she was mad at him rather than directing her anger toward the one person she shouldn't.

Richard was a dangerous man who would stop at nothing to see her destroyed should he find out who she was.

Thane may still not accept that she was his mate, despite all the signs clearly saying differently, but he had sworn to protect her; and that was exactly what he planned to do, even if it upset her.

"He's not long healed from a severe wound. I would rather not injure him further whilst he still heals. He is very useful to me, and I don't want him dying, yet," Richard confessed.

Anya hesitated to agree, confusing him. Surely she wanted to see him again, wanted them to use her rather than use violence against him.

Thane cocked his head to the side, watching her twiddle her thumbs.

The door. Of course she'd be afraid to go along with him. He'd know what she was the moment she couldn't pass through.

From her description, Thane thought he might know a way around it which would allow them both to pass, but only if she hadn't left out any important information, and he had the time to pull it off.

"Will you assist us, Miss Shaw? Or will I have to resort to other means to show Mr Marrok?"

She continued to glare at Thane but nodded and walked toward them.

"Wait," Hugh called, jumping to his feet and grabbing her arm.

Thane stepped forward before he got control of himself, causing both Richard and Hugh to stare at him.

"I haven't finished talking with her yet."

"You'll have time after we're done. This is far more important than whatever you have to say to her." Richard insulted, turning away from him, his face red with rage.

Hugh groaned loudly dragging her close briefly, slipping what looked like a small dagger into her hand. "For protection," he whispered, then smiled and kissed her cheek.

Who did he think she needed protection from?

"Wait," another boy chimed in, walking toward them. His breath reeked of whiskey, his speech slurred. "She should stay with us. I don't trust him." The boy wrapped his arm around Anya's waist and looked pointedly at Thane.

Thane was close to snapping when he nuzzled near her neck. She was clearly uncomfortable, shoving him back and trying to break free from his hold. But before he had a chance to react, the unexpected happened.

Richard flew past him and grabbed the boy by the scruff of his jacket, bringing him within inches of his face.

"She's coming with me and Thane whether you like it or not, Chase. You should learn to hold your tongue and not touch what doesn't belong to you."

For once Thane actually agreed with Richard, but something didn't feel right. How had he managed to move so quickly? Even Thane struggled to keep up with his movements. And Hugh, his face paled, his heart racing.

From the moment he'd met Richard, Thane suspected there was more to him than met the eye, always hearing stories about him growing up. But never had he expected them to be true.

Thane had followed him for weeks, hoping he would slip up and show himself for what he really was, but nothing happened. Now he moved faster than humanly possible, that same nothingness dulling out all the other scents around him. Something was definitely wrong about all of this.

# Chapter 22

As they made their way through the corridors, Anya searched the space around her for somewhere to hide or run away from this, but there was no escape. If she couldn't get through that door, Richard would know. If she ran, he would grow suspicious. What was she going to do?

What about Thane? He wouldn't be able to pass through either.

She looked at him and narrowed her eyes.

How could he remain calm at a time like this? Was he not worried at all?

He may have a lot more practice than her at controlling his emotions, but sometimes he hid them too well.

So much for them making progress. She felt like screaming. Especially when they rounded the last corner. That ominous red glow made her heart race with each step closer, her breathing rapid and irregular. What were they going to do?

She turned to Thane once more praying he'd have a plan, only his face was pale, the muscles in his jaw now clenched.

Great. Now he shows some emotion, but not what she was hoping for.

"Do you have the key?" she asked Richard, grasping at straws.

Maybe if they were lucky he'd have forgotten it somewhere, giving them time to work out a plan or run. He might know then that they weren't human, but they would be outside, free from capture or death.

"Yes of course. I always have it on me. The only other person with a key is Hugh."

That wasn't entirely true. In Hugh's haste, he'd forgotten to take back the key he'd given her before. She still had it. It was the only reason she'd attempted to get in there by herself.

Anya was out of ideas, and the door was just ahead of them. Each loud step on the marble floor echoed inside her head as they seemed to move in slow motion.

Richard tugged the key from his pocket and reached a hand for the lock. The key turned with a click.

Anya held her breath, waiting for what was about to happen when she suddenly tripped, landing in a heap on the floor by Richard's feet.

She turned behind her, looking for what had tripped her, only to see Thane's foot tangled with her own, a small smile curving his lips. He winked down at her.

Did he have a plan? She hoped so.

Anya stayed on the floor, grasping her ankle in the pretence it was twisted, remembering the feeling well.

Richard stared down at her, gritting his teeth and rolling his eyes, but still he crouched down and tested her ankle.

Anya continued the lie, making out it was too painful to put pressure on, gasping when he lifted her gently to her feet. She'd expected nothing but annoyance from him, not a helping hand.

When she turned back to Thane, he shrugged and smiled, making her stomach flutter and her anger disappear.

With Richard's attention back on the door that was no longer glowing, Anya leaned into Thane and whispered so only he would hear her. "What did you do?"

He turned and glared, obviously not wanting to discuss it in front of Richard, leaving her again with more questions.

"Hurry up," Richard snapped over his shoulder, already descending the spiral staircase.

With a deep breath Anya edged forward, peering into the darkness, wishing he'd light a torch as Hugh had.

With each step, the darkness seemed to swallow them, until she could barely see her hand in front of her face.

Anya reached her hands out, searching for the wall to help guide her lower, testing each step with her foot. Still she stumbled. Bumping into Richard, or being caught by Thane behind her.

She hoped they were almost there, but with no way of knowing, or seeing the bottom, she relied on the men around her.

The sounds of their footsteps on the concrete, and Lucas's heavy breathing below were the only sounds she could hear over her own heart beating.

What had Richard done to him?

Anya forced her eyes closed, desperately trying to hold back her tears before Richard saw. When she reopened them, her vision flickered in and out of focus.

She didn't understand at first. Then she remembered how Thane could see in the dark. She must be able to as well. *'One of the many advantages to being a shifter,'* Thane had told her.

Thane's hand grabbed her shoulder, spinning her around. He leant his face close to hers and shook his head.

What was wrong?

Anya stared into his eyes, confused, until she saw the

reflection of her own glowing in the darkness. She had to control herself, learn to keep her emotions in check around those that meant her harm.

Thane tucked her behind him, keeping a hold of her arm as he led her down the steps.

He didn't need to, she could see fairly clearly now, but she didn't tell him that, savouring the comfort of having him touching and protecting her.

As they rounded the last bend, she stopped dead in her tracks.

Lucas was on the floor, lying completely still, his chest rising and falling rapidly.

She couldn't see the injury Richard had mentioned earlier, but she knew that was the reason for his struggle.

Moving closer to the bars, she came face to face with his glowing green eyes, shining bright like an emerald in the sunlight. Hauntingly beautiful. So much like Thane's in intensity. They swirled with different emotions as he sat up and moved toward her.

"What do you want, Richard?" he snarled, looking past her.

"I want you to give us a little demonstration. I brought the girl to make you a little more compliant."

This time he didn't hold back his growl, lunging at the bars, barking words in a language she didn't recognize. To her surprise Richard replied, calm and laid back.

It was only when Lucas gripped tight on the bars that she noticed the deep welts in his wrists, the bite marks on his arms.

He'd tried to break free the only way he knew how, but it hadn't worked.

Anya covered her mouth to stop the sob from escaping.

She wanted to go to him, comfort him, but she couldn't, not with Richard there to see.

"Come here," Richard called to Thane, leaning back

against the wall, relaxed as though he were threatened like this every day.

Thane stepped out of the shadows, his face solemn and serious. He nodded but she couldn't tell whether it was to Richard or a greeting to Lucas.

He continued to walk forward, stopping just behind her, placing a firm hand on her shoulder, an attempt to move her behind him once again. Anya resisted, trying to push his hand away. He couldn't tear her from her dad, not now she knew who he was, but Lucas whined, his eyes seeming to plead with her to listen.

She moved away watching Thane step within inches of the bars.

Lucas stood up straight for the first time, coming eye to eye with Thane.

She hadn't realised how tall he was. Most of her previous visit he'd been seated or slouched before he changed into a wolf.

Watching him now, he studied Thane with curiosity, cocking his head to the side, his eyes flickering to life once again. There seemed to be a silent communication between them as they stood there face to face. It was an overwhelming experience to watch, making her chest hurt, and her eyes fill water.

"You're a brave one," Richard commented, placing his hand on Thane's broad back. "Brave, or foolish."

"The wolf can't hurt me when he's shackled in silver chains."

"He may not be able to break free of them, but he can still cause damage if you stray too close. My scar is proof of that," Richard said, pointing to the nasty scar that ran across his face.

Lucas smiled wide, flashing his sharp canines, obviously pleased by his handy work.

"I'll bear that in mind."

"Very well," Richard muttered, making his way to the staircase, "I'll leave you here for a few minutes whilst I grab some things from my office. I trust you'll keep Miss Shaw safe while I'm gone, Thane? "

"Of course."

"And Miss Shaw? Do make yourself useful and ask the big bad wolf to shift for us. It'll save me having to use the tools I'm about to retrieve."

Anya nodded, unsure how else she could respond. It would be better for him to shift and save himself the torture he'd undoubtedly endure otherwise, but she didn't want to be the one asking him. All she wanted to do was be close and talk to him, free him if she had chance so she could hold him. The last thing that crossed her mind was asking him to shift for Richard's benefit.

"Why did you bring her here, Thane? " Lucas demanded when Richard closed the door behind him with a deafening bang.

"She's stubborn, I wonder who she inherited that trait from," Thane teased, glancing back and smiling over his shoulder toward her.

"She's not safe here," Lucas croaked, turning to look at her. "You need to run. They're suspicious of you already. It will only take Richard a matter of time before he has proof. He always gets what he wants."

Was that what all of this was about? A test to see if she would pass through the door, giving him the proof he needed?

It didn't matter now. They went through without Richard knowing the truth. But she wasn't prepared to leave. Not without Lucas.

"I can't leave you here, not now I know who you are. What I am."

Lucas whimpered low in his throat, barely audible to her ears, she wasn't sure she had truly heard him until she saw a tear roll down his cheek.

"I cannot protect you, Anya, and I fear Thane will be greatly outmatched. You need to run before they learn who you are."

"I won't leave you!" she cried, unable to contain the tears any longer as they rolled down her face, burning hot against her cheeks, the salt bitter against her lips.

"He's right, Anya, it's not safe for you here. I've heard rumours all night about Richard finding Lucas's long-lost daughter."

Anya didn't understand how the hunters knew what she was. She hadn't found out herself that long ago. There was no way she had slipped up and made a mistake around them.

"How?" she managed to ask when all other words escaped her.

"You look so much like your mother. I'm sure that's why Richard has been suspicious since the start."

Anya knew she was spitting image of her mother with her burgundy hair, and small frame, but her face was more like Lucas's now she looked at him. Especially now she knew who she'd inherited the green eyes from.

Surely not even Richard would condemn her on looks alone.

She tried to remember all her meetings with Richard. All the times she could have given him reason to distrust her. Nothing stood out.

"I'll do all I can to free you. I won't stop until I do," she insisted, making her way toward the cell to hold him.

He stretched his arms out as far as he could, straining against his shackles to hold her close while she sobbed.

"I know you will," he muttered, burying his face in her hair. "I'm proud to call you my daughter. You've grown into an amazing woman."

The tears streamed down her face forcing her to cling to him, never wishing to let go, or leave him here.

"Be safe," he whispered, releasing her and stepping back into the darkness of his prison.

"But Richard's expecting me to ask you to shift."

"I will when he returns. I promise you I'll do it without the need of force, after all, both the witnesses have seen me shift before."

She couldn't argue with his logic. Of course Richard would have seen him shift over the years, and Thane, well he was Lucas's student for a long time, as well as his friend. He would have seen him in his wolf form many times. She on the other hand had only seen him change once, but she hoped she would see him do so again. When he was free, and could run through the woods like he no doubt longed to do.

Anya said her farewells to Lucas, nodding when he asked her not to return.

She couldn't promise she wouldn't come back to see him, she would find it difficult to stay away, but she needed him to believe she was safe.

With her foot on the first step, Thane grabbed a hold of her wrist, spinning her around.

"I'll come find you when I'm done. Tell you if I learn anything. Just, be careful."

She nodded again, unable to speak past the lump in her throat, forcing herself to run up the stairs, not daring to look back.

# Chapter 23

The shrill sound of chimes rang out from Thane's pocket. A new message from Richard, informing him that plans had changed. Instructing him to return to the party after Anya's 'sudden departure'.

Thane had no intention of leaving. Not yet. Instead, he stepped toward Lucas's prison, and took a seat on the floor in front of him. Bowing his head slightly when Lucas joined him on the other side of the bars.

"I'm sorry it was Anya who had to find you here, that I allowed her to come back."

Lucas sighed, mimicking his seated position. "I can see she has spirit, just like Amelia. You couldn't have kept her away."

"I never stopped searching for either of you," Thane admitted, hanging his head in shame.

"I know, but in doing so, you've destroyed your own chance of a life, and the happiness you deserve."

Thane didn't argue, knowing it would be futile to try. He knew the last few years had been tough on him. That he had become more secluded and more hateful. But some people still managed to break through that barrier he'd built around himself.

Lucas had always been one to see through his defences. It made sense that his daughter would be able to do the same.

"I can smell her on your skin, Thane. I could smell you on hers the moment she stepped into the cellar, before I realised who it was standing before me."

"I tried to push her away, to keep her from this life."

"It's better she learns about it now, rather than later. She needs to know how to protect herself. I trust you'll teach her well."

Thane knew it was coming. He'd already discussed it with Edwin, knowing she needed to be taught how to embrace her gift and learn to control it. He just didn't expect to be the one to teach her. He didn't think he would be strong enough to handle seeing her shift for the first time; if it turned out that she was able to. Her glowing eyes were enough to threaten his control. Even now, remembering that piercing green shimmer, his chest ached, and his groin throbbed. Being the one to teach her would only end badly between them. But he didn't think he had the strength left in him to fight the pull.

Suddenly, both men heard the door at the top of the stairs close and lock, shortly followed by heavy footsteps echoing down the narrow stairwell and bouncing around the circular room they sat in.

Richard was coming back, hoping to speak with Lucas, alone.

Thane looked around him, searching for a place to hide.

In the back of one of the cells, he saw a gap just big enough for him to fit, between the frame of an old bed, and a hole in the wall.

Squeezing between the broken bars of the old cell was difficult, and required a lot of adjustment, but he couldn't fail.

Finally he pushed his torso through, catching his arm on the jagged metal where the bars had been broken, causing him to wince with the pain. The cut was deep and no doubt dirty, but he couldn't afford to worry about it now.

Seconds after he took his hiding position, Richard rounded the last bend and stepped onto the grimy floor, his boots thumping and crunching on the debris littered on the ground.

Thane slowed his heartbeat and quieted his breathing, hoping that Richard's hearing was not as keen as his own.

Lucas made a loud noise, gaining Richard's attention when he walked toward Thane, causing him to stop and turn.

"Ah Lucas, it seems you were spared tonight. How considerate of the young Miss Shaw."

Lucas growled, turning his back on Richard to play with a sparkling chain Thane hadn't noticed him holding before.

It had to be a gift from Anya. The chain resembled the one he'd seen around her neck several times.

Another layer of ice surrounding Thane's heart fractured, leaving him wanting.

"Now now, no need to get grouchy. You know what I want, why not make this easier on yourself and give me her name."

Lucas remained silent, playing the pendant between his thumb and forefinger, the shiny metal glinting as the light caught on it.

Thane finally realised what she had given him. Not just her chain, but the key to this room. All he needed to do now was break free of the shackles binding him. A task Thane was only too happy to help find a way of achieving.

"Not to worry, I'm sure we're already closing in on her, but if she turns out to be nobody of importance to you, Lucas, I'm sure Hugh will have his fun with her, or maybe I could."

"Go to hell," Lucas spat, jumping to his feet and pulling against his restraints.

"You will never get her name from me, no matter what dirty tactics you try. I would rather die."

"And you will, once I'm finished with you—" Richard paused to move closer to the bars before adding, "—you know, the lovely Miss Shaw looks an awful lot like Amelia, wouldn't you agree?"

Lucas remained silent, barely reacting as he continued to stare into Richard's face. A wise decision, even though Thane knew it was killing him to think Richard was so close to finding her.

"I wouldn't know. I can barely remember her face."

"Don't lie to me, Lucas," Richard growled, rattling the bars. "I know how close shifters are with their mates. You would never forget her face, even if you'd been here a hundred years."

Lucas just continued to stare at him, pulling his lips back over his teeth and snarling.

"You know she's dead though, don't you? That your child is now alone and defenceless, just waiting for me to find her?"

It was Thane's turn to hold in a growl as he thought of Richard anywhere near her.

He was wrong. Anya was not alone. Since the moment Erebus had found her, she'd been protected. Edwin took her in as his own, the Guard claiming her as one of them. And now she had him.

Lucas on the other hand growled deep and loud, lunging toward the bars. Gripping them tightly, he gnashed his teeth in Richard's face.

"Perhaps when I find her, I'll allow her to live so she can be mine."

Lucas dashed his hand out so quickly that even Richard was caught unawares, his throat clamped in Lucas's vice-like grip. His teeth elongated into fangs, dripping with saliva, rage swirling wildly in his glowing eyes.

"She would never be yours," Lucas spat, chucking Richard to the floor.

Richard quickly scrambled to his feet and dusted himself off.

"Just as Amelia refused your affections, she will do the same."

"I will enjoy killing her in front of you when I find her, or perhaps I will take her as my plaything even against her will. That would be worse than her death for you, wouldn't it?" Richard laughed, picking off the remaining debris from his jacket.

Lucas turned his back on him, obviously having heard enough. But Richard remained, walking in the opposite direction, toward where Thane hid.

Thane feared he might spot him as he squinted into the dark, but instead of continuing toward him, Richard took a seat on the bench outside the door.

"You know. If you'd just give me the names I require, you and your child could be free. After all, none of them have come searching for you. It's a good trade," Richard offered, shrugging his shoulders and holding out his hands in a nonchalant manner.

"I will never give you our leaders' names, Richard. My daughter will understand and know you're lying."

"You're such a disappointment, Lucas. I had hoped you would break sooner or later, but if anything you've become more stubborn. Maybe you've outlived your usefulness after all."

"Then kill me and get it over with."

Thane's heart was in his throat waiting for Richard to move, to attack. He would have to stop him if he tried. It wouldn't matter if he gave himself away, he couldn't allow him to kill Lucas. Except Richard didn't move. He tilted his head back and laughed.

"You never change do you, Lucas? Even after all these years, you wish for death. I'd have thought you would want to be with your child," he laughed again and pushed to his feet, this time headed for the stairs. "Don't worry, I'll find her for you and bring her here. Then I'll decide what to do with her."

Still not getting the reactions he hoped for, Richard sighed and began to climb the stairs, calling a pathetic goodbye over his shoulder.

When Thane heard the door slam shut and the lock click in place, he emerged from his hiding spot.

"You should go, Thane, before he comes back and finds you here. You need to protect her, keep her from him," Lucas insisted, shoving the key in Thane's hand as he leant in to say goodbye.

"I can't take this, Lucas."

"How else do you expect to get out of here? Richard locked the door behind him and will expect it to be locked next time he comes"

"But this is a gift from her, a means for your escape," Thane pleaded, shoving the key back toward him.

"Until you find a way for me to break these chains, I am stuck here with or without that key. You need it more than I do, and if Richard finds the door unlocked, he'll assume she is to blame."

Thane nodded, taking the key offered to him and rested his forehead against Lucas's.

It was a brief touch, but it was something that meant a lot, marking their friendship.

"I will not rest until I free you."

"I know, just like I know you'll take care of my girl."

Thane turned, heading for the steps with a pain in his chest.

He didn't want to leave him down there alone, but he knew he couldn't free him. Not yet. He needed to break that chain.

"And Thane?"

Thane paused, looking over his shoulder with his foot poised above the first step.

"You cannot resist the call. I tried, and it almost destroyed me. I never got to spend much time with her—" Lucas croaked, swallowing the lump in his throat. "Don't make the same mistakes I did. Enjoy the time you have, as fate is a cruel mistress and she will take her from you forever."

Thane ran up the steps, Lucas's final words echoing inside of his mind.

He was right. Thane had tried so hard to push her away, to keep himself at a distance when he didn't trust her. But she proved she was loyal and found her way into his heart.

Would she still want him when she learnt what he was capable of, why the Guard's all feared him?

She may have the spirit of a warrior, but his past was painted in blood.

# Chapter 24

After almost two hours of sketching on Thane's doorstep, Anya's patience was wearing thin.

She thought Thane would have been home by now. She didn't remember it taking this long when she saw Lucas shift for the first time. What if something had gone wrong? What if Thane was now stuck down there with Lucas?

Anya leaned her head back against the door and looked up at the night sky.

It was no use worrying. She'd just have to wait longer, or go home and call it a night.

A faint sound of footsteps echoed down the alleyway in front, startling her and making her flinch.

It was probably Tynan again. In the last hour, he'd passed by several times, stopping to chat or watch her draw before he left, only to come back again.

At first she'd thought nothing of it, but by the fourth time, she knew he was up to something. Either he was lonely and wanted someone to talk to like when he kept dropping by her house, or he was waiting for Thane.

Anya couldn't help but smile as he passed her yet again with a big grin and a shy wave.

After how they met, she never would have expected that in just a few weeks they'd become friends. There was just something about him she couldn't stay angry at. Whether it was his witty charms or his relentless apologizing.

Giving up, Anya pushed to her feet and hugged her sketchbook to her chest.

She glanced over her shoulder once more before Thane's house disappeared from view and smiled.

No matter how much Thane tried to push her away, she could see him softening toward her.

When she had leant back in Hugh's arms earlier, Thane's eyes had flashed to life, even if it was only for a brief moment.

Could it be that he was jealous?

It didn't make sense. Why would he send her away with Hugh if he was jealous of her being around him? Perhaps it was anger instead, or disapproval because of him being a hunter.

Why couldn't he just tell her how he felt, and what he was thinking?

When Anya finally arrived home, it was well past midnight.

Her modest little house looked deserted and dark, another cruel reminder that she lived alone.

Perhaps she should move back with Edwin. At least then she would feel loved and protected. But was she ready to trust him again?

She sighed and breathed in deeply. Why did it have to be

dark? Anya hated the dark. But she couldn't leave her light on all the time.

That same faint sound of footsteps echoed in the alley behind her, forcing her to spin around.

Surely Tynan hadn't followed her home, not this late at night.

She watched, waiting to see who appeared, listening for more sounds. Nothing. No shadows moved toward her. No unnerving feeling that someone was there, and no more noise.

She shrugged her shoulders and turned back to her door, rummaging around in her bag for her keys.

Perhaps if someone had taught her how to use her abilities, she might have been able to decipher what the sound was.

The noise sounded once again, making her pause her search. Only this time it grew louder as something seemed to approach from behind.

Anya spun around and listened, waiting to see who would emerge. The sound changing from steps to a moan, nothing like she'd heard before.

Curious and concerned someone was hurt, Anya stepped forward, the moan turning into an inhuman snicker.

Soon realising her mistake, she spun and bolted back toward her door.

The laugh behind her grew louder, almost mocking like it enjoyed the chase.

Giving up with her bag, Anya searched her pockets for her key, when a large hand gripped her shoulder, spinning her around on the spot.

His eyes were glowing bright blue, like Thane's. No, not like Thane's. They didn't seem right, didn't look human.

He leaned in close to her face and inhaled deeply. So close, she could smell his putrid breath and the citrus gel in his hair. A shiver travelled through her body making her cringe and back away from the man in front of her. He smiled a menacing smile and moved closer, taking a strand of her hair between his fingers and bringing it to his nose.

"You smell divine," he croaked, his voice more animal than man. "No wonder Thane likes you."

"Y—you know Thane?" she managed, praying that he meant her no harm. "Is he alright? He's not home yet."

"No idea. Haven't seen him for a while."

The man moved closer still, his huge body pressing against hers.

Anya tried to back away, but her back hit against the wooden door, the handle digging into her spine.

"You know you should never run from an animal, especially one that likes to hunt," he smiled that same terrifying and menacing smile.

"What are you?"

He stood back astonished, looking down at her through furrowed brows.

There was something about him, something different from all the other shifters she'd met. Something dangerous.

"What do you want from me?"

"Now my little wolfy, that's the question you should be asking."

"How do you know that?"

"I can smell it on your skin like you should be able to tell what I am."

He leaned forward, offering his thick neck in front of her face. "Take a sniff."

Anya did as she was told, fearful that if she refused it might offend him in some way. Still she couldn't guess what he was. His scent unexpected and strong, combining with the citrus of his hair.

He shuddered and moaned, placing one of his strong

hands on her hip, the other around her throat in a threatening hold.

She didn't struggle. It would be futile to try. Just answered him honestly, "I still can't tell."

"Such a shame," he replied, his eyes glowing even brighter as he pulled her closer.

His erection pressed into her abdomen as his hand slid down her hips, skimming over her thighs.

Anya pushed further into the wood behind trying to escape him, still fumbling in her jacket pocket for her keys.

"That won't help you."

He looked down at her hand and grabbed a hold of her wrist, pinning it by the side of her head on the door, leaning in close to her neck.

A loud growl sounded behind the man making her heart stop. Just how many were there?

He spun on his heels, holding her behind him as the growl grew louder.

Anya peered around him to see a large black wolf climbing up the steps toward them, snarling. His sharp teeth bared.

"T—Thane. I thought you were busy," the man stumbled, taking a step back into her.

Thane snarled louder, edging closer to the man, his hackles raised and his eyes like granite.

"What? I didn't know."

"Don't lie to me," Thane growled, snapping his teeth shut.

"I'm sorry. I was just testing what she knew."

"Liar," Thane roared, drool dripping from his razor like canines. "You're trying to take what's not yours again."

"Wait, Thane, don't do this," the man begged as Thane opened his mouth to bite.

"Stop," Anya shouted, moving between the men, holding Thane back.

"I think you should leave now," she said to the man,

hoping he would never come back.

"Yes. Leave, Duncan."

"I'm sorry, Thane. I really didn't know."

Duncan shifted into a jaguar, much like Tynan, only his pelt matched Thanes in colour, his eyes wilder as he ran away quickly, not daring to look over his shoulder as he disappeared into the darkness.

Anya turned back to Thane still in wolf form, staring her in the eyes.

She crouched down in front of him, placing her hands on his face.

This close, she could see the scar that cut across his jaw, marking him the same as the man.

"Don't growl at me," she snapped when she heard a deep rumble coming from his chest. To her surprise he whined and lowered his head, rubbing his cheek against her hand.

"Thank you for saving me again, Thane," she sighed, leaning her forehead against his.

His fur was soft, tickling her nose in the gentle breeze. She wrapped her arms around his neck and moved closer to his warmth.

He shifted back into a human and picked her up in his strong arms.

Taking the keys from her hand, he carried her inside and up the stairs. Her heart pounded in anticipation until her hand brushed against something wet on his arm.

"You're bleeding," she gasped, spotting the deep laceration on his forearm. "What happened?"

"Nothing. I can barely feel it."

She traced her fingers around the top of the wound and saw it was red and inflamed.

Thane closed his eyes and sucked in a breath through his clenched teeth, stopping himself from crying out in pain.

"I thought you said it didn't hurt?" she teased.

Thane reopened his eyes and glared at her obviously displeased that she had seen him in pain.

Memories of him in the arena flooded her mind. She'd been too far away, surrounded by hunters she didn't trust, unable to go and help him as she had wanted, but now things were different. He was in her home and nobody was there to see her aid him.

"Let me clean it for you. Please."

"I'll do it later when I get home."

"It already looks infected. Don't be so stubborn."

He raised his eyebrow and smiled.

Thane may be stubborn, but so was she, and this time she wasn't going to take no for an answer.

She gently ran her fingers over his arm, noticing lots of little cuts, bruises and scars across his neck and bare chest.

She gasped as her palm grazed over his searing hot flesh.

"Thane. You're—"

"Yes. It's a side effect of the shift. Try not to look down."

Anya bit her lip, trying not to think of him naked, holding her against him as she forced her attention back to his eyes. No longer the ominous navy she had seen downstairs. Now they glistened a pale, ice blue that reminded her of a glacier, both beautiful and deadly.

Suddenly he placed her on her bed and turned away, heading for the door.

She sat up quickly. He wasn't getting away that easily. She needed to make sure his wound was clean. But she was at a loss for words when his bare behind caught her attention, her hands itching to touch and feel his golden skin beneath her palm.

"You know, it's rude to stare," he called over his shoulder, pausing by the door to flash her a devilish smile.

She hid her face behind her hands as blood rushed to her cheeks.

He rarely smiled, but whenever he did, it took her breath

away.

Anya stepped toward him, intent on forcing him to stay, to let her take care of him until he turned to face her, that wicked gleam never leaving his face.

She needed to clean his wound, to take care of him knowing he'd be too stubborn to do it himself, but all she could think about was placing her hands on his body.

He sucked in a deep breath, shuddering as her hands landed on the solid ridges of his stomach. Inching lower. Needing to feel his warmth. Enjoying having his scent wrapped around her.

"W—what's this?" she asked as her hand brushed over raised skin.

It looked like a tattoo, the dark ink forming symbols that seemed familiar. Only, each symbol was raised as though it was under the skin rather than a part of it.

"Tattoos react differently with our skin where we shift. So we use a different method that's passed down through our generations."

Anya continued to stare down at the symbols on his skin, tracing her fingers along the edges of each of them. She could feel his stomach muscles tensing as her hand moved lower.

Suddenly he snatched her hand away with a sigh, holding it in the air by her head. His eyes burned brightly. It was impossible to resist glancing down at the impressive length of him.

"Don't," Thane whispered in a voice laced with arousal.

Anya bit down on her lip and reluctantly pulled her hand back, trying to think of anything to take her mind off the hunger she suddenly felt for him, the deep ache between her thighs intensifying.

"What do they mean?" she asked, her voice deep and husky.

"They're runes to protect me and those around me. Symbols that help me keep control and remember my past."

The mere mention of his past dimmed the passion in his

eyes, yet he continued to stare into hers with a look so intense she felt a shiver tingle down her spine.

She longed to ask what happened to him, but she didn't want to push him away, not when he was finally letting her close. Not running from their intimacy.

"Why is there a gap here?" she asked, her eyes drifting south once more, spotting a gap in the pattern decorating his lower abdomen.

"My mate will fill that gap."

Her heart felt like it stopped. The thought of this beautiful man belonging to another was too painful to bear. She'd already fallen for him, and there was nothing she could do to stop it.

Anya lifted her eyes to his and gasped. His face was mere inches from her own, that bright glow filling her vision.

Suddenly she found herself pressed up against the door frame with his lips on her own, one large hand fisted in her hair, tipping her head back to deepen the kiss.

She moaned into his mouth and clenched her hands tight against his chest. His kiss soft, yet passionate, and so very unlike him. His hold on her possessive, and almost needy.

Just as fast as the kiss had started, he pulled back whispering, "I'm sorry," in her ear before he dashed out of her room, shifting back into a wolf as he leaped down the stairs.

Everything happened so fast, leaving her stunned in silence, staring after him.

Sighing, she perched on the edge of her bed, her heart racing and her stomach twisting into knots.

She never had a chance to ask him what happened with his arm, or what he'd learnt from Lucas.

# Chapter 25

Thane had gone to Anya's the other night with the intention of telling her what he'd learnt from Lucas. To explain to her why she needed to stay away from them as they grew more and more suspicious of her. Instead, he'd found Duncan on her doorstep, getting far too close for his liking.

The young Guard had always rubbed Thane the wrong way, trying his best to undermine everyone in a higher position than himself.

It was no secret that he wanted to be top dog, craving the title Thane was supposed to inherit. A title Thane didn't even want. It was Lucas's, not his. But when he saw Duncan place his hands on Anya's skin, something inside snapped, demanding he take her, and claim her for his own. No shifter, vampire or any other creature of Lore would dare touch her then. Only he couldn't go through with it. Not yet. She needed to know the real him first.

Thane sighed loudly, leaning back into his chair.

"What's up?" Tynan asked, glancing over his shoulder from the video game he played on the TV.

"I can't think how to break Lucas's chain. It needs to be something inconspicuous."

"No, that's not what's bothering you," Tynan replied, pausing his game to turn and face Thane with his arms resting over his crossed legs.

"You've been moody these last couple of days."

"Well moodier than normal," he laughed when Thane raised his eyebrows.

"Is it Anya?"

"Why do you assume it's her?"

"Only she can make you this tense and grouchy."

Tynan was right. Thane knew he had a fiery temper, but not even Duncan could get under his skin like she could. Every time he was around her, he found it increasingly difficult to control himself.

"Why do I keep torturing myself with her?"

"She's your mate, Thane. You know you can't resist it, why bother trying?"

"She deserves better," he sighed.

"You're a good person, Thane. What happened to your family and the events after wasn't your fault. Anyone would have done the same. Let her decide whether or not she wants to be with you."

"I killed so many people, Tynan. I doubt many would have reacted so badly. Only Lucas was able to talk me out of it."

Thane had been on the brink of being classed a rogue. Lost to the wolf for years, killing anyone who stumbled too close. Not only were guilty lives lost, but also innocent people, and those of fellow Guardians that Thane had never had the opportunity to work with. No doubt they had all come to put an end to him, yet Lucas hesitated, believing he could reason with the wolf. He hadn't been wrong.

"Yeah, but the amount of good you've done since outweighs the bad. It's our job to kill the hunters and rogues, we can't always help when innocent people get caught up in the fight. We've all saved more than we've killed."

Thane rested his head back against the chair and sighed again.

He didn't care how many hunters he killed when he knew they'd kill indiscriminately. It was the innocent people and his own kinds blood on his hands that bothered him. He'd become a monster the moment he gave in to his desire for vengeance, and he still felt like a monster now. Nothing he did could ever erase what he'd done. Anya deserved something more. Someone who could protect her. Someone who she wouldn't have to fear losing control.

"Thane?"

"What?" he groaned, lifting his head to look across the room at Tynan.

"You said you needed an inconspicuous way to free Lucas. How about a strong acid that would eat through the chains?"

"That could work. It would need to be powerful enough to work in a small dosage though so I can hide the vial. What would be strong enough to do that? It's a thick chain," Thane explained, leaning forward in his chair, excited they may have a lead at last.

"I don't know," Tynan shrugged, scratching his head as Thane groaned, slumping back once again. "But I do know a place where we can find out."

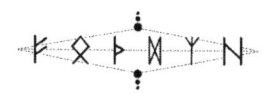

---

After a short walk through the busy town, they arrived outside a small book store which Tynan insisted had what they were after. Thane was skeptical. The store looked tiny.

"Wouldn't a library be better? They have more books after all."

"Nah. This place is deceiving. I came in the other day and they have tons of books. It's, cosy. Plus this would be more private."

Thane couldn't argue with his logic. A small book store like this couldn't attract too many customers. A library on the other hand could have tons. All of which posed the risk of others overseeing what they searched for.

A little bell above the door chimed loud and shrill, making Thane's ears ring as he stepped through the glass doors, coming to stop when he saw the magnitude of people inside.

"So much for privacy," he muttered, frowning when a group of young boys pushed past him in a rush to get to the counter. He righted his footing and growled loudly causing them all to turn to him.

"Sorry," they muttered as they squirmed away from his murderous gaze.

Before he would have laughed at their cowardice, now he pitied them.

He could feel himself softening because of her. A dangerous thing when he needed to remain vigilant. He couldn't afford to let his guard down, especially in a place as busy as this.

He tried to ignore the other customers, engrossed in his search while Tynan sat in the corner, propped up against the cash register, but it was impossible. One old lady kept hovering around him, occasionally commenting on the books he picked up, making him suspicious. Another asked him if he needed help with anything. Even a group of younger girls he hadn't noticed upon entering tried to flirt with him and gain his attention, standing close and purposely brushing past him.

This was all very new and strange to him. He was used to people keeping their distance, whispering about him as though he were unaware.

"Need a hand?" a feminine voice asked from behind him. A soft and alluring sound that raised every hair across his neck and arms.

Thane spun around to face her, conscious of what he could say to her after the distance between them when he kissed her three days ago.

He found himself at a loss for words, but not because of feeling awkward like he feared. No, she was dressed like something out of a fantasy. Her shirt was tight, straining to stay shut around her ample breasts, the top few buttons left open giving him the slightest peek of her black lace bra beneath.

Thane clenched his fists tight to restrain himself from reaching out and touching her. His eyes roamed lower, to a sinfully short black skirt that stopped halfway between her knee and her bottom. A small slit on the left leg showed a dream catcher tattoo on her leg he'd never seen before.

Thane continued to stare, savouring the sight of her, feeling a hunger to caress her skin and taste her flesh.

"Do you want my help or not?" she asked, placing her hands on her hips, though he could see the colour blooming in her cheeks.

All he could do was nod, unable to think or speak a coherent sentence with her standing in front of him like that.

"What are you looking for?"

"A book on acids," Tynan replied for him, walking toward them and placing a kiss on Anya's cheek.

"Acid? All right, let me see what we've got," she replied with a smile, patting Tynan's chest as she made her way back to the cash register.

Thane turned to Tynan and raised a brow, curious as to when the two of them became so close.

Had he known she worked here? From his huge smile and

casual shrug, Thane knew the answer.

He thought it was only Edwin who interfered in his life, trying to bring the two of them closer.

"Depending on the amount of detail you're after, we have several books that might be helpful," Anya told him as he approached. "The chemistry books are the most detailed, where the encyclopedias have brief descriptions."

"The chemistry books will do fine. Where are those?" Thane asked, speaking to her for the first time.

"Here," she replied, pointing to an overflowing shelf. "Want anything else?"

In his head, Thane asked her to kiss him, to let him take her right there. His groin ached painfully as he adjusted his tight jeans.

"I don't know where to start," he admitted, settling for the half-truth rather than his desires.

"My shift will be over in a few minutes, then I'm all yours," she smiled, heading back to the register once again to serve a young boy.

Thane wanted that to be true. Wanted her to mean those words in another way, but he couldn't subject her to that, not when she didn't know what she was getting herself into.

He watched her work while they waited. She seemed to enjoy her job, but the thought of her wearing such an outfit on a regular basis, surrounded by young boys and men infuriated him.

As he glanced around the compact store, he felt a growl escape his throat when he spotted the boy she was serving looking down her blouse, and another ogling her legs. Did she not notice that almost every male here was looking at her with hunger in their eyes?

A group of boys gossiped behind him, leering at her.

Thane walked over, and leaned against the shelving, purposely knocking into it so a loose book landed on one of them. When the boy turned and opened his mouth to curse at him, he paused snapping it shut again. Thane couldn't contain his smile.

"Looking at anything interesting, are you?" he sneered, leaning casually against the shelf.

"We were just leaving," one of the boys announced.

"I didn't know she had a boyfriend," another of them whispered to his friends with a frown.

Thane liked that other people thought she was his. It put a smile on his face knowing that he'd scared them away. Hopefully they'd think twice about coming back to stare.

Perhaps he wasn't going soft after all.

Halfway back to the desk, he froze. In front of him stood Anya, arms crossed over her chest, with an eyebrow raised above one eye, Tynan smiling wide behind her.

"What was that?" she demanded.

What could he say? He couldn't tell her he didn't want them looking at her. That he didn't like any other male's eyes on her body. He was becoming too jealous and possessive already.

"Nothing," he lied, walking past her and elbowing Tynan in the ribs as he continued to smirk.

"Do you always get this many people in here?" he asked, unable to keep the bitterness from his tone. He'd expected it to be quiet when he saw it from the outside. He couldn't have been more wrong.

"Yeah, it's always busy on a weekend, though Mrs Baldwin complains it's quiet during the week when she's by herself."

"Not surprising," Thane huffed, looking toward the old woman she pointed out. The same old woman that kept following him.

Anya laughed, rubbing his arm with tenderness before crouching down to search the shelves.

He'd slipped up, admitting to her he was jealous, but the sound of her laughter put the smile back on his face.

"Why acids?" she asked.

"I can't discuss it here," he whispered in her ear, taking an indulgent breath by her neck.

"Why didn't you just look online?"

"Ty suggested coming here. Now I know why," Thane grumbled, looking pointedly at Tynan, whose grin just widened further. Thane would have to teach him a lesson later.

"I don't know how to say this, but if what I think you're searching for is correct, you won't find anything in these books," Anya replied with a solemn look on her face. "No chemistry book will help, or I would have told you sooner."

"What do you mean?" Tynan frowned as he stepped closer.

"Maybe we should discuss this somewhere more private?"

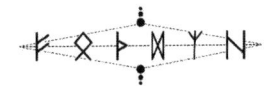

---

"Make yourself at home," Thane told Anya as they all entered his house, "I'll—"

"I'll make some drinks. You two can go to the living room. Just don't unpause my game," Tynan interrupted, beating Thane to it.

Thane shook his head, but led the way, making himself comfortable on the sofa, stretching his arm across the back cushions.

Instead of sitting in the armchair like he'd expected, Anya sat beside him, curling her feet beneath her and clasping her hands together on her lap.

"What were you saying about the acid?" Thane asked, needing to fill the silence.

Why did he feel so awkward? He was never nervous like

this, especially around women. It was usually them that steered clear of him.

"I was just saying that no conventional acids will be able to eat through the silver chains like I assumed you were after."

"That was what we were hoping for."

"There are a few acids that will dissolve the silver, but that will take hours which you just won't have. Not only that. They give off a noxious gas that in such a confined area could cause problems."

"It would draw too much attention," Thane sighed, slouching back into the cushions, rubbing a hand across his face.

He had hoped it would be something simple, instead he found himself at yet another dead end. What was he going to do? He needed a way of breaking those chains. Brute strength wouldn't work on such things. He could see they'd been strengthened by a spell, meaning Lucas wouldn't be able to break free. Even both of them pulling together was unlikely to do a thing. The acid had been his only lead.

"What about magic?" Anya suggested, shuffling on the sofa so that she faced him.

"What?"

"Well, before I wouldn't have thought about it, but surely a witch or something would know a way to break them?"

"It's possible, but I doubt the witches I know would be able to help."

Heleana was an incredibly talented witch, but she used her powers to heal and to foresee the future. He doubted she would know such a thing. Then again, she might know someone who did.

"What about Erebus?" Tynan suggested as he entered carrying three drinks.

"Erebus?" Anya asked, knitting her eyebrows together.

"He's a demon," Thane answered, running his hand through his hair.

Maybe Tynan was onto something. Erebus was likely to ask for something in return, but what would that matter if it helped Lucas? Anya would finally have her father and he would see his friend free once more.

"How could a demon help? Do they have magic?"

"Yes. Very powerful magic."

"He's a Guardian just like us. Only, being a demon means he tends to stay on his own plane. He won't like being asked to come top-side. But it's worth a shot, right?" Tynan asked, taking his seat on the floor in front of the TV.

Thane considered Erebus a friend, but he and Lucas had never seen eye to eye.

Would he help, knowing who they were trying to save?

# Chapter 26

Anya grew tired after a long and disappointing day.

When Thane and Tynan had turned up at the book store, she'd assumed they'd come to tell her their plan, but like her own searching, they'd come up empty-handed.

Who was this Erebus they spoke of? Why did his name sound so familiar?

Suddenly a loud knock sounded at the door, making her jump out of her skin.

"That's probably Thane. Let him back in while I kill this boss," Tynan spoke around a mouthful of cake, making her chuckle.

"Hey," she called as she opened the door, expecting to come face to face with Thane.

Instead, a tall, muscular man with eyes like fire stared down at her with a sly grin.

"You must be Anya," he replied, his voice soft and lilted as he looked her up and down. "You've certainly changed over the years."

Anya continued to stare at him, unable to move, or speak.

"Don't panic. I'm not here to eat your soul," he joked, trying to put her at ease. It didn't work.

Never had she expected to come face to face with a demon.

He was nothing like she'd imagined. Not that she knew what to expect. Just, something different. Perhaps it was because Tynan told her that demons stayed on their own plane, that they didn't like coming '*top-side*', as he called it. But this man in front of her looked like any other man you might see walking down the street. Except for those eyes. His eyes seemed to reflect the flames of hell, shimmering all different shades of orange, red and yellow, reminding her of the face from her memories.

How was it possible that she knew this demon?

"Is Thane here?"

"No," she replied, shaking her head vigorously. "He left about an hour ago. He didn't say where he was going, or when he'd be back."

"Erebus," Tynan called from behind her, pushing past to embrace the man before them.

"Since when were we on a hugging basis, cat," he mocked, tapping a hand across Tynan's back.

"Don't play coy. You know you missed me."

"Like a hole in the head," he replied with a smirk, rolling his eyes. "Where is Thane? He said this was important."

"He left to speak with Edwin."

To her surprise the demon growled, the fire in his eyes intensifying.

Did he not like Edwin? Or was he annoyed that Thane had left?

"He should be back soon. Come in and I'll let him know you're here."

Anya didn't know why she felt so uneasy around him. But as she sat watching him and Tynan play a game, acting like old friends, she couldn't get comfortable. She squirmed in her seat, fiddling with her hair and the hem of her skirt.

Why was his presence bothering her more than any other person she'd met? He seemed like a nice guy. Friendly and playful. She doubted Thane or Tynan would be friends with someone who wasn't. But there was something about him that put her on edge.

"Do I bother you?" he asked, spinning around on the floor to face her.

Anya had been so absorbed in her thoughts, she hadn't even noticed Tynan exit the room, leaving her alone with him.

"No," she lied, sinking into the cushions further.

"Don't lie to me. You're nervous. Why?"

Anya shrugged her shoulders, unable to give him a clear answer. Truth was, she didn't know why he bothered her.

"Perhaps I should come back later," he suggested with a sigh.

"No," she blurted, sitting up straight in her chair. "I'm sorry, but we need you to help free Lucas."

"I see. So that's why Thane called me," he commented, scratching his stubbled chin. "Lucas and I never really got on. Why would I want to help free him?"

"Surely you wouldn't leave one of your own at the mercy of a hunter?"

"But he's not one of my own, is he? I'm a demon. He's a shifter."

Anya didn't understand. How could he leave a fellow Guardian in the hands of a hunter? Surely he knew what they were capable of. What could Lucas have done to make him hate him that much?

"He's still a Guardian. I thought you protected one another?"

"Tell that to your dear old dad," he retorted, scrunching his nose up in disgust.

"How did you know?"

"That's he's your dad? I keep up to date with my work, even from different planes. You never know when war will involve us all."

She supposed that made sense. Knowledge was power after all, and this man seemed to radiate power like a storm. She felt sorry for anybody who ended up on the wrong side of him.

"Then you must know that I'll do anything to see him free."

Anya expected him to jump at the chance to have her in his debt, but instead he shook his head, pinching the bridge of his nose between his index finger and thumb.

"I doubt there is much you can do for me, little Wolf."

"No, but maybe I can," Thane growled from the open doorway, making Anya flinch.

How could he have come in so silently that neither of them seemed to notice?

Anya turned to Thane as he stood, gripping hold of the door frame with one hand, a menacing power coming off of him in waves.

Was he angry with her for speaking to the demon without him?

"Ah, just the man I was waiting for."

"Erebus, why are you here? You were supposed to meet me at headquarters."

"And have to suffer one of Edwin's lectures? No thank you," he replied, batting his hand in dismissal. "Besides. I wanted to see how much the girl had grown before I agreed to anything."

How was it possible that he remembered her, yet all she could remember from him was the fire in his eyes? Who was he?

"Well now you've seen her, you can go," Thane growled,

taking a step toward them.

Anya was confused. She thought they were friends. So why didn't Thane want him here? Maybe her inkling had been right. Perhaps the demon did mean to harm her.

"Well, it's a good job I did come here first. Seeing the determination despite her fear has swayed my decision," Erebus commented, turning to her with a sly smile. "I will help you free Lucas. But, only if you agree to help me when the time comes."

"Deal."

"Not you, sugar. Him," Erebus commented, turning back to Thane, crossing his arms over his chest.

"I'll be in your debt."

"Wait," Anya called, jumping to her feet and taking a step toward Thane. "You don't know what he's asking for. Shouldn't you find out first?"

"I know what I'm doing, Anya. We need him. And I know what he'll want in return," Thane shrugged, turning his attention back to Erebus. "Things are in turmoil down in hell, aren't they? Are you sure you want to bring in an outsider?"

"I don't have a lot of choice, Thane."

"Then you can count on my help whenever you need it."

"Good. I'll be in touch with a spell to break him free," Erebus replied with a smirk, standing and heading toward Thane.

Thane held out his hand, placing it against his chest, halting him in his tracks.

"You have a week, tops, otherwise our deal is off."

"Don't fret. I know just the man I need to pay a small visit to."

# Chapter 27

Anya was going out of her mind with boredom and worry after spending the last four days at home. Alone.

Leaning her head back against the soft cushions of her sofa, she sighed and shielded her eyes from the bright morning sun.

She wanted to go for a run in the hopes of curbing her boredom and working out some of the tension stiffening her muscles, but she didn't dare. The feeling of being watched hadn't stopped since she'd returned home from Thane's the other day, even though she remained indoors.

She was scared to venture outside alone and didn't want to ask for help. She already assumed that Thane thought of her as weak, and she was determined to prove him otherwise. Always asking others to help wouldn't strengthen her argument.

Anya caught a glimpse of her reflection in the TV and gasped as her eyes flickered from their usual green to a dim yellowy brown. That wasn't normal. She knew what she was now, but she'd never seen her eyes that colour before. She needed to learn how to control her emotions before someone dangerous noticed what she was, but how was she to learn when she wouldn't ask for help?

Anya groaned and slumped down further into the cushions.

Maybe the journal Hugh had given her would teach her something new.

She lifted her arm from over her eyes and peered across at her backpack thrown in the corner by the TV. But what if it was a trap? Maybe it was Hugh who had figured out what she was. He was the one who spent the most time with her after all. It made sense he'd be the one informing his dad about her.

But she had to know what was in that journal. Some deep feeling was egging her on, telling her it was important. Her inner wolf perhaps?

Slowly, Anya pushed out of her chair and crouched down in front of her bag, pulling the journal free and tracing her fingers along the leather jacket.

She didn't get a chance to debate whether she should read it or not before a loud knock sounded at the front door, making her jump out of her skin.

Stuffing the book back into her bag, Anya sprung to her feet and headed to the door.

She stretched her hand toward the doorknob and hesitated.

What if it was the person responsible for making her feel uneasy? Had they seen her pull the journal free?

Anya pushed the door open a crack and peeked around the edge.

"Hey," she greeted when she spotted a familiar face.
"I've been asked to fetch you."
"What for?"
"Nothing to worry about," Tynan smiled, combing his

fingers through his golden locks, "Edwin's called a meeting of the Guard and Thane's insisting you attend. Erebus has come through with a plan to free Lucas."

Had the demon really come through so quickly? What could this spell he'd acquired entail? She needed to know. She also needed to check on Thane. What if the demon already asked for his help?

"But I'm not a Guardian," she whispered, twiddling her thumbs.

"No, but Thane said you deserve to be there and nobody will argue with that. But I warn you some of the Guards aren't friendly."

"I'm sure I'll manage. After all, I deal with Thane."

"Yeah, that's true," Tynan chuckled, draping his arm across her shoulders.

Anya wasn't afraid of the Guardians. She knew that Thane, Tynan and Edwin would never let them do anything to her. No, she was afraid to go outside, even if she had Tynan with her. The feeling of someone watching her had finally vanished, but in its place was dread. Something deep down insisted that she was in danger, but from what she didn't know. What if that danger lurked outside in the alleyways or in the shadow of the trees?

Anya chewed on her lip and took one last glance outside, before grabbing her jacket hooked on the railing.

Anything had to be better than staying here alone. Tynan would protect her from whatever threat was lurking nearby, wouldn't he?

"You'll be fine," Tynan reassured her, pulling her toward him as she shrugged into her coat.

Being this close to someone she had learnt to trust, someone she cared about filled her with comfort and confidence.

Perhaps she was panicking over nothing. Maybe it was just her nerves playing tricks on her, after all, the thought of being surrounded by so many unfamiliar faces did unnerve her.

"Do I need anything else?"

"Nope. Let's go." Tynan didn't wait for a reply, just took a hold of her hand and pulled her down the steps.

On the walk to Edwin's, Anya felt her nerves kicking in again.

This would be the first time she'd seen him since their argument over a month ago. She wasn't sure what she was going to say to him.

She still loved him as much as she always had. He would always be a father figure to her, but she wasn't sure whether she forgave him for his deceit. It was Thane that had insisted she be there, not him. That hurt.

Then there was Duncan, the man who'd forced himself on her. A man Thane had chased away. What if he was there too? Would he stay away, scared of Thane? Or would he wait for her to be alone to try his luck a second time?

Tynan warned her that not all of the Guards were friendly, and even Thane had told her something similar in the past. What if there were more people like Duncan, just waiting for her to be alone, to scare or hurt her?

Anya shook her head, trying to push the fears from her mind. It didn't matter what or who they were, she had people who would protect her. All she had to do was make sure she was never alone with anyone.

"What's wrong?" Tynan asked, slowing his pace to walk alongside her. "You're never this quiet."

"Sorry," Anya mumbled, spinning a stray lock of hair around her finger, "just thinking."

Tynan stopped, turned around and held her by the shoulders. "You have nothing to worry about. Erebus has found a way to get Lucas out, and Edwin has a great idea for a distraction. Your dad will be free soon."

Her heart skipped several beats.

She might finally be able to hold her dad properly. Talk to him without looking over her shoulder. Help him become healthy again. She would finally have a family. But why did she feel so unhappy?

Was it guilt because of how things were with Edwin? No, that wasn't it. She knew in her heart that she would always love Edwin, no matter what. So what was bothering her?

"Will you and Thane leave once Lucas has been freed?"

It was a question she dreaded the answer to, but she needed to know.

She may have her dad back, and in time she knew she would forgive Edwin, but Thane and Tynan had come to mean a lot to her. Especially Thane. She feared she loved him. A foolish thing to do, but she just couldn't control her overwhelming need for him in her life.

"I plan on sticking around. But I can't speak for Thane," he paused, looking over his shoulder at her. "With Lucas found, Thane won't need to travel so frequently, but he likes his space and this town holds a lot of painful memories for him. I'm not sure if he'll want to return or help with the hunters."

"I guess Thane hasn't found the reason for the hunters gaining strength and numbers yet then?"

Tynan shrugged in response.

It surprised her that Thane hadn't told him anything. Surely he must have found out some information since joining them. He was a Guard, he would know what to look for. And Tynan was his friend. Why would he not confide in him? Anya used to share everything with Keri, right down to the last detail. But since she'd come back, things had changed. Keri had joined the hunters and become a killer. But even before she learnt that she didn't feel the same about her. Anya no longer felt like she could trust her.

Would she capture her? Or kill her if she found out what she was? Had she told anybody else about Edwin's secrecy and strange friends? Surely not. They would have come for him already if that was true. Maybe Keri had dismissed or forgotten Anya's ramblings.

As they continued on their way, Anya couldn't help but notice how quiet everything was.

Usually this stretch of road was full of people everywhere, pushing and shoving around the market. Today, nothing. Even the stalls weren't open.

Tynan seemed to notice as well, constantly checking over his shoulder and flinching at every sound. Could he sense something she couldn't?

"I don't like this," he whispered, taking a step closer to her side, "It's too quiet and something doesn't feel right."

"You feel it too?" she asked, glancing over her shoulder toward a dark alleyway, "like someone's watching?"

"No. It's something else."

Anya turned and scanned the horizon for anything out of the ordinary, trying to concentrate on the feeling to see if she could pinpoint the source. The action was so difficult and unnatural. She wasn't used to her heightened senses and didn't know how to control them.

Straining to see further, her vision blurred in and out of focus as she stared ahead at a black mass in the distance. Her eyes refusing to focus on the shadowy figure. Unable to decipher whether it was human or not.

"Ty?"

"Shh," he snapped, covering her mouth with his hand, pulling her back against his chest.

Anya stopped struggling and listened. Footsteps headed toward them, the sound bouncing off of the narrow streets around them. It sounded like a group of people.

"You need to run Anya."

"But—"

"Trust me, I'll be fine. I'll be more likely to get injured if you stay here because I'll be worrying about you."

Anya nodded, turning around quickly to run the rest of the way to Edwin's, hoping she reached his house before whoever was approaching caught up.

She ran straight into Hugh's arms, falling back into a heap on the floor, rubbing her arm where she'd landed. She pushed to her feet and frowned.

"Sorry Anya," Hugh sighed, pressing something sharp into her arm.

Looking down to see what was causing the pain, she saw the needle buried deep in her skin, making her sway on her feet. Bile filled her throat as her vision blurred, but she couldn't fight it. Darkness crept into the corner of her eyes.

"Anya!" she heard Tynan roar as she drifted to sleep in Hugh's arms.

# Chapter 28

As Thane sat in the meeting room, surrounded by people he tolerated at best, an overwhelming feeling of dread washed over him.

Sitting up straight in his chair, his eyes glowing bright, he searched the room.

Nothing was out of place. Nobody giving off any unusual vibes, but where was Edwin? More importantly, where was Tynan with Anya? It wasn't like either of them to be late.

"Something wrong, wolf?" Duncan smiled, causing Thane's hackles to rise.

Thane jumped out of his chair and wrapped his hand around Duncan's throat, squeezing hard, his claws and fangs elongating to deadly points.

"Put him down, Thane. You know he only likes to wind you up," Edwin instructed upon entering the room, limping slightly on his left leg.

Thane watched him all the way to his chair. Only when he was seated did he release Duncan and walk toward him.

"Don't ask—" Edwin commented when Thane stood over him, arms crossed over his chest, waiting for an explanation. "I had a small run-in with a couple of hunters, but don't worry, they've been neatly disposed of."

Thane didn't like it. If Richard knew those men had come to Edwin for information and neither of them returned, his suspicions would grow leaving Edwin vulnerable to another attack. He may be a good fighter, strong and well trained, but Richard had numbers, and Edwin was growing old. He couldn't fight for long.

Thane sighed, taking a seat next to him, slouching back in his chair waiting for Tynan to appear.

Edwin had told Thane he didn't want Anya to attend the meeting, fearful of the other Guards, but Thane insisted. It was a meeting about Lucas after all, she had a right to be there. If any of the others, especially Duncan, got too close or said something unacceptable, Edwin should put them in their place. He was their leader.

Thane watched the other men and women, noting their impatience when Edwin didn't begin.

"Do we really need to wait for the pup? She's not a Guard and has no right to be here," Duncan muttered to another member, making him laugh.

"Careful Duncan, I can only control Thane for so long. You know as well as I do, he isn't one to listen to sense."

Both men went silent, bowing their heads.

"Thane?" Heleana whispered beside him, taking her seat. "Is it true, Anya is your mate?"

Nothing slipped by Heleana. She'd been a healer to the Guardians for years, always managing to find out information before anybody else. The one person in this room, aside from Edwin that Thane actually cared for.

"How long have you known?" he sighed.

"The moment I made you that mask."

Interesting he thought, turning to question her further. He knew she was a gifted woman, often seeing things before anybody else, but this was extraordinary, even for her. Whoever ended up being her mate would be a lucky man.

"How—" he began, pausing when he caught sight of Tynan staggering into the room, alone and injured.

Thane jumped to his feet and met him halfway across the room.

"Thane!" he cried, collapsing against him. "T—they took her. I tried to stop them, but there were too many."

Heleana rushed to his side, taking Tynan off of him to inspect his wounds. The way she moved, the way she ran her hands over his body reminding him so much of Anya, his heart clenched.

"Where?" he managed to ask, anger lacing his voice turning it deep and gravelly.

"There were too many, Thane, you won't make it by yourself."

"Where?!" he growled.

Nothing Tynan could say to him would talk him out of going after her.

"Near Oleander's. They ambushed us. They were just so quiet, I don't understand it."

Thane didn't wait for him to finish before he sprinted from the room.

He refused to believe she was lost, that he couldn't save her before it was too late. He would not lose her now, not when he hadn't told her the truth. How much he needed her.

He ran fast, his muscles protesting against him as he forced them to work harder than he ever had in his human form. He would not fail her, or Lucas. Not again.

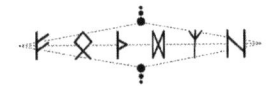

When Thane reached the tavern, he could still smell her scent on the wind.

He scanned the area, looking for any clues who had taken her. He knew the hunters had been involved, but who was the one to give the order?

In the distance Thane spotted something glisten on the floor. Fisting the metal in his hand, he growled. It was a chain he'd seen on the boy, Hugh. Anya must have grabbed a hold of it when he took her.

"Thane," a familiar voice whispered from behind him, "come here."

He followed the faint sound of Oleander's voice, finding him hidden beside his cellar.

"There are still some of them left, I've been watching them. Two strayed close enough for me to take care of, but I can see four more."

"Where?" Thane growled, his teeth already sharpening in his mouth.

"Two on the corner by the flower shop. One up top," Oleander pointed to the man on the roof, pausing to search for the last man. "The other is coming this way. He must have heard you."

Thane needed vengeance, needed to kill them all. How dare they take something that was his.

He waited, crouching down ready to pounce on the man as he rounded the corner.

Claws slashing out, Thane grabbed him by his throat, snapping his teeth shut just inches from the guy's face.

"Where is she?" he demanded.

"I don't know what you're talking about," the man pleaded, scratching at his own neck to loosen Thane's restricting hold.

"Liar," Thane roared, squeezing his fingers tighter.

"Shh, the others will hear you," Oleander commented close to his ear, like a whisper on the breeze. There one minute, gone the next.

"I didn't see, just knew we were here to find someone, maybe get our first kill."

Thane recognized the man from the arena. One of the new recruits who had competed against him. Perhaps he was telling the truth.

"Then you're no use to me," Thane shrugged, clenching his hand even tighter and flexing his claws on his other hand ready to slash down.

"Wait!" the man choked, coughing and spluttering when Thane loosened his vice-like grip. "I might be able to get you inside, to find out more information."

"I don't need you to get in."

"Richard's gone on lockdown. Everybody is to report in and out at the gate. You'll never get past them alone."

"That's where you're wrong."

Thane was finished talking to the man. He may have proved helpful by letting him in on the tightened security, but that meant little to him. Richard wasn't suspicious of him yet, and he would walk in right under their noses.

With the first man disposed of, Thane spotted Oleander on the roof with the second, drinking from his neck until he sagged in his arms.

Two down, two to go.

Thane stalked the men, watching as they grew more and more restless.

All of them were new recruits. This couldn't be the work of Richard. He would never send rookies to do such an important task. This had the boy written all over it, but why? Thane knew the boy had feelings for Anya, knew he wanted her to himself, but to kidnap her? What was he thinking?

He growled low, infuriated for not seeing this coming.

One of the men heard him, flinching and aiming a gun his way. He elbowed his friend in the side and pointed for him to flank around the area Thane stood. Thane laughed. It would do them no good with only two of them left.

Thane rested his back against the stone wall behind him, crossing his arms over his chest, waiting.

"What are you doing here?" one of them asked, appearing around the corner.

"Didn't know Hugh asked you to join this exercise?" the other commented.

"He didn't," Thane smiled, his fangs glistening in the sun and his claws protruding from his fingers.

As quickly as they noticed, their necks were sliced, blood pooling at their feet before they fell in a heap on the floor.

"Nice work, Thane. I'm impressed."

"I'm not done yet."

"You'll need help getting her out of there if that's where he's taken her."

"I work better alone."

"Don't be so stubborn. You might get past security but you won't get out with her. Let me help you."

"Why? What's in it for you?"

"I want revenge just like you do, but for different reasons."

Thane knew little about Oleander's past, only that his bride and child had been killed by hunters, but he thought those responsible had all been killed. Perhaps he'd discovered something new. A command from a higher member. Whatever the reason, Thane was grateful for the assistance. He was going to need it.

Thane and Oleander sat outside the hunter's headquarters watching as men and women came and left.

The man earlier hadn't lied. Richard had put extra men on security. It was going to be difficult to sneak in, and impossible to get her out if she was inside. Maybe Richard was involved after all.

Tightening the hold on his emotions, Thane straightened his back and headed toward the gate, leaving Oleander to sneak over the fence while the guards were distracted.

"Halt," the man on watch commanded, stepping in front of Thane, blanching of colour when he looked hesitantly up. "What's your name?"

"Thane. Richard will be expecting me."

"Ok. Your name's here. Go on through."

Thane nodded, pushing his way past before the man had a chance to move out of his way. He was pissed, and god help anyone who got in his way.

Once inside the gates, Thane met with Oleander by a concealed door around the side of the main building. He'd spotted it on an earlier visit making a note to keep it in mind for later.

Thane was surprised at how fast and stealthy the man moved. He'd heard that Oleander was a good fighter, faster than most shifters, but he'd never seen him in action before. Impressed, Thane slipped through the door first, motioning for him to follow once he knew the coast was clear.

Nobody was in sight. A complete contrast to the teeming numbers of people patrolling the perimeter. It was just too easy to make their way through the halls, making Thane suspicious.

"It's no good, Thane," Oleander whispered, following his gaze as they passed the newly glowing door that concealed Lucas. "We can't risk freeing him with so many hunters around. It'll be hard enough to free the girl."

"She could be down there with him. Why else would they have so many men here and nowhere inside?"

"A trap perhaps? Or maybe Hugh set this all up so that nobody would notice he and Anya were missing?"

Thane hated to admit it, but Oleander had a point. This was all too easy and stunk of a trap. He couldn't risk falling for it in order to free Lucas earlier than planned. He had to stick to the task at hand. Anya's safety came first. Lucas wasn't in any immediate danger. She was.

Thane scrubbed a hand over his face and sighed, the stubble across his jaw scratching his palm. He needed to find her and tell her how much she meant to him. What she was to him.

"We need to find Richard," Thane insisted, clenching his fists tight.

"What good will that do?"

"I don't think the order came from him. The work is too sloppy. He'll be furious if anybody has interfered with his plans and might just slip up and tell us where we can find Hugh."

"It's worth a shot. He doesn't seem too fond of his son anyway."

Thane nodded, explaining to him that he had gained Richard's trust whilst here, hoping to get close enough to Lucas so he could find a way to free him. Now his deceit had another purpose.

Stomping down the corridor toward the main hall, the same overwhelming sensation Thane had felt earlier washed over him. He knew it was her then, that she was in trouble. He had to make this quick.

"Richard?" he practically growled as he burst through the heavy doors.

"Thane?" Richard flinched, jumping out of his chair, "I wasn't expecting to see you today. What's wrong?"

"Where is Hugh?"

"I'd like to know that myself," he grumbled, slouching back into his chair, spinning the pen he held between his two index fingers. "He informed me of an attack so I doubled my men and pulled back several on hunts. Yet nothing has come of it."

Thane wanted to punch something. Anything. He knew Hugh was responsible for this, but to fool his own dad. The boy had guts. Now Thane and Oleander were in the middle of a feud between two hunters. Stuck in a place surrounded by people who would kill both of them if they found out what they were.

Thane turned, expecting to see Oleander just behind him, but the damned vampire wasn't there. Thane hoped he was waiting outside so Richard wouldn't see him. If he wasn't, he would be stuck here, alone.

"What do you want with Hugh?" Richard asked, regaining Thane's attention.

"He's taken something that belongs to me and I want it back."

"That was indeed foolish of him. He always was a stupid boy. Weak, just like his mother. Not a fighter or a leader like ourselves."

Thane wasn't so sure he agreed. The boy had to be brave to stand against his father, the notorious hunter. Richard had never lost his mark, until now, and it was his own son that was responsible. If Thane hadn't been so furious, he might have been impressed.

Richard watched him, scratching his face, and tracing a finger over his scar.

"Send the boy back to me in one piece once you've retrieved your possession, won't you?"

"I make no promises."

"This is why I like you, Thane. Your honesty," Richard laughed, resting his hands behind his neck.

Thane smiled to himself as he left the room. What a fool Richard was. Nobody would have guessed that he could be won over so easily. Perhaps he wasn't the big bad hunter everyone believed him to be after all.

Thane stomped down the halls, clenching his fists tight.

He was still no closer to finding her. This whole trip had been a waste of time. When he found the boy, he would make him pay. If he'd so much as laid a finger on her, Thane would make sure he suffered before he killed him.

All this time he'd been watching Richard, never expecting Hugh would be the one to pose a threat.

"Why didn't I see this coming?" he grumbled to himself, feeling like a fool. Now it was too late. The only times he'd seen Hugh was at the pub and here. He had no idea where to start looking.

# Chapter 29

Anya awoke half in a daze. Slowly she opened her eyes and glanced around the room she lay in.

"W-where am I?" she asked, rubbing at her eyes as she took in the small, dark space, wondering how she'd got there.

"Somewhere safe," a quiet voice replied.

Anya searched the room for that voice, trying to focus on the sounds of rustling she could hear as they moved in the distance, but there was no mistaking who that voice belonged to.

"What did you do to me?"

"You'll be fine once the effects wear off. It was just a mild tranquillizer to make you a little more compliant."

She couldn't believe it. Hugh had injected her and taken her somewhere. No doubt he planned to kill her.

How did he know where she would be? How did he find out?

Anya sat up, rubbing her aching arms and legs, feeling

battered and bruised. Had she put up a fight? Or was it the effects of the drug?

Oh god. Tynan. Had they killed him?

Her heart clenched as tears filled her eyes, but she squeezed them shut. She couldn't let him think she was afraid.

"How long have you known what you are?" Hugh asked her.

Anya remained silent, unable to talk past the lump forming in her throat.

She searched the room for any means of escape, hoping that as soon as her body stopped feeling sluggish, she could make a run for it. She may be a novice and not know how to control her abilities yet, but she knew if she pushed herself hard enough and focused, she would be faster than him.

Hugh walked out of the shadows and gripped her chin between his fingers, holding it firm. "How long?" he demanded, his face too close to her own, his eyes hard and steady.

"Just over a month," she spat, rubbing at her sore jaw when he finally released her.

"After you found out about us? That doesn't make sense."

She nodded, confused by what he was saying.

"Why would they wait so long to tell you? Did they not know either?"

Anya wrapped her arms around her middle as Hugh continued to ramble on to himself.

"How did you find out?" she finally asked, unable to remain silent.

"I've known for a while. It doesn't matter how I found out," he sighed, moving closer to her. "Richard's been following you since he found out you were back in town. He's been suspicious of you from the get-go."

Hugh kicked a small wooden table in the corner, causing it to collapse and make a loud bang on the floor. "I told him he was a fool, but I guess that was me in the end."

"I'm still the same person now as I was when you met me. It's just now I know what I was all along," she whispered, trying to reason with him.

"I know that. It doesn't matter."

"But—"

"Shh," he snapped, staring behind him for a few minutes.

Her heart was racing in anticipation as Hugh began to fiddle around in his jacket pocket.

"What are you doing?" she squealed, retreating as far back as she could. But instead of the knife or gun she'd been expecting, he pulled out his phone and told someone they could come in.

She prayed it wouldn't be Richard. Hoping that she still had a chance to win Hugh over. She was completely defenceless and could barely move, but she could still speak and would try her best to make him see sense.

Yes, she was half shifter but that didn't mean she was a monster.

Slowly, she pushed to her feet, determined to prove she was strong. That she wasn't afraid of him, even though inside she trembled. Her body felt heavy and her vision blurred, making her eyes water and burn, but still she pushed herself, leaning against the wooden wall when her legs wobbled below her.

Hugh turned to her and raised a brow, but smiled, his eyes glinting in the flickering light above them.

"Impressive. That tranq should have kept you out for a few more hours."

Anya just stared at him, frowning.

"There was always something different about you. Something unique," he continued, cocking his head to one side watching her try to stand by herself. "I guess I was right after all."

Thane told her that he believed she was a healer, not that she really understood what that entailed, but apparently it made her more approachable. Maybe Hugh had mistaken his attraction to her as that of a comfortable feeling.

"Do you plan to kill me?"

"No. I'm supposed to tell Richard if I find out anything," Hugh groaned, rubbing at his temples. "I'm not meant to interfere, but I don't think I can stand by anymore."

"What do you mean?"

Before Hugh had a chance to answer, Keri burst into the room wrapping her arms around Anya.

"He hasn't touched you has he?"

"No I haven't," he bit back, heading toward the door. "Just watch her until I get back."

"Yeah, yeah," she groaned, waving her hand in dismissal.

Anya smiled, grateful for Keri's concern. Perhaps she hadn't changed too much after all. Maybe she wouldn't want to harm her for being different like she'd feared.

A loud bang sounded as Hugh exited the small building, shortly followed by the sound of a car engine.

Keri stood and peered through the small window, smiling wide when she turned back to face Anya.

"Can you walk yet?"

"I don't know."

"Come," Keri commanded, linking her arms with Anya's and pulling her toward the exit.

"What if he comes back?"

"Don't worry. Richard is furious with him. He won't be back hours," Keri replied, peeking around the doorway.

"Quick. Hugh has a couple of thugs on patrol so we need to move before they circle back."

Nodding, Anya followed Keri out of the house and into the darkening woods.

Still, she didn't recognize where she was, but she could smell something familiar as a strong unnerving feeling crept along her skin.

"Where are we?" Anya asked, needing to know so she could tell the Guards its whereabouts if they asked her.

"The last place any shifter would look. Right under their noses."

"What was that?"

Anya ducked and dodged thorns and low branches before colliding into the back of Keri. She hadn't even notice her come to a stop in front of her.

Anya fell to the floor, scratching her arms and legs as she landed.

Keri turned back to look at her, her eyes wide and glassy, flashing crimson in the setting sun.

No. That can't be right. Why would her eyes change like that? She must be seeing things. A side effect of the drugs Hugh had given her.

Shaking her head, Anya pushed to her feet and wiped the debris off her clothes.

Blood trickled down her arm, dripping onto the ground by her feet.

"Let me see," Keri asked in a taut voice, snatching her arm and pulling it close to her face for a better look.

"Just surface scratches," she commented, still holding onto her arm in a vice like grip.

"Keri?" Anya asked, watching as she continued to study her cuts, licking her lips and tightening her grip.

Something wasn't right.

Keri inched her face closer to the cut on Anya's arm, her eyes definitely glowing a sickening scarlet.

Anya froze as a wave of fear washed over her for what was about to happen. But Keri paused, squeezing onto her arm tight, making her squirm under the pressure.

"Why did you have to cut yourself," she groaned, trying to

speak around canines that had grown several inches longer, "this makes my job so much more difficult."

"Y—you're a vampire?"

"Way to point out the obvious," Keri drawled, rolling her eyes.

"Since when?"

"Now let's see," she replied in a snarky tone, tapping a finger on her chin, "I was attacked by a shifter, just like you, who left me for dead. Lucky for me, I guess, that some vampire happened to pass and decided it would be a waste not to turn me."

What could she possibly say to something like that? It made sense that Keri would hate her kind if that was how they'd treated her, but they were supposed to be friends. They weren't so different after all.

"Your blood smells so sweet. So tempting. I've never tasted a shifter before."

"You can fight it, Keri. We're friends."

"I don't want to fight it," she roared, slamming Anya's back against a tree, the vibrations travelling down her spine taking her breath away and making her vision waiver.

"You act like you're completely innocent, but you must have known. Ever since you've returned you've been distant and wary around me. Don't make out that you still care."

"But you're like me. We should be sticking together, helping one another like we used to. If the hunters find out what you are, they'll kill you."

"That's where you're wrong, chick. Richard already knows what I am. He's the one who spared me when he came across me in the midst of turning."

"That doesn't make sense."

"Doesn't it? Richard isn't human himself. I guess he pitied me. And now," Keri paused, pressing something sharp into Anya's leg, making her cry out in pain, "I'll bring you in as an offering of my loyalty. He's been searching for you, '*the long-lost daughter*' for years. How he'll praise me when he realizes I was the one to find you. So very clever hiding it from me all this time."

Anya's heart raced, the pain in her thigh spreading down her leg.

How could Keri be so cold and heartless? She was supposed to be her friend, and all she could think about was getting in Richard's good books.

"Do you realise how hard it's been trying to catch you? You'd already be his if that stupid wolf hadn't interrupted me. And that damn hottie taking you home after I spiked your drink. What a waste."

Her body trembled at the thought of being at Richard's mercy, just waiting for him to kill or torture her.

All this time it was Keri's presence she'd been feeling.

Suddenly she caught a faint scent in the breeze. A mild aftershave tickled her nose

A twig snapped in the distance.

Keri must have heard it too, turning her head in the same direction, scowling into the shadows of the trees.

Please let it be Thane, Anya thought to herself, praying that somehow he knew where Hugh had taken her.

All this time she'd been scared of Richard and Hugh, fearful of how much they knew, when the person she should've been afraid of was Keri. The one person who seemed to know exactly who and what she was.

"Show yourself. I know there's someone there," Keri called, pointing a small dagger out in front of her.

No sooner had the words left her mouth, when a tall and slender man emerged from the trees, his eyes like liquid mercury as he circled around them.

"You really think you'll hit me with that, Keri," he snickered, his voice seeming to bounce off the trees, coming from all directions as he disappeared from sight once more.

"Y—you can't kill me," Keri stuttered, the unsteady rhythm of her heart echoing in Anya's ears as she searched around nervously. "You sired me."

"You're such a disappointment, Keri. Killing you would be a mercy."

"The council would be furious."

"When they find out you've been working for the hunters, they'll reward me for disposing of my own mistake."

Anya didn't know what to do. Here she was, covered in cuts, with a vampire on either side of her. But as she looked at the male, she couldn't help but wonder who he was, and why she thought she recognised him.

"Don't come any closer," Keri begged, pulling Anya in front of her and holding the stained dagger to her throat, "or I'll kill her before you reach me. I know you're here for her."

"Actually, I'm here for you," he replied, his voice a whisper on the breeze, "she's just an added bonus."

Keri squeezed Anya's shoulder tighter, pressing the knife deeper into her neck, making her choke.

"You think lover boy will reward you knowing you're responsible for killing his prize? The one person he's been searching for these past twenty-plus years?"

"Shut up," Keri screeched, searching around her once everything was silent.

Did this other vampire mean to save her, or was he planning on finishing what Keri had started? Anya's heart pounded loudly in her chest, causing her ribs to ache and her legs to wobble.

If only she hadn't been so stubborn to ask for help. She might have been able to control her abilities better and fight her way free, running from them while they fought one another.

Keri lowered her knife a fraction, peering around the tree behind them, searching for the man. No sooner had her head turned, was the man upon them, lifting Keri off her feet by her throat, his eyes now tinged red.

"W—who are you?" Anya asked, her hands and voice shaking as she scrambled away from them.

"I'm here to help you Anya, but you need to keep back. Your blood is hard to resist."

Anya looked down at her arms and frowned. The blood was already beginning to dry and heal where the cuts were shallow. Then she remembered the stinging sensation in her leg from where Keri had stabbed her with something sharp.

A strong burning sensation travelled down the length of her thigh, causing her chest to tighten and her body to sway. Looking down slowly, she noticed blood soaking through her jeans. Could feel it rushing down her leg beneath the fabric, making her head woozy and her ears ring.

"I—"

"Your body blocked out the pain because of your need to run. You're bleeding quite badly."

Anya leaned back against a tree, unsure what to do. How was she supposed to get away now?

"Do you have your phone, Anya?" the man asked, tightening his grip around Keri's throat as his eyes seemed to glow brighter and more deadly.

She shook her head, remembering that she'd felt for it earlier and found it missing.

The man growled loudly in Keri's face when she struggled to free herself, drawing Anya's attention, her fangs protruding from her mouth once again.

"In my back pocket, you'll find my phone. Use it to contact someone to come and help you," he instructed, breaking her concentration.

"But—"

"I won't hurt you, Anya. I'm in control right now, but you

need to be quick."

Hesitantly, she pushed herself away from the tree, feeling the throb in her leg as it protested under her weight. There was no chance she would ever find her way out of this wood, let alone find her way home, or somewhere safe. She had no choice, she needed that phone.

Slowly Anya reached her hand toward him, brushing her fingers across his thigh. He tensed, his eyes flashing silvery red. So beautiful and mesmerising.

He squeezed his eyes shut and told her to hurry, breaking her free from the trance his eyes had put her under.

The moment she took a step back and unlocked the phone, the man vanished with Keri still in his grasp.

Was he going to kill her?

Anya stared off into the distance where they'd disappeared and sighed, swiping away a tear that rolled down her cheek.

Keri had wanted to take her to Richard, a man Anya feared more than anybody else. She'd even threatened to kill her in order to save herself. Those weren't the actions of a friend. Anya needed to remember that. She couldn't afford to feel sorry for her. Right now she needed to find a way of stopping the blood she could still feel trickling across her frozen skin.

Anya pulled the belt out from her jeans and used it to tourniquet her leg, helping to stop the flow of blood still staining her jeans, turning them a strange colour.

She looked down at the unlocked phone she'd taken from the vampire and swore.

No signal.

"Great," she groaned, hobbling toward another tree to lean against, "now what?"

# Chapter 30

Thane paced back and forth in front of Edwin's desk, waiting for some direction.

"You're going to wear a hole in my carpet soon, boy."

Thane turned his head to glare at Edwin without stopping. His jaw clenched tight.

It had been hours since Hugh had taken Anya, and he was still no closer to finding her.

He'd exhausted all of his ideas searching and decided to come to Edwin to see if he had any clues on where to go next. Standing here waiting for him to search and contact some of his spies was grating on Thane's nerves.

He needed to find her. He could feel her distress as though it were his own.

"I'm going as fast as I can Thane. I'm sorry."

"If he hurts her—"

"I know. But you won't be the only one who wishes to

seek vengeance should that happen," Edwin snapped, pushing to his feet, leaning his palms on his desk as he stared at Thane. "She's the closest thing I've ever had to a daughter and I won't let anybody hurt her."

Anya and Edwin had hardly spoken since she'd found out about Lucas. Thane could see how much it pained him to see her so distant, but he remained silent, allowing her to come to him when she was ready.

Thane felt a pang of guilt for losing his patience with possibly the one man who understood how he felt.

Twenty-seven years ago, Edwin's only son had disappeared, supposedly taken by the hunters. A year after that, his mate was killed, and with it his chance of a family. Anya was the closest thing he had to a family, and now she was missing. It had to be eating him up alive.

Tynan was right, he was a fool. A coward even for pushing her away, when all he wanted to do was pull her close and lose himself in her touch. If he'd just given into his feelings, let himself close to her, the bond between them would have grown.

He could feel her now. Knew she was afraid and in pain, but he couldn't locate her. It was as though there were a wall between them. A wall he no doubt built.

Thane growled loudly, plonking down in a chair beside him, holding his head between his hands.

"I don't understand how the boy found out," he grumbled into his hands.

"You said yourself that Richard was already suspicious of her. We all suspected that's why the hunters were growing in numbers. I guess we were right."

"Yes, but as far as I could see, Hugh and Richard didn't get along. Richard also seemed clueless that Hugh had taken her."

"Are you sure he wasn't lying?"

"Yes." Thane had watched him carefully when they spoke.

He could tell by his steady pulse and eyes that Richard had been telling the truth. In fact, Richard looked just as pissed off with Hugh as he was.

"Someone else must have known."

"Maybe," Edwin replied, scratching his bare chin, "but I'm sure the boy won't hurt her. It's clear he has feelings for her and wouldn't want to cause her harm, even if he now knows what she is,"

"That just makes him more dangerous," Thane argued, leaning forward, placing his hands on his knees, "you said before that he finds it difficult to control himself. If he's touched her—" Thane clenched his fists tight, blanching them of all colour. His bones popping loudly with the pressure.

"You called for me, Edwin?" a strident voice called, infuriating Thane further.

He wasn't in the mood to deal with Duncan now, baring his teeth as he walked past, causing him to flinch and move away.

"Yes. You've been watching Hugh for sometime. I want a list of places he usually visits to help narrow down our search," Edwin demanded, his tone commanding like the leader he was.

"Let him have her. Maybe then Richard might back off for a while and—"

Thane cut off the rest of his sentence, lunging at him and pinning him to the floor by his shoulders, his teeth itching to bite him.

"We don't leave our own, Duncan. You know that," Edwin replied, stepping around his desk.

"Maybe we should give you up in her place. I'm sure Richard would love to see you after the chaos you've caused him," Thane snapped, pressing his elbow down into his throat.

"I'll list all the places I remember, mark them on the map."

"Wise decision, Duncan. There's a map on that table over

there. You can start straight away."

Thane stepped back, pulling him to his feet and pushing him toward the table Edwin had pointed out.

Soon Duncan would learn who was in charge and stop challenging those above him.

As an adolescent, new alpha of his pack, he was volatile and constantly testing his limits. But all he'd achieved so far was to piss off a lot of the wrong people.

Thane could see him becoming a strong leader, but he needed a firm teacher to knock him down a notch or two.

As soon as Duncan had finished with the map, Thane snatched it from under his nose and shoved it toward Edwin. He was unaccustomed to this area now and would need Edwin to tell him where to start.

"Here are the places you've already checked Thane," Edwin commented, placing a different colour marker on the map, several of those overlapping with the ones Duncan had placed.

Thane leaned against the desk, studying the map closely, watching and waiting for his next location, unaware that Duncan had joined him, standing close to his side, one hand resting palm down on the table, the other on his hip.

"It's true then. She really is your mate, isn't she?" he asked with a sigh.

Unable to take his eyes off of the map and Edwin's hand, Thane nodded.

"I think I know how Hugh found out about her," Duncan informed him, moving in closer to whisper in his ear. "Keri."

Thane stood up straight, turning to face him. He furrowed his brow and cocked his head to one side. "How would she have found out?"

"They've been friends for years. Seems logical that she'd notice before anyone else."

No. There had to be more to it than that. Edwin had

known Anya since she was four, a long time before she ever met Keri, and he still refused to believe she would be able to transform like the rest of them.

Someone had to have told her, or she was one of those watching Anya.

"Be careful around her. There's something not right about her. Besides her being a vampire."

"She's a vampire?"

Thane had only seen Keri a couple of times. Once at the party, again at the pub, and those few times he'd passed her in the hall. But every time he'd seen her, Hugh was there.

He'd been busy focusing on him, he'd barely even noticed the girl who Anya used to call her friend.

Was this girl the one she kept sensing around her? Or was it Richard like Thane had first thought?

"Yeah. One of Oleander's if I'm not mistaken."

Suddenly the mobile phone on Edwin's desk chimed to life, buzzing and vibrating across the table. Oleander's name printed up brightly on the screen.

Thane didn't hesitate to answer when Edwin seemed preoccupied by his work.

"Oleander?" he asked in a clipped tone.

The vampire had disappeared on him with no notice, leaving him surrounded by hunters. He'd better have found something important to be ringing them now. He had a lot to answer for if Keri was indeed his.

"T—Thane?" a faint voice called, bringing him to his knees.

"Anya?" he choked, his heart leaping into his throat. She was ok.

"Where are you? Where's Oleander?"

"I—I don't know," she replied, her voice sounding faint and strained. "I'm in a wood I don't recognize."

"Stay where you are. I'll come find you as soon as I locate the signal from his phone."

Thane passed the phone to Edwin, turning on the loudspeaker as he jumped onto the computer, still listening to her speak, telling himself over and over that she was ok, that he would find her soon.

"Anya are you all right?" Edwin asked, his voice quivering as he finally let a tear fall in his relief.

"I don't know."

"Did Hugh hurt you?"

"No. He didn't seem to know what to do with me."

"He's been brought up by a powerful hunter. It's no surprise that he doesn't understand what's going on and his feelings. You're supposed to be the enemy after all, yet to him, you're just an innocent girl that's done nothing wrong," Edwin continued to waffle on, but Thane was growing worried. He hadn't heard Anya reply for a while now.

"Got a signal," Thane shouted already headed for the door.

He had to be quick. He could feel her energy fading, which could only mean one thing.

"No," he growled, pushing himself as hard as he could, transforming with no hesitation as he sprinted to where the signal pointed him.

He might need to carry her home, but he knew he'd be quicker at tracking her as the wolf. She was all that mattered right now. He would just have to fight off anybody he came across.

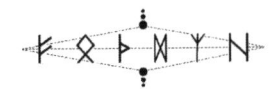

Edwin's voice was lulling Anya to sleep as he spoke in a monotone voice.

She knew she had to stay awake, but the wound was becoming increasingly painful and her body was beginning to lose the battle.

She'd pushed herself too hard in order to find a spot with signal so she could get help. The bleeding hadn't stopped. In fact, she'd made it worse.

A simple stab wound shouldn't bleed this much, unless she'd hit something vital, or Keri's blade had been tipped with something poisonous.

"Anya?" Edwin shouted down the phone, his voice ringing in her ears "Are you still there?"

"Anya?" he shouted louder.

"I—I'm still here," she rasped, her breathing becoming increasingly difficult. Her head throbbing.

"Don't lie to me this time. What's wrong?" Edwin asked, his voice shaky and rough like he was holding back tears.

"Bleeding—" she replied, feeling a pang of guilt at not having gone to him sooner.

The tranquillizer Hugh had given her must have worn off as she started to walk around. Now she could feel every stab of pain and the burning sensation with every step she took back in the direction she'd come from.

She needed to find the dagger Keri had dropped, see if it had been poisoned like she feared. Thane would need to know how to treat her wound when he found her. The dagger would help.

Anya fell to her hands and knees, the phone forgotten on the floor by her side. The sounds of Edwin's shouts becoming distant and faint as she drifted in and out of consciousness.

Her hand began to sting as it collided with something cold and metallic, blood oozing from the new cut across her palm. She looked down at it with a frown, her eyes blurring when she tried to focus on the shining metal.

Her vision turned black as she fell to the ground, her hand just millimetres from the sharp object.

# Chapter 31

When Thane arrived, Anya was lying lifeless on the floor.

Transforming back, he rushed to her side, checking her pulse, his heart in his throat.

She was alive. Just. Her pulse was weak, and her faint breathing irregular.

What could have happened in the minutes it took him to get here?

Thane searched her body looking for a wound of some kind to help him figure out what was wrong. Rubbing his hand over her legs, his hand came away wet and stained.

Gently he turned her onto her side, he saw the blood still oozing through her jeans.

"No," he cried, recognizing the discolouration of her blood. She'd been poisoned. But with what?

He searched the ground around her, looking for anything out of place, anything toxic to a shifter that would cause this. He saw nothing, not until he crouched by her face.

Next to her hand, something glittered under the falling sun. A dagger. He frowned. That wasn't the cause of the wound on her leg. The cut across her hand, maybe. Had she taken the dagger and used it to defend herself?

Growling loudly, he bent over and gently picked her up, cradling her against his massive chest.

His heart ached as he looked down at her sickeningly pale face.

Without knowing what the poison was, they wouldn't know how to treat her.

Thane roared up at the sky and ran back toward Edwin's praying he wasn't too late.

Heleana would think of something. She had to.

The run back took far too long for Thane's liking, but he couldn't shift into the wolf, not with Anya in his arms.

He sprinted through the back doors he'd left open in his hurry earlier and dashed into Edwin's office.

"Thane," Edwin shouted, bursting into the room by the other entrance. "What happened?"

"I don't know," he croaked, barely holding his emotions in check, "she was like this when I arrived."

Allowing Edwin to examine her, Thane pulled on a pair of jeans Edwin had tossed toward him when he entered, before joining him by her side.

Edwin's concern mirrored his own when he saw the blood dripping onto the desk, painting it a purple-blue.

"Do you know what it is?" Thane asked, taking her hand in his own, checking her pulse, careful not to get in Edwin's way as he worked the blood between his fingers.

"I'm not sure. She's obviously been infected with

something toxic to us to make her blood react this way, but I can't tell what with."

"Heleana?"

"Still in the meeting room, worrying about you after you rushed out so quickly—"

Thane didn't wait for him to finish, darting from the room before he completed his sentence. He needed to find Heleana. She would know what was wrong.

Thane burst through the doors, startling several people inside.

"Heleana?" he shouted, standing in the open doorway. The doors crashed into the walls on either side of him. "Where is she?"

"I'm here, Thane," she called, pushing her way through several people standing in the way.

"What's wrong? Were you injured?"

"Come quickly."

He didn't wait for her, rushing back to Edwin's office to be by Anya's side. He couldn't stand being away from her, not when he thought he'd lost her. But this was not the end. He refused to give up on her.

"Oh god. What happened?" Heleana exclaimed entering the room behind him.

She rushed to Anya's side and placed her hand on Edwin's shoulder, nodding for him to stand aside and give her the room she needed to properly assess her patient.

"What happened, Thane?"

"I don't know. She was on the floor like this when I found her. She had Oleander's phone," he replied, placing the phone on the desk by her feet.

"The poison in her is reacting with her blood quite quickly. I don't know if I'll be able to work out the cause in time to save her."

"You have to," Thane demanded, squeezing his hand tight

around her arm.

"I'll do my best, Thane, but any idea on the cause would help speed up the process."

"There was nothing I could see, just a dagger that looked clean and a lot of natural debris."

"Pass me the dagger," she asked, holding her hand out toward him.

He pulled the blade from Anya's pocket where he'd hidden it earlier, passing it to her by the hilt.

"You'll need to remove her jeans for me to have a proper look," Heleana commented as she took a seat by Anya's side and began to study the dagger carefully.

She sniffed at the metal, cut the tip of her finger, and even tasted it, all to check if the blade was the cause.

"You're right Thane, it isn't the dagger, but the dagger is definitely a hunter's blade, it bears their mark."

Heleana stood and draped a blanket over Anya's lap to keep her warm.

Thane took a step back, allowing Heleana the room she needed to work. Every muscle in his body protested with the need to be close to Anya, touching her to make sure she was still there.

He found himself pacing once more, trying anything he could to work off some of the tension he felt stiffening his muscles.

"Thane, Edwin has gone to research in the library. Go help him, it will give you something to do while I stop this bleeding," Heleana paused, watching him as he turned to stare at her, ready to snarl if she forced him to leave.

"Thane, I need to know what toxin is doing this if I have any chance of saving her. The best thing you can do is help me find it. I know how hard it is to be separated from her, especially like this, but you must."

She was right. Damn it she always was.

He nodded, making his way slowly out of the room after

placing a kiss gently on Anya's forehead.

He would find out what this toxin was even if it killed him, but he wasn't going to the library to study. No, he was going straight to the source.

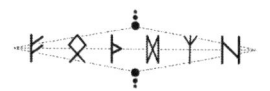

ᚠ ᚨ ᚦ ᚾ ᛦ ᚾ

Thane had successfully made it past the guards on the gate and into the building for a second time.

It didn't take him long to find the one person he wanted to see.

"Back so soon. Did you find Hugh?"

"No," Thane snapped, just barely keeping control of his emotions and his instincts to cause damage.

"You must have just missed him then. He's in the library at the moment, moping around like a child. You'd think he'd be used to my disappointment by now—"

Thane nodded, walking past Richard before he could utter another word.

If there was anybody better to question about this, it was the bastard who took her.

Opening the door with a deafening crack, Thane stomped into the library, his canines already elongated beneath his lips.

"What have you done to her?" he demanded, spotting Hugh huddled over some books in the corner. He could smell her delicious scent on his skin, rubbing his wolf the wrong way.

"W—what do you mean?" Hugh asked, scrambling to his feet, backing away from Thane.

"Don't play stupid with me. Anya. What did you do to her?"

"Nothing. Anya's fine, she's with Keri."

Thane slumped back against the wall, the cool stone chilling his flushed skin.

Perhaps Duncan had been telling the truth after all. What was he going to do now?

"What aren't you telling me?" Hugh asked, taking a hesitant step toward him.

Thane's eyes darted in his direction, pinning him to the spot and making him gasp.

"You're a shifter too, aren't you? Like her."

Thane didn't respond. He didn't need to. Hugh could think what he wanted. It didn't matter anymore. If she died, he would destroy every hunter here, or die trying.

He braced himself, ready for Hugh to scream for help, or attack, only too happy to kill him if he tried. After all he was the one responsible for Anya going missing in the first place. Then he'd left her with Keri, who had likely been the one to poison her. But instead of doing the expected, Hugh just stood still, staring at him.

"Why aren't you attacking me?" Hugh asked.

Thane wanted to, but he knew it would be a waste of time when Anya lay dying elsewhere. He needed to find out what the toxin was so Heleana could start treating Anya properly.

Thane turned to walk away, not caring that Hugh still approached him. It was obvious the boy didn't know what had happened to Anya. He was no longer of any use.

"Wait," Hugh called as Thane went to step out of the room.

Thane spun around and grabbed a hold of Hugh's collar, losing his patience with his constant interruptions.

"I don't have time for you," he growled, baring his teeth, making Hugh flinch.

"What's happened to Anya? You wouldn't have come here for no reason. What were you hoping to find out?"

"She's been poisoned," Thane sighed, seeing no reason

not to tell him the truth. "We're not sure what was used as the symptoms are nothing like any toxin we're accustomed to."

"How's that possible? She was fine when I left her. Keri had just come in—" Hugh frowned, scratching his head. "No. It can't be."

Hugh slumped down in a nearby chair and brushed his hand through his short hair.

"How could I have been so stupid? She'd been pestering me for months, insisting I do something about her. I thought she was just worried because they were friends. Obviously, I was wrong."

Thane slipped from the room, the wolf rearing up inside of him, wanting to claim blood.

The boy was right, he was stupid. Anyone would have suspected her if she kept bringing up the subject. How could he be so dense?

Thane growled and clenched his fists, trying to keep his emotions under control. It wouldn't serve him well to shift now. He needed to help Anya first. Needed to do everything in his power to make sure she survived.

"Thane. Wait," Hugh called from behind him. "I might be able to help you."

"Help me?" Thane growled, never slowing his pace as he stormed through the corridors. "You already said you had no idea anything had happened. How could you possibly help me?"

"I care about her too," he shouted, finally bringing Thane to a stop. "I know I shouldn't. I know that I should be killing her, but the truth is, I can't. I've never killed anyone before and I doubt I ever could."

Thane turned to him and raised a brow.

Was the boy really such a novice? How could that be possible when he was Richard's son?

"I'm a disappointment to Richard. He hates me, but I don't care. I don't agree with what he says and does. I really want to help," he pleaded, moving closer.

"What could you do that I can't do myself?" Thane asked, curling his lips back over his teeth in disgust.

"I've heard Richard talking about a new weapon against the Lore. I'm not sure what it is, but if we can gain access to his office, we may be able to find out more about it. It might even be the toxin you're looking for."

Thane studied Hugh for a few moments, trying to figure him out.

If it was true that Richard had come up with a new weapon against them, it was his job as a Guardian to find out. But Anya came first. He needed to put her safety and her life before anyone else's. She was his main priority, his mate, and he refused to lose her. But could he trust the boy not to be leading him into a trap?

# Chapter 32

They'd been hiding outside Richard's office for ages, waiting for him to leave. The time was ticking away quickly. Every second Thane spent away from Anya, became more painful until he was struggling to remain still. He needed to get back to her, had to make sure she was safe. But he couldn't leave, not until he found this weapon that could prove to be the one afflicting her.

"Here," Hugh whispered, motioning for Thane to join him by a small crevice in the wall.

"Maybe I should lure him away so you can take a look."

"No. I don't know what I'm looking for," Thane snapped, gripping the boy's arm and pulling him back into the darkness around them. "I'm not happy about waiting either, but you're stuck with me until I find what's wrong with her. Understood?"

Hugh nodded, gulping loudly.

Thane turned back to the door and watched, trying hard to ignore the buzzing of his phone as it rang in his pocket. He couldn't risk answering in case Richard heard, or came out and spotted them. He'd have to check who was calling once they were finally inside.

"Maybe, I could—" Hugh started, until Thane placed his hand across his mouth, glaring down at him. Hugh furrowed his brow, turning his attention back to the door.

Richard emerged his phone against his ear, shouting at someone about their duties.

It was obvious the boy hadn't heard Richard move inside, headed toward them. He was lucky Thane was there to stop him from getting caught if this had been his plan when he took Anya.

When Richard's voice finally faded, Thane released Hugh and headed to the door, running his fingers along the edges, searching for any traps or triggers that Richard may have set.

"What are you doing? I've come here loads of times." Hugh asked, placing his hand on the doorknob.

"Wait," Thane insisted, having felt something odd near the hinges.

After a few seconds of fiddling and picking at the wood, Thane pulled out a wire and smiled smugly.

"All right. Can I go in now?"

Thane nodded, still smiling as he pushed his way past, throwing the wire into the bin by the desk.

"What are we looking for?"

"I'm not entirely sure. It could be anywhere."

"What?" Thane roared, shoving Hugh back against the door using his forearm. "You led me here not knowing what you were looking for?"

"I only heard rumours."

"So this could be all for nothing? You really are stupid aren't you?"

"Wait. Let me just check his computer. I'm sure I'll find something that mentions it if it's true. Then we'll know whether it's worth searching for."

Thane growled, but released him, removing his phone from his pocket as Hugh rushed to the desk to begin his search.

"You've got until I finish this phone call to find something. Otherwise, we're leaving."

Hugh nodded and began frantically typing at the computer.

Edwin picked up on the second ring. "Thane. I've been trying to get a hold of you since you ran off," he began. Thane was relieved that his voice sounded calm and steady. Nothing bad could have happened yet.

"Heleana has managed to slow Anya's heart to stop it from spreading the poison around her body so quickly. It should keep her stable for a few hours longer, but we need to find the cause."

"I'm working on it," Thane sighed.

"What's your plan?"

"Thane. I found something," Hugh exclaimed, jumping out of the chair and pointing frantically at the screen.

"Who's that?" Edwin asked, ignoring the ringing of another phone in his office. "Hugh? You went to the hunters. Are you stupid? If they'd killed you, who would've saved her then?"

"Hugh told me about a new weapon Richard has found to use against us. He wasn't lying," Thane replied, staring at the screen before him. "He's found a way to mix two poisons that usually have no major effect on us and made them stronger using aconite?"

"Wolfsbane," Edwin gasped. "We're in trouble if he's managed to mass produce it."

"Let's hope this was a prototype to see how things went."

"Yes, but unfortunately for us, they've used it on someone still learning their abilities," Edwin sighed, "if it had been used on one of us, it might not have been so effective."

"I'm not so sure. I'll email this file to Heleana. Make sure she gets it."

"I will. Call if you need anything else. And Thane. Be

careful."

Thane took pictures and forwarded the file to all the healers he knew, hoping that if the drug had been spread among the hunters, they would have some way of fighting it, before he deleted all traces of the drug from Richard's computer. If nothing else, it would slow them down at producing more.

Leaning back in the chair, relieved that he'd finally found out what was affecting Anya, he could sit and regain control over his emotions. Heleana would be able to find an antidote.

"We need to leave before Richard returns. If he finds us here, he'll be furious."

"Did Richard know you took her?"

"No. I didn't tell anyone other than. Shit—"

Thane rested back against the plush chair and sighed. If Richard knew about Anya, then he would've known about Thane too. But why would he have let him leave if that was true?

"When did you tell Keri?"

"Only when I asked her to come and stay with her. I don't think she knew I'd taken her until she got there. I was only trying to protect her."

"From what? If you thought Keri was nothing but human?"

"What? Keri is human."

"No. She's a vampire."

"That's a lie. I'd have known."

"Like you knew I was a shifter you mean? Your precious organisation is full of deceit," Thane sneered, wrinkling his nose in disgust.

"I already told you I'm not like the rest of them. I've never agreed with them. Why do you think Richard hates me?" Hugh insisted, clenching his fists. "I took Anya to protect her from him. I've known what she was since before she did and I wanted to save her from him. He's been suspicious of her since the moment she returned, just waiting for an excuse to take her for himself. He was so proud when he thought I'd won her. But it was all a lie."

"To keep her safe?"

"Yes," he sighed. "I knew she didn't want me from the first time I met her at the party. The only reason I persisted at the pub was because I liked her and I was drunk. But it worked. Richard thought I was interested and pushed me to pursue her."

"He was in love with her mother," Thane informed him, leaning forward in his chair.

"I know. Amelia. He killed all those responsible for killing her, you know. Not that it makes him any less guilty for her death. He was the one who organized the kidnap of them both. Little did he know that the one who held them hated him."

"How do you know all this?" Thane asked, intrigued. If Richard hated his son, why would he share such information with him?

"I read," Hugh shrugged. "I hated Richard. He stood by and let my mum die. He even blamed the shifters for her death, but I found out that was a lie too. It's why I stopped hating your kind," he continued, rubbing at his temples.

"I come here often and read through his files, learning all the stuff he wouldn't tell me, feeding the information to your alliance through another source."

"You're the one responsible for informing us on how many hunters have joined recently?" Thane asked, impressed by the deeds this boy had done for them. Maybe he wasn't so bad after all.

"Lucas still hates me though. I don't know why. I've always tried to pass him food and water when nobody was around, but he refused it."

"Lucas is stubborn," Thane smiled, jumping to his feet and heading to the door.

"Wait. Where are you going?"

Thane ignored Hugh, nodding to other hunters so they

wouldn't suspect him as he continued through the halls.

He was going to free Lucas. Anya needed family around her, and he had a right to see her when she was fighting for her life.

"Thane. Wait. You can't," Hugh begged, grabbing a hold of his arm in a vain attempt to stop him as he headed toward the cellar.

"Watch me."

"But Richard's already furious, and you don't have an antidote for this new weapon yet. Maybe I could ask him about it?"

"Brilliant idea. Why didn't I think of that?" Thane drawled, rolling his eyes, "oh yes, because he'd know you found the information from his computer, and he'd know you had help passing his trap. You really are a moron."

"I didn't think he scared you?" Hugh murmured.

Thane gripped Hugh's collar and lifted his feet off the ground, moving within inches of his face. "I'm not scared of him. But I am freeing Lucas whether you like it or not. He has a right to see his daughter."

"I-I don't have my key."

"What are you so afraid of?" Thane asked, lifting the key from around his neck.

"I told you. He hates me. He'll kill me."

Thane shook his head and pushed Hugh to the side, slotting the key into the lock. The magic from the runes sent agony across his hand.

The barrier had been repaired, meaning there had to be a witch among them. Perhaps that was how Thane couldn't sense who was following Anya. Witches didn't give off a specific scent, just a sense of power. That, or their witch was especially talented at cloaking spells.

Thane growled and released the handle. He doubted it would be so easy to break the circuit a second time.

"You can't pass, can you?" Hugh asked, hopeful.

Thane studied the markings, noticing his scratch from before. A new rune had been placed over the top, now glowing a bloody red since Thane touched the door.

He flexed his fingers, allowing his claws to slice through his skin and picked at the rune. The glowing continued like he thought it would.

"Damn it," he growled.

"How did you get through before?"

"I broke the spell by removing a rune, breaking the circuit."

"I assume it isn't working this time?"

"No. The loop must be the other side."

"So. Now what?"

"There are only two options really. Either I destroy this door causing a lot of noise, or you go down there and let him out," Thane shrugged, smirking when Hugh's face blanched of colour. "Personally, I prefer the second option."

"No," Hugh shrieked, waving his hands out in front of him. Shaking his head, "not happening. No way."

Thane knew he wouldn't be happy going down there alone to let out Lucas, fearing his own life, and rightly so, but there weren't many options.

"Me freeing him won't help if we can't break the spell. He'll be stuck on the other side of the door."

"Lucas will be able to break the loop from the other side unless you have a blade that you can use to scratch off the runes to allow me through?"

Hugh patted down his clothes, searching for anything he could use, and bowed his head in defeat when he came up empty-handed. He sighed before taking a step through the door, looking back over his shoulder as he went.

"What about the chains?"

Thane dug around in his pocket and tossed him a vial of

liquid with a note inside.

Erebus had come through just in time. Maybe someone had seen this all coming. The damned demon could have warned him if that was the case.

"Give this to him, with the key," he instructed.

"Leave it in his reach, then run if you value your life. Perhaps I'll be able to talk him out of killing you once he reaches the top."

"W—what is it?"

"A powerful spell to destroy the chains."

Hugh nodded, taking the vial and gulping audibly before disappearing into the darkness of the stairwell as he rounded the first spiral.

Thane hoped he would be quick. They needed to get back to Anya.

He pulled out his phone, feeling the need to check on her again.

It took far too long for Edwin to answer. There had to be something wrong.

"Sorry, Thane. We have a little bit of trouble here. Seems that Oleander made his way back after losing Keri in the woods, only the girl has sent a welcoming party."

Thane swore loudly, punching the wall beside him causing the plaster to crack, littering the floor with dust.

"Is she safe?"

"For now. Some of the boys took her upstairs and locked her in my room along with Heleana and Tynan. She's well protected, and Heleana insisted the move had no negative effect on her. She's working on an antidote as we speak. I just hope she manages it before it's too late."

"I'm in the middle of freeing Lucas. He has a right to see her."

"You're right. He needs to see her in case the worst should

happen—"

"Don't say that," Thane roared, cringing when he realized he could have drawn more attention to himself. Hopefully the hunters remained on guard outside. "She's not going to die. I won't let her," he continued, this time much quieter.

"I'm sorry Thane. Of course, you're right. We'll all do our best to make sure of it. Just be careful, and watch your back as you head here."

Thane hung up the phone quickly as he heard a noise coming from the stairs. The words muffled, making it impossible to understand what was being said, but he could tell it was Lucas who spoke. He sounded furious, banging loudly on the bars as he collided with them, no doubt lunging for Hugh.

Did Lucas know something he didn't? Could he feel Anya's panic stronger than he could? Maybe he could just smell her on Hugh's skin like Thane had.

The sound of the glass vial clinking against the stone floor broke him free of his thoughts, shortly followed by a loud roar and heavy footsteps echoing as Hugh took Thane's advice to run up the stairs. Perhaps the boy wasn't so foolish after all.

Thane didn't have to wait long until he saw Hugh's pale face appear around the bend, his hands shaking as he ran past him and caught his breath.

Only seconds later, he heard the metal thud of Lucas's chains crash to the ground as he roared loudly.

They waited for several minutes, wondering why Lucas remained still. Neither of them had heard a sound since the loud roar he released earlier.

"Lucas?" Thane called down the steps, continuing to stare down into the darkness.

He noticed Lucas's green eyes glowing before he saw his shape shadowed in the limited light. He looked furious and ready to kill.

"Lucas?" Thane asked, unsure why Lucas looked so crazed, even though he too felt like going on a killing frenzy.

"He's touched my girl. I can smell her on his skin."

"I took her but I didn't hurt her, I swear. Why would I free you if I meant you harm," Hugh pleaded, peering around Thane, using him as a shield.

"Let me deal with this," Thane told Hugh, pushing him further behind him so he was blocked from Lucas's view.

"Lucas. You need to scratch off the runes until the glowing stops, then you'll be free to leave. The spell's been recast and it's stronger."

Lucas eyed the frame, following what Thane could only assume were more runes.

One by one, Lucas scratched his claws across the frame, erasing each and every part of the spell. With each swipe, the glowing dimmed until it ceased altogether.

Smiling menacingly, Lucas stepped through the doorway, his eyes black as onyx, and focused on Hugh.

"You need to come with me, Lucas. I'll explain on the way."

"You want me to let him live?"

"Yes," Thane sighed, hanging his head in shame.

He knew Lucas had been through a lot, but if all that Hugh had said was true, he was innocent. Thane was through with having innocent people's blood on his hands.

"I wanted to kill him as much as you until I learnt more. You know I'm right. Please, Lucas. She doesn't have long left."

Lucas's eyes finally returned to Thane, the darkness slowly receding, leaving behind his emerald green eyes that were so much like Anya's, it pained him to look at them.

"Let's go."

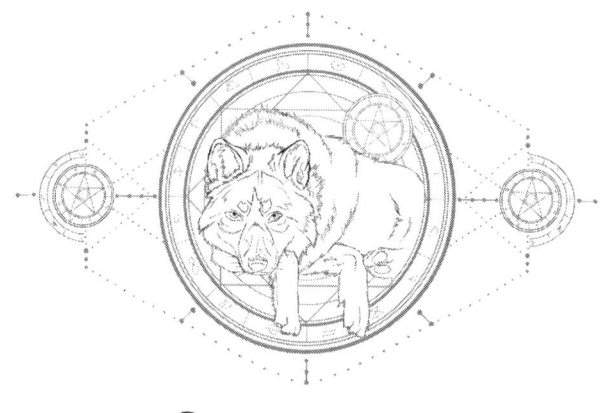

# Chapter 33

It wasn't easy with so many hunters around, but they finally made it back to Edwin's in one piece.

Hugh knew a lot of secret entrances and gaps in the walls, none of the others seemed to notice. Once again the boy had surprised him, helping them rather than turning them in or screaming for help.

Thane blew out a breath at the sight before them. Edwin hadn't been exaggerating when he'd told him things were bad. Below he could see masses of hunters swarming all over the building, other members of the Guard fighting them off and pushing them back.

"How are we going to get through? There's too many of them for us three," Hugh asked, scanning the horizon as he counted the hunters.

Lucas growled, still irritated by his presence. Thane couldn't blame him, he wasn't too fond of the boy either, but he had proven to be useful more than once. He owed the guy a lot if his searching paid off and Anya was saved.

"We shouldn't even be bringing you inside," Lucas snarled, peeling his lips back over his elongated canines.

"Edwin told me to bring him," Thane assured him, trying to calm the situation before they drew attention to themselves. "He's been helpful so far and could well have saved Anya's life. He freed you too, don't forget, Lucas."

"Only because you made him. It was through no doing of his own free will."

"I am here you know," Hugh grumbled.

Thane and Lucas both snarled at him this time.

The boy was grating on Thane's nerves, even if he had helped him. By no means did he consider him a friend, but Edwin was convinced that he could get him to leave the hunters. If everything the boy had said earlier was true, he had no doubts that Edwin would succeed.

Hugh hated Richard, and the hunters, or so he claimed. Why would he stay with them if he was offered a place by their side instead?

Returning his attention back to the job at hand, Thane studied the movements of the hunters, working out the patterns of their patrols and gauging their weapons.

There were easily thirty people surrounding the outside, another seven or so fighting up close, but those were being taken care of without any real danger. The ones posing the most threat were those on the outskirts carrying bows and guns, shooting at anyone who exited the house. Shifters, vampires, and witches alike, fighting alongside one another like they had many years ago.

"You brought him too?" Lucas spat, looking down at the battle in Edwin's garden.

"Erebus is the one who brought me the spell to break you free," Thane growled, spotting Erebus before Lucas had chance to name him, "without him, you'd still be in chains."

Lucas sneered but remained silent, knowing he wouldn't win this argument. Thane knew he wouldn't be happy to see the demon, but he owed him his freedom and the chance to see his daughter without bars between them. Erebus had come through on several occasions when they needed him, and here he was yet again, fighting by their side despite their differences.

Thane watched on, deciding their best form of attack.

"Lucas, if you take out the few up the back. You won't be as strong as you used to be," Thane pointed to the five or so men he could see in the bushes, their rifles pointed to the ground below.

"Hugh, I'll trust you with the few in front of us here. They won't expect you to attack so take advantage of it. We might learn to trust you if you do this well," he continued, still hesitant to give him a large enough role that he could sway things in favour of the hunters. Thane still wasn't sure whether he trusted Hugh. But for now, he had to make the most of what he had.

"I'll take those at the front."

"There's a lot there. Would I not be better use helping you?" Hugh asked, peering over and frowning at the number of people Thane would be left to deal with.

"Thane is a good fighter. They'll be no problem for him."

"I've seen him fight, I know he's good, but they have weapons designed to kill your kind," Hugh pointed out, crossing his arms over his chest in defiance.

"I fight better alone. And like you, the first group won't see it coming until it's too late."

"Then let me tell you what sort of weapons they'll likely be using."

Hugh listed off the types of guns they held, and the ammo they used. Thane wasn't surprised that they had such powerful ammunition against them. So many things that could cause serious harm, or stop their healing, but it did surprise him that so many of them didn't seem to know how to use them. These hunters were all novices like the ones who had gone along with Hugh when he took Anya.

In the distance, all three of them heard a roar as another shifter fell to the floor, a gaping wound in his side from one of the men close by with a gun. That same shooter pointing and cheering down below, waiting for approval.

"No time for chat now, we need to take these guys out. Let's move," Thane commanded, dusting himself off, ready to put on his hunter facade.

Each of them left in their separate direction. Lucas stuck to the shade of the trees until the last minute, attacking in his human form, his claws and teeth ripping the men apart as he partially shifted.

Hugh strolled casually up to the three men not far from where they had hatched their plans. Not one of them pulled a weapon on him, just greeted him and pointed to some of the men below struggling with some vampires.

Hugh nodded and took the gun offered to him, aiming it at a vampire, a man Thane didn't recognize.

Thane braced himself, ready to stray from his path to deal with his treachery when Hugh spun around and smacked the closest to him around the face with the end of his rifle.
The other two were too slow to notice he had attacked them instead of their enemy giving Hugh the advantage. He bent down quickly, retrieving a small dagger from the now unconscious man's body and slashed the necks of the other two.

Thane nodded his head with a smirk. For someone who hated the idea of killing, the boy did it well. He was young, but he was fast and knew how to use his charm and cunning, much like Tynan. If trained right, he would become a decent fighter.

Thane crouched just in time as a bullet whizzed by his head, directed below at a group of shifters. He spotted Duncan among them, dodging at the last minute before taking hold of one of the hunters attacking, using him as a human shield.

The sooner Thane took out the men in front of him, the better.

Casually he walked over to them, waving when they turned their weapons on him.

"Oh. Sorry Thane. Didn't know it was you," one of the men called, lowering his weapon.

"That guy is too quick, nobody can hit him," a female called behind him, pointing down at Oleander as he jumped and dived past attacks.

Thane sighed, not having noticed the woman before. He hated killing females, but he couldn't let her live knowing she was here to hurt Anya, his friends, and his brothers in the Guard.

"He's been hit with an arrow. It's only a matter of time until he starts to slow down."

Thane saw Oleander fight earlier. He knew a scratch like that wouldn't slow him unless they'd managed to hit something vital, or lace the arrowhead with poison.

Having had enough of them shooting at his friends and colleagues, Thane circled around the back of them, looking for a weak spot.

A few of them were lost in their task, they wouldn't notice him attack right away. A few more looked his way, curious what he was doing. The others would notice him quickly.

Mind made up, Thane watched the man a few steps in front of him, waiting patiently for the perfect moment to attack.

He lunged, knocking the man off his feet, his claws slicing their way through his chest as he jumped onto the next guy, digging his sharp teeth in through his throat.

Thane was on the fourth guy when he felt a burning sensation from his hip as a blade sliced through the muscle.

He roared, swinging his huge arms around, knocking the girl he had seen earlier to the floor. She held her hands up in surrender hoping he would show her mercy. He didn't. She had come here to kill them, and then sliced a silver dagger through his flesh. She didn't deserve his pity, or his mercy, but he would kill her quickly, not allowing her to suffer as he had with some of the men previous to her. Taking her head between his hands, he broke her slender neck with a sickening crunch.

It was too easy. He could feel his fur prickling beneath his skin, the wolf wanting to be free and kill everyone around him.

"Thane," he heard someone shout behind him, causing him to spin just in time to miss a sword across his back.

He dodged, sliding across the floor, knocking over another hunter in the process.

Using Duncan's trick, he held the flailing man in front of him, using him as a shield as another man joined in, swinging his sword at him. The man didn't last long, his limbs cut from his body in seconds, but it gave Thane enough time to right his footing. He threw the corpse at the others and knocked them flat, then rushed forward and took both their swords, stabbing them in the chest.

To the right, Thane spotted another man running toward him, a small sphere in his hand.

Hugh screeched another warning, telling him to cover his ears, but it wasn't enough. The grenade landed just yards from his feet, causing him to fly through the air with the explosion. The sound piercing through him as sharp as any blade, knocking the wind from his lungs.

Thane held on to his ears, wincing as they continued to ring loudly. He could see Hugh shouting at him again, but he couldn't hear the words over the loud hum.

He spun, looking for a threat, but saw nothing until he turned back to Hugh, locked in combat with one of the men Thane had fought when being tested. The guy was big and strong, but incredibly slow. Hugh took several powerful hits to the face and torso before he managed to find a gap in the assault, removing the dagger from his jacket, digging the small blade into the guy's heart.

With his ears still ringing loudly, blood slowly trickling down his face, Thane limped toward Hugh, patting him on the shoulder as they headed down the hill together to meet Lucas.

"Are you alright?" Lucas asked Thane, the sound still muffled by the ringing, "You got sloppy. What happened?"

"Nothing. I'll be fine," Thane lied.

How could he tell Lucas that he was close to losing control at such a crucial time; that the wolf wanted to take charge and make everyone pay for coming anywhere near his mate? It wouldn't matter if they were friend or foe, the wolf would have been lost to his bloodthirst and need for vengeance.

"How about you?"

"Fine," he grumbled, holding a hand to his ribs as he turned to Hugh, "I guess you came in useful after all."

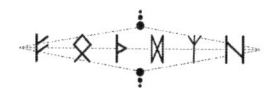

ᚠ ᛜ ᚦ ᚾ ᛉ ᚾ

The three of them strolled into Edwin's, but none of them joined in the cheers with the other Guards at their victory, all too concerned about Anya to celebrate yet.

Thane and Lucas made their way upstairs to Edwin's room, leaving Hugh behind in the study. Neither of them wanted him around her yet. He may have aided them in battle, and in their escape, but he was still guilty of taking and leaving her in the care of a traitor. Not only was she supposed to be Anya's friend, but she also wasn't human and she'd decided to join the hunters rather than her own kind.

"I'll give you some space," Tynan whispered, excusing himself from Anya's room when they entered. She was in safe hands now. Neither of them would let anything bad happen to her.

Thane watched on with his heart in his throat as Lucas made his way over to her side, taking her hand in his. Her skin was pale against his warmer tone, he lifted it to his lips. Love and tenderness were in his every move as he gathered her in his arms.

"Lucas, I need to check her blood pressure again," Heleana whispered, obviously uncomfortable asking him to move aside.

Lucas didn't respond, just moved up to her head, still squeezing her hand.

Thane wanted to go to her too, to hold her safe in his arms and never let go, but this was Lucas's time and Thane blamed himself for her being like this in the first place. If he had just protected her better, not pushed her away, or even if he'd gone and got her himself, this might not have happened. Not that he could blame Tynan. He knew he cared for her and would've protected her as best he could.

"Thane?" Lucas called, finally taking his glassy eyes off of her ashen face, "It's not your fault."

Lucas always had a way of knowing what Thane was thinking, whether it was because he could sense his energy change, or he too had felt something similar, Thane didn't know.

"I failed you. Both of you," he replied, hanging his head in shame.

Usually Thane wasn't comfortable admitting his failures in front of anybody, but he'd always felt comfortable telling Lucas everything, and Heleana was used to hearing any Guard's problems, just not usually his.

"You freed me just like you promised to do, and she's still alive now thanks to your speed and determination. She'll pull through. She's a fighter. Just look at her."

Thane did just that. Looked at her. She seemed so peaceful, her hair fanned around her pale face. Her full lips shiny and plump. He longed to see her smile and laugh. Prayed she would get the chance to hold her father in her arms and know him as a free man.

"I'm proud of you, Thane," Lucas whispered with a smile, gripping his arm, "not just as a mentor, but as a friend. I couldn't think of anyone better for my girl."

Thane's heart broke as he continued to watch her, refusing to look at Lucas. He didn't want him to see the sorrow in his eyes or the despair he felt when he thought of losing her. Lucas had felt the pain of losing his mate, he didn't need the reminder, didn't need to see that Thane had finally lost the courage to believe she would make it.

"Her blood pressure seems stable," Heleana remarked, placing a hand on Lucas's shoulder. "I'm hoping that the antidote I've managed to scrape together works, but I won't know more until morning. "

"Thank you," Lucas replied for both of them when Thane's voice refused to work.

How was it possible that Lucas was faring better than him?

Thane joined Lucas, crouching down above her head, cupping her face in his hands and resting his forehead against hers.

"It's so good to have you back, Lucas," Heleana remarked, stroking the back of her fingers across his cheek before she left the room, closing the door quietly behind.

Thane lifted his head and watched Anya's chest rise and fall shallowly, savouring the touch Lucas offered him as he rested a hand on his shoulder.

"I was hoping to be freed under different circumstances," Lucas mumbled, trying for a joke.

"The meeting we had planned when this all started was about freeing you. Hugh just happened to take her at the worst possible moment, allowing this all to kick off," Thane replied, scowling at the door. "A strong part of me still wants to kill him."

"What made you stop?"

"He told me that he was trying to save her from Richard. He had no clue she'd been poisoned. He was also responsible for finding what the poison was so we could treat it. We'd have had no chance of saving her without him."

"In some ways, he did the right thing. If they'd attacked with her here, she would undoubtedly wish to join the fight."

"Better that than her being like this. I could have protected her if she was by my side."

"Then you would have both fell. Take it from me, we're always sloppy when we're worrying about something else. I saw you fighting earlier. You weren't concentrating."

Lucas was right. Thane had been too busy thinking about Anya, worrying that some of the hunters may have slipped through and made it to her. The wolf had been close to seizing control. Also worrying about Hugh, concerned that he would betray them and fight alongside the hunters. But the boy surprised him, killing some of his own men, helping and warning Thane when he was in trouble. He'd also swallowed his fear and freed Lucas. Maybe he should cut the boy some slack.

"I treated her badly, Lucas," Thane sighed, brushing the hair from her face, "I pushed her away and made her hate me all because I was too afraid to let her in and forget the past."

"I may not have known her long, but I doubt she hates you, Thane. The way she looked at you before was the same way Amelia looked at me. Anger evident in her frown, but warmth and longing in her eyes."

Thane looked up at Lucas and saw his own grief mirrored in his eyes.

He'd lost his mate, as had Edwin. He didn't know how either of them coped. Sitting here now, watching her suffer and struggle to fight death, he felt himself breaking apart.

"She'll pull through. Just don't give up on her," Lucas reassured him, squeezing his shoulder tight before he exited the room, leaving Thane alone with her.

Thane sat in silence, just watching her, hoping that any second now she would open her eyes.

He sighed, pulling up a chair by her side and resting his head against hers as she continued to sleep.

Why hadn't he started training her already? Perhaps if he'd stopped fighting the call, he would've been able to teach her how to control her abilities and she would have been able to put up more of a fight against Hugh when she was taken, or against Keri when she drugged her.

Thane growled, deep and long.

When he found Keri, he would rip her throat out and watch her struggle for breath, savouring the sight as she panicked. The wolf's voice rumbled in his chest with agreement.

A loud knock sounded at the door, breaking him free of the spiralling rage that was slowly sucking him under, putting him on the brink of losing control.

When he looked down at the side of the bed, he saw deep gashes in the wood where he'd dug his nails in deep.

"Come in," he grumbled, slouching back in his chair, rubbing a hand through his matted hair.

"Still no improvement?" Oleander asked, peering around the door.

"Heleana said she's stable but she won't know how effective the antidote is until morning."

"It was lucky you got there when you did. I'm sorry I didn't notice the poison when I was there."

"How could you have? It's nothing we've seen before. Besides, you were preoccupied with Keri."

Thane hadn't forgotten that Oleander had been the one to find her. If he hadn't stopped Keri when he had, would she have bitten her, unable to control herself around all the blood?

"How did Keri manage to escape you?" Thane asked, furrowing his brows between his eyes as he remembered how fast and silent Oleander fought.

"I was sloppy and she took advantage. I won't let that happen again."

"She's the reason you insisted on joining me when I went to the hunters, isn't she?" Thane asked.

He nodded, brushing his jacket to get rid of some imaginary dust. A nervous habit, Thane knew from watching others.

"She begged me to save her life after she'd been bitten and left to die by a shifter," he shrugged as though it was nothing to sire a new vampire, though Thane knew it took a lot of power and energy to do.

"That explains her hatred for us," Thane groaned, rubbing his hand across his nape, his muscles solid and full of tension.

"I'm sorry I left you alone back there. I sensed Keri nearby and had to take the chance of following her. I should never have changed her in the first place."

"No. Don't apologise," Thane insisted, looking him in the eye. "If you hadn't left and found them when you did, Anya might not even be here now."

"Keri's still a young vampire. She's foolish and makes simple mistakes. I'm sure we'll catch her again soon."

Thane grumbled, the sound coming from deep in his throat.

"If I find her again, Thane, I'll call you," he began, taking a step toward him. "It's my job to put her down, but I will honour your need for vengeance and allow you to make her suffer first."

"What about the council?" Thane asked, knowing that any vampire death or termination had to go through their council so they could keep track of their people.

"Let me deal with them."

# Chapter 34

Thane knew that Edwin worried about him being alone. Every now and then he sent someone in to check on him, but all he succeeded in doing was pushing him closer to the edge.

Watching over Anya, listening to their mindless chatter was grating on his nerves and making him tense. He didn't want to listen to their nonsense or their small talk. He wanted to be alone so he could get control of himself. The wolf was pacing inside his mind, his fur scratching impatiently against the inside of his skin, demanding to be set free. But he couldn't give in, couldn't be weak.

He needed to remain by her side to prove to himself that she was still here. The second he believed he'd lost her, everything would be over, and god help anyone who got in his way.

"Thane?" Tynan whispered, poking his head around the door.

Thane wanted to growl and demand he leave, but he knew by the lack of eye contact that he didn't want to be there either.

"I don't mean to bother you, but Edwin and Lucas want to discuss what happened and what to do next. They want you there."

This time Thane did growl, loud and deep.

He understood their concern and the need to take action, getting to Keri before any of the hunters found her, but he couldn't leave Anya. Not yet.

"I told them you wouldn't be happy about the idea. Perhaps I can try and buy you some more time?"

"If Edwin wants my point of view on what happened, and my ideas, he can come to me. I will not leave this room until I know she is well. It's better for everyone this way."

Tynan nodded and left without another word, leaving him alone once more with her, but for how long? Edwin would likely return himself and demand he attend their meeting, but what was the point? If anything happened to Anya, any plan they put together would be pointless.

If for some reason she didn't pull through and began to deteriorate, his mind would be lost. He'd storm the hunters and take out as many as he could before they overcome him. Any Guard's or innocents that got in his way wouldn't stand a chance.

Thane was right, it didn't take Edwin long to rush into the room with a stern look on his face. Only he didn't come alone. Marching into the room behind him were all the Guards he'd expect to see in a meeting.

"Seeing as you won't leave, we'll bring the meeting to you," Edwin commented, pulling up a chair in the corner of the room, motioning for the others to take a seat around him.

Thane was grateful that Edwin had listened and not demanded he leave her side. He was also grateful that he'd sat further away so that they weren't all surrounding her. What he didn't appreciate was seeing Duncan stroll into the room with a smug look on his face, or Hugh who shortly followed behind, his hands visibly shaking as he crossed the room.

At least the boy felt nervous being forced into a small area full of Guardians that would likely kill him, but that didn't change the fact that Thane wanted him nowhere near her. Not whilst she slept and had no say. And certainly not after he'd taken her. A stupid move on his behalf, even if he claimed to be protecting her.

Anya was Thane's to protect, not his.

But even though having Hugh there put Thane on edge, nothing could stop the growl escaping his throat as Duncan stepped too close.

Thane jumped to his feet and stood between the jaguar shifter and Anya, blocking his view of her frail and defenceless body.

"Duncan, sit down. Now," Edwin roared, pushing out of his own chair with a panicked expression on his face. "I don't want any bloodshed in this room while the girl is healing. You understand me?"

"Should have thought of that before you decided to bring them in here," Thane growled back, never taking his eyes away from Duncan.

"For once, I'm not here to cause problems, Thane. I wanted to apologize for what I said before about handing her to them. And I wanted to do it in front of everyone so you'd know I was sincere."

Thane furrowed his brows between his eyes as he continued to stare at Duncan standing before him.

Never had he expected the young alpha to bow his head and admit he was wrong, especially not in front of an audience, many of which followed him around like lap dogs.

Thane couldn't help but feel suspicious as to why he'd decided to say this now, but as he'd said, why else would he admit his faults in front of everyone?

"I've been speaking with the hunter," Duncan continued, scowling at Hugh as he took a seat on the floor by Edwin. "We think we know a few places to look for Keri. It's not much, but I hope it might help."

It was one thing for Duncan to cower below another alpha, but to admit he'd discussed something so important with someone many would consider the enemy? Thane was at a loss for words. Maybe Duncan really had done some growing up after all.

"Well I think that's a load of bull," one of Duncan's usual lackeys, Bjorn a bear shifter chimed in, crossing his arms over his broad chest.

"How can we be expected to trust the word of a hunter?" he sneered, turning away in disgust. "He could be leading us all into a trap, killing a mere new recruit to win us over."

"I have more reason to hate the boy than anyone," Lucas interrupted, shoving at Bjorn, "but I saw him fight up close. He was nauseated killing someone who I can only assume was his first. Not only that, he rushed to Thane's side when he saw him in trouble, buying him enough time to react. Without the boy's help, the battle could have ended very differently."

Thane finally turned from Duncan, reseating himself beside Anya as he watched on, detached from the whole argument.

All he and the wolf were concerned with was making sure Anya was safe. That she wasn't going to die. Watching her, he whimpered quietly.

Never would he have guessed how much she would come to mean to him, but sitting here now he couldn't bear the thought of not having her in his life. He needed her. He would not give up on her.

Thane forced his attention away from her, and back to Duncan who hadn't moved from his spot several feet away.

What if Bjorn was right and Hugh was setting a trap for them?

Thane didn't care. He would happily risk being caught, or even killed if it meant he got to Keri first.

Since the attack, it had been quiet. No more hunters. No more Guards being tailed around town. It made sense that Keri had worked alone, promising some new recruits their first kills just like Hugh had when he snatched Anya. If Richard had known, he would have sent in more hunters by now, attacking them whilst they were weakened. But like Hugh, Keri had sent novices to do a real hunter's job. Not one of them had survived. The only living hunters that knew of the attack were Keri and Hugh.

Thane turned to Hugh, watching on as the rest of the meeting continued without his input. He was restless, his eyes flitting to each Guard around him, terrified, and rightly so. Any one of the men and women surrounding him could kill him in seconds before he had a chance to even blink. There was no way the boy was that good an actor just like Lucas had said. He also wasn't that smart. Thane doubted that even Richard would have set up something quite so elaborate.

Hugh noticed his staring, blanching of colour and trying to look anywhere but his eyes. Thane wondered what he saw as he looked at him. He knew the wolf was riding close to the surface, but could he see it?

"There's no point going over and over the same points," Edwin grumbled loudly, drawing Thane's attention once again as he pinched the bridge of his nose and tapped his foot on the floor.

"We need some direction."

"We need to concentrate on our defences," Bjorn insisted, glaring in Hugh's direction.

"That's pointless. We've seen no signs of another attack. We need to attack them whilst they're distracted," a witch Thane didn't recognize called, speaking up for the first time.

Thane's head was hurting as each side argued what should be their priority, but so far as he could see, they were all wrong. The death of so many new recruits wouldn't have gone unnoticed by Richard, but it made sense he wasn't in the loop. Not yet.

"You're all missing the point," he sighed.

Each of the Guards turned to him and waited, a smile on Edwin and Lucas's faces. Hell, even Duncan smirked at him as he finally joined in the debate.

"Once Anya is well, the priority should be finding and silencing Keri."

"Just let her die so we can get on with it. I doubt the antidote will work anyway, after all, it was sourced from a hunter."

Thane leapt across the room, knocking Bjorn flat on his back, pressing down on his neck with all his weight.

Lucas and Edwin both growled, jumping to their feet.

"The antidote will work. We've already begun to see progress, even if it is slow," Heleana commented calmly, trying to hold the others back.

"Be careful what you say, bear," Lucas snarled. "If I didn't know better, I'd say you wanted her to not pull through."

While those around him continued to argue, Thane saw red, all logic leaving his mind. All that mattered to him was starving the air from Bjorn's body as he applied more pressure. Muffled sounds tickled at his eardrums, but it didn't matter, the wolf was in control. He could feel someone tugging at his arms as all colour drained from the bear shifter's face. Still he didn't stop. Deep down, Thane knew he should let go, but the wolf ruled him now and no one would get away with talking about his mate that way. She would pull through and she would show everyone here just how strong she was.

"Thane," someone's familiar voice echoed in his ears, "don't do this. He's not worth it. Think of Anya."

Thane blinked several times, his vision fading in and out of focus, staring down at Bjorn's discolouring face.

"Don't become the monster you fear you are. You're better than this. Stronger." The voice was Heleana trying to calm him and make him see reason, but why should he care? If Anya didn't make it, he would become the monster he'd always tried to rein back.

Suddenly Thane felt a caress inside of him, surrounding his fracturing heart as it squeezed gently. There was no mistaking the powerful touch of a mate's embrace. Somehow, she was clinging to him, letting him know she was still there. Maybe she was more aware of what was going on around her than they thought.

As quickly as he'd leapt across the room, Thane was back on his feet, heading back to Anya's side to hold her hand in his. The pull inside of him to return to her side overwhelming the wolf's need to kill.

"Perhaps you should leave now, Bjorn," Edwin growled, pulling him to his feet and pushing him toward the door, "We'll talk about you stepping down from your position later."

"What? He's the one—"

"Don't test me," Edwin snapped, his eyes changing to a hollow white that only happened when he was really angry. "Nobody would have blamed Thane for not stopping after the remark you made."

"She's my daughter too, bear. I hear you wish her dead again and I'll finish the job myself."

Once more, Thane drifted into his own world, staring helplessly down at Anya's pale face.

How could she lay there so peacefully with all this commotion around her?

He cupped her cheek in his hand and rested his head against hers, listening to the steady beat of her heart. A single tear fell from his eyes as a gentle hand squeezed his shoulder.

"She'll pull through, you'll see," Heleana whispered, moving to the other side of the bed to check on her vitals for the third time today.

"I know she will. She's a fighter," he replied, hoping he was right.

Thane's eyes grew heavy as he lay his head beside Anya's, watching the rest of the meeting continue without him. He didn't want to fall asleep, afraid he might miss Anya awaken, but all the events over the past couple of days were beginning to take their toll.

He closed his eyes and just listened to the steady beat of her heart, lulling him deeper into sleep. He squeezed her hand and brought it up to his face, resting his cheek in her palm. So delicate and small, but it was warm and comforted him more than he could have imagined. Holding onto her seemed to anchor him, calming the wolf.

His eyes snapped open, the sounds of shuffling and heavy footsteps woke him.

Everyone was leaving, filing back out of the room as quickly as they'd entered.

"Duncan?" Thane called, as he went to leave.

Duncan spun on the spot, and stepped to the side, snatching Hugh by his collar when he tried to leave.

"You want info?" he asked, still holding onto Hugh as he stepped closer.

"When she wakes. I am going to find Keri, and I want you two with me. You know where to start looking."

"You want me with you?" they asked in unison, looking to each other and raising their brows.

"I thought you still wanted to kill me," Hugh spoke first, straightening his collar when Duncan finally let go.

"Part of me still does," Thane admitted, stretching his arms above his head to loosen his tightening muscles, "but you've already proven useful, and I don't agree with what Bjorn says."

"I'll help all I can. It's the least I can do."

"Look, Thane. I respect you and believe you'll be a great leader, but do you really think we'll be able to work together? We've never really seen eye to eye."

"No, we haven't. But that needs to change," Thane sighed,

placing Anya's hand down gently on the bed beside her before he stood. "If we're to beat the hunters and keep this alliance going, we need to work together. You're strong, and you're smart, but you have a big mouth."

"Thanks," Duncan snorted, crossing his arms over his chest.

"You'd be a good alpha if you weren't so pigheaded."

"Yeah, yeah," he dismissed, waving his hand in the air, "So what's the plan?"

"Same as before. Wait for Anya to wake, then our search for Keri can begin."

# Chapter 35

Thane hadn't slept in two days. He just kept waiting and hoping Anya would wake up any second since Heleana gave her the all-clear, insisting that she would recover soon. He could feel her energy and her life force growing stronger, but still nothing happened.

A week after he'd found her poisoned in the woods, Thane finally drifted to sleep. He dreamt of Anya. Dreamt of how they had shared a kiss in his room, except the dream didn't end there. Instead of him walking away like he had, he stayed and began to undress her, caressing her soft body beneath his fingers.

A light touch against his fingers interrupted the image, just as she was pulling his shirt over her head. He growled, the sound rumbling in his chest. He nudged whoever was trying to wake him. He didn't want this dream to end, not yet. Whoever it was could wait.

Thane swatted at their hand and rolled his head to the side, trying to get comfortable as he leaned against the bed Anya slept in.

Again he felt a brush, this time with a little more force, yet still weak and delicate.

Thane cracked open his eyes with a grumble, about to shout for whoever it was to leave him be when he realised whose hand was resting on his.

"Anya?" he called, his throat rough and gravelly, squeezing her hand in his.

She stirred, moaning quietly as he leaned over her.

"Heleana," he bellowed, knowing she wouldn't be far away.

Seconds later she burst into the room, closely followed by Lucas, Edwin and Tynan.

Lucas rushed to her side, grabbing a hold of her other hand, the others remained at a distance. Heleana checked her over, opening her eyes to see if they responded to light and checking her reflexes.

"She's waking up," she called, smiling wide and placing her hand on Thane's shoulder.

Thane couldn't help himself. He took a hold of her and crushed her in his arms, spinning her around and nuzzling her neck.

"Thank you," he whispered against her, "thank you so much."

Heleana just smiled, stroking his cheek before resuming her position by Anya's side.

When Thane turned back to Anya, he saw her eyes were open, glowing just as brightly as her father's next to her. Her teeth now sharp and her claws protruded from her fingertips.

Thane crouched by her side, taking her hand in his once more, bringing it up to his lips and resting her palm against his cheek.

Her eyes seemed to flash brighter, but her claws retracted, as did her canines.

Surely that wasn't jealousy? Thane couldn't help but smile.

"Hi honey. I need to check a few of your vitals, but as soon as I'm done, they're all yours," Heleana smiled, motioning to all the men around her. "Be gentle guys, especially you two," she added pointing at Thane and Lucas.

Anya's eyes followed Heleana's finger from him to her dad, freezing when she spotted him. Tears welled up in her eyes looking up at a man she must have thought she would never see free. Tears flowed down her cheeks, her eyes now burning a pale green.

"Shh," Lucas cooed, placing his hand on her forehead before moving his head close enough to lean against hers.

Her tears continued to fall as she closed her eyes and remained still, biting on her bottom lip.

"Can you feel this?" Heleana asked as she began to test each of her reflexes, seemingly happy with her progress, only frowning once.

"Your leg is taking a little longer to heal than usual. It's most likely because of the poison still working its way out of your system, and trying to heal all the other cuts and scrapes you had. Just keep it rested for a while, all right hunni," Heleana smiled, placing her equipment back into her pockets.

Anya didn't hesitate to try and sit up as soon as Heleana left the room, swaying when she lifted her back off the bed. Thane was there, ready and waiting, holding her arm to keep her steady.

"How long was I asleep?" she asked, her voice hoarse.

"Almost eight days ago now," Edwin replied from behind, causing everyone to turn to him. "We were afraid you wouldn't make it."

"I never believed that," Lucas and Tynan said in unison.

"She's too stubborn, like her mother," Lucas continued, smiling wide when he turned back to her.

"I know someone else like that," Thane muttered, causing

Lucas to smirk.

Anya took her arm back from Thane and wrapped both around Lucas's neck pulling him closer, burying her face against his chest.

Thane felt at a loss, wishing she would hold onto him, but could he blame her for not? He'd pushed her away for so long. Could she ever be happy being his?

"I've waited such a long time for this," Lucas whispered, holding her tight.

"We'll leave you two alone for a while," Edwin announced, turning to leave.

"Wait," Anya argued, gripping onto his sleeve before he had a chance to move far. "I never told you that I forgave you and that I'm sorry."

Edwin cupped her cheek in his hand and smiled, stroking his thumb across her cheek as more tears fell.

"I know child. I'm just glad you're safe. All I ever wanted was to protect you."

He leaned forward and placed a kiss on her forehead, whispering *"I love you,"* as he squeezed Lucas's shoulder and ushered Tynan and Thane out of the room.

Thane wanted to stay by her side, determined to never leave it again, but Anya and Lucas deserved some time alone.

He sighed, allowing Edwin to move him outside in silence, not daring to look back over his shoulder in case he changed his mind.

Now Anya was awake. He had other things he needed to take care of.

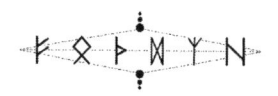

Anya couldn't believe her dad was finally here, by her side where he should have been all these years.

Her heart broke as she held onto him, knowing how much suffering he'd been through. How much he must miss her mother.

"I'm sorry," she mumbled against his soft mahogany hair.

"Shh," he whispered, stroking the back of her head with his large hand, "you have nothing to apologise for. You're here now and you're safe. Without you, I'd still be stuck in that place with none of the Guards knowing where I was."

Lucas pushed her back and held her at arm's length, smiling down at her from his superior height as he sat beside her on the bed.

"I hear you're tough as nails, just like her."

"I don't know about that," she grumbled, looking away from those eyes that saw too much.

Anya could barely remember her mum, but she knew she had fought for her safety as hard as she could, risking her life to save that of her child. Anya doubted she could ever be that strong.

"I was there when you told Richard no, remember? People don't say no to him very often."

She remembered how she told him she would never join them, the look of disgust and disbelief contorting his evil face.

"I hear you even put Thane in his place a few times. How many people can say that, I wonder?"

Anya smiled. The shock on Thane's face when she stood up to him that first time. He hadn't been angry. No, he smiled, proud of her backbone. His words still sent shivers down her spine as she remembered how closely he whispered them in her ear.

"How did they get you out?" she asked, trying to change the subject before her face turned scarlet, "I was on my way to the meeting when—"

"Shh. Don't think of that now. Just concentrate on getting better,"

Lucas interrupted. "Thane and an unexpected friend broke me free, using a powerful spell to destroy the chains binding me," he smiled, pulling out her chain from under his t-shirt, revealing the ancient-looking key dangling close to his heart.

"This truly was one of the best gifts I have ever received, after the gift your mother gave me. Thank you, my daughter."

Her heart jumped into her throat, tears pooling in her eyes as she looked into his mournful face when speaking about her mum. She knew the gift he spoke of was her, she could tell by the way he looked at her with an undying love.

Not caring about the pain or the healer's advice, Anya leapt into his lap, wrapping her arms tightly around him. Her vision blurred and her lungs burned from overexerting herself, but it was worth it just to hold him close. The only thing that would have made this moment perfect was if her mum was here too.

"I'll be sure to thank Thane and your unexpected friend later," she murmured against his shoulder.

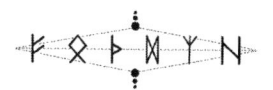

---

After another forty-eight hours of rest, Anya was going out of her mind. She was more than ready to get up, and out of this room.

A few visitors had stopped by since she woke, mainly her dad and Tynan. Even Oleander, the vampire who'd taken Keri away had come to see her, apologizing for not noticing the poison and for allowing Keri to escape him. She couldn't believe Keri was still out there, just waiting to try and get to her again.

Everyone gave her their perspective on what had happened, explaining how the hunters had attacked Edwin's home while she was unconscious. A few of the Guards had fallen in combat, and the person responsible was Keri.

She didn't understand it. How could she have ever felt guilty for thinking less of her? Keri was not her friend. She doubted she ever truly was. Even now her blood boiled at the thought of what Keri had done, what she'd put her family through.

Then she thought of Thane and how he had not come to see her by himself, even though everyone told her that he hadn't left her side once Lucas was free and the battle was won. Why was he avoiding her?

Anya was through with waiting. She wanted answers, and she knew exactly where to get them.

As soon as Heleana finished her exam, checking over all her vitals for the fifth time today, Anya pushed the covers off her legs, slowly spinning them over the side of the bed. Her head was still fuzzy, her legs tingling from lying still for so long, but she couldn't keep still any longer.

She grabbed a hold of the dressing gown that was piled by the bed, covering her short nightdress, and made her way into the hall, beginning her search for Thane.

She didn't know where he would be. Whether he'd be awake or sleeping. She followed her instincts knowing deep down that she would find him.

Strolling down the corridors, she swayed on her feet, her vision blurring in and out of focus, yet she wouldn't give in. She propped herself against the wall, using it to aid her travel until she reached a door she was sure Thane was behind.

Reaching her hand out, she hesitated.

What if he was busy, or he didn't want to see her? There must be a reason he was keeping his distance. Would he shout and tell her to leave?

"You can come in, Anya," his voice called through the door, making her shiver and her stomach flutter.

"How did you know I was here?" she asked entering the room and closing the door behind her so she could lean against it, not wanting Thane to know she was still wobbly on her feet.

"I can smell you, remember?"

Of course he could. Anya sighed and rubbed her hands up and down her arms. How foolish of her to think it was anything more than his heightened senses.

"What's wrong?" Thane asked, looking her from head to toe, warming her chilled skin with his hungry eyes. "Shouldn't you be resting?"

"I've had enough rest to last me a lifetime," she snapped, suddenly feeling very guilty, until Thane laughed, easing her worry.

"I guess you have. So why did you come here?" he continued, leaning back in his chair, his muscles stretching deliciously tight when he placed his hands behind his head.

She longed to go to him. To stroke her hands over his body as she had done before, but she couldn't, not yet. She couldn't let him see how weak she still was. He would demand her to return to her room, and she wasn't ready. She needed her answers, but more importantly, she needed to be near him.

"I wanted to thank you properly for helping free Lucas," she finally replied, realising she'd been silent for too long.

"There's no need to thank me. I did what anyone would have done. Besides, he had a right to see you."

All of those she cared about had believed she might die. When she'd passed out in the woods, she thought she might too, but here she was. It shocked her how much effort everyone had put in to save her when she wasn't a member of the Guard. She owed Heleana for all of her hard work and tireless effort. She also owed her an apology for becoming jealous when she saw her nuzzling with Thane.

At first, Anya had thought she was flirting with him, but later she'd realised her mistake. It was something that shifters did for comfort, allowing skin contact with those they trusted and cared for. Being one of the few healers among the Guard, Heleana was trusted by all. Still, Anya couldn't help but feel a little jealous as she remembered that look of comfort and happiness on Thane's face as he held onto her. She longed for him to hold her close, a spark of happiness lighting up his beautiful eyes.

"Lucas mentioned someone else helped you?" Anya commented, hoping to distract herself from her thoughts before she gave herself away. She also wanted to know who this person was that apparently helped them.

Thane sighed, rubbing a hand down his face. She knew that nobody was telling her for a reason, knew that it had to be someone other than Erebus, otherwise Tynan would have said something already, but she hoped Thane would be the one person who would tell her. He always told her the truth, even if it wasn't what she wanted to hear.

"Sit down before you fall down, Anya."

"I'm fine. I shouldn't stay long. Someone might notice me missing."

"So you are supposed to be in bed still?" he teased, causing her to blush and fidget with the hem of her dressing gown.

"Come on, Anya. I can see you're swaying on your feet. I know you're supposed to be in bed still. Please sit down."

The way his voice broke as he pleaded made her heart skip a beat, knowing he really had worried about her and still was, even if he had been avoiding her.

"Where?"

"Sit on the bed. At least then, if anyone asks, you're still resting in bed," he joked, a hint of mischief in that smile of his. Anya couldn't help but smile with him, happy to see this more playful side to him.

She'd come here in hopes of answers to the questions everybody else seemed to be avoiding, as well as a need to be near him, but all she wanted now was to wrap herself in his arms and just rest by his side. Her answers, the hunters, and all the bad things could wait.

"I want you to answer me honestly, Anya. Then I'll be honest with you," Thane began, turning his chair toward her on the bed. "Did Hugh hurt you when he took you?"

"No, not intentionally."

"Good," Thane nodded, leaning forward on his elbows, inhaling deeply.

"He's the one who helped me free your dad when I couldn't pass through the door. He took the spell and key down to him," he paused, allowing the information to sink in before continuing, "He also helped us against the hunters when they attacked. Killing three of them, and warning me when I became sloppy and missed an attack. It was lucky he was there."

Anya didn't understand. How could Hugh, the same guy who had taken her against her will, be the person who had stood alongside them and fought against his own people? Nothing seemed to make sense.

"I don't get it," she said with a frown. "Why would he take me, then help later?"

"You'll have to talk to him tomorrow and ask him yourself, but he claims he was trying to save you. Not hurt or kill you, when he took you."

Thane moved toward her, crouching down on his haunches and taking her hands in his, holding them close to his chest. She wasn't sure whether he realised what he was doing as he rested them against the drumming of his heart.

"Have they told you everything that happened?" he asked, stroking his thumbs over the backs of her hands.

"No. I've heard little bits and pieces from different people. Nobody seems to want to tell me anything."

"So you came to me?" he asked, dropping her hands and

standing above her.

Anya nodded, feeling bad admitting she'd come here for answers that nobody else would give her. She wanted to tell him she was also here because she couldn't stop thinking about him. That she had sensed him nearby the whole time she was unconscious. Wanted him to know that she loved him, knowing he may never return her affections.

"I'm happy to tell you what happened, but I think they're only holding things back to protect and stop you from worrying."

"I know, but I have a right to know the truth."

"Yes, but not right now. You need to rest before you faint. Your colour has changed since you've been here."

"I don't want to go back to that room. I'm fed up with being in there," she grumbled, turning her face away from him so he wouldn't see her eyes filling with unshed tears. She wanted to remain by his side, surrounded by his comforting scent.

"Then stay here."

Anya turned back, gaping up at him like a fool.

That was the last thing she'd expected him to say. Usually he pushed her away for reasons she didn't fully understand, but something was different about him now. He seemed broken and raw, his emotions out of control. Was this why he'd stayed away?

"You don't have to," he spoke into the silence that fell between them.

"No, no, I want to. I just… wasn't expecting that."

Thane sighed and sat beside her on the bed. She turned to face him, tucking her healed leg beneath the other.

"I know I've not been that kind to you, Anya, but like everyone else, I was trying to protect you."

Anya thought of all her meetings with him in her head, from the first time she saw him at the masquerade ball, until now. He may have been rude to start with, brushing her off, and being arrogant, but ever since that first night, he'd helped when most people would've left her. How could she possibly think he was a bad guy? He'd caught her when she fainted, on more than one occasion. Stayed with her when she was afraid. Always telling her the truth, and holding her when she needed comforting. He desired her as much as she did him, she could see it even now, but for the first time, he wasn't pushing her away and saying no.

"Why?"

"My past haunts me, Anya. I thought it best if I pushed you away, but I realised how stupid I was when I saw you lying so still in the woods," he paused, looking away from her as his voice cracked. "I thought you were dead."

Anya took his face between her hands and forced him to look at her. His eyes shined azure as a small animalistic whimper escaped his throat. She stroked his cheek and cocked her head to the side as a tear rolled down his cheek.

Thane pushed her hands aside and pulled her toward him, wrapping his huge arms around her, and holding her tight. "You're mine, Anya," he whispered in her ear, "my mate."

Anya didn't know how to respond, his words ringing around inside her head. Was it true? For a while now, it was all she had hoped for. To be his. She knew he cared for her, why else would he have done the things he had, but to be his mate? It was a dream come true.

"How long have you known?" she asked, tears filling her eyes.

"Since the moment I met you," he sighed, "I just refused to believe it until recently. Pushing you away because it was easier than admitting I was wrong. But when I found you in the woods, I knew I couldn't deny it any longer. I couldn't face losing you."

"Was the thought of me being your mate really so bad?"

"No, don't say that," Thane pleaded, crushing her against his chest, "I was just angry with fate for giving me someone I thought I couldn't protect."

"I don't understand. You didn't know anything about me when we met. Why would you think I needed protection?"

Thane sighed, letting her go to rub a hand across his stubbly jaw.

"I think it's time you knew the truth. Why I'm feared by the rest, and why I don't let anybody close."

# Chapter 36

"My mum was the healer of my pack, my dad the alpha," Thane began, watching her as he spoke to gauge her reaction to his story. "When I was only six, nothing more than a pup really, humans moved near our territory."

At first, they'd thought nothing of it, after all, the humans had as much right to be there as they did.

"As more people moved in, our pack grew, just as the human town did. Everything was going well and everyone was happy."

He could remember every face from his pack. Every family, but those that stood at the forefront of his memories were his parents, and his sister, Neela. She was his twin and his best friend. Their eyes were the same shade of blue, her pelt the mirror of his own. Just picturing her beautiful face made him want to weep.

Anya moved closer until her legs brushed against his, offering him her comfort. He knew she was meant to be a healer, he'd known from the moment she'd treated Tynan. The way her hands moved, the way her energy made every hair on his body stand on end when she focused her ability. Even now he could feel a gentle caress against his skin even though her hands remained on her lap, unaware of what she was capable of.

"M—my sister," he struggled, battling to keep control of his emotions, her name difficult to say out loud.

Without hesitation, Anya took hold of his hand, bringing it onto her lap, rubbing her thumb absent-mindedly over the back of his skin, giving him the strength to carry on.

"Neela was my twin, but we were best friends too. We used to travel up to the human town together and play with the other children our age."

"What was she like?"

"She was incredible. Not a single dominant or cruel bone in her body. A maternal female like our mother, through and through. She often followed her around, watching how to care for the others, learning what it meant to be a healer, and when she wasn't following mother around, she was glued to my side."

Though he struggled to say her name after bottling it up for so long, he felt at ease talking about what an amazing person she'd been. Remembering all the wonderful things she'd done in such a short life. If only he'd been strong enough to protect her.

"You all got along with the humans?"

"Yes, in the beginning."

Thane could feel himself becoming numb, the wolf fighting for control over his mind. It didn't want him to feel pain and suffering, just wanted to take over and consume his thoughts with blood and revenge, eradicating all traces of emotion. He shoved the wolf aside, needing to continue, to explain to her why he was this way, and why he kept her at a distance for so long.

"One day, Neela and Lizzy, a human girl from the town, were fooling around in the woods between our homes, when suddenly I heard a scream."

He'd known it was Neela straight away, feeling her fear and anxiety as though it were his own, but he couldn't understand why. Not at first.

"Lizzy began to scream too, the sounds of their cries fading as they moved further away. Another friend of ours, Philip, came running into our pack shouting about a madman carrying a rifle."

"A hunter?" Anya gasped, squeezing his hand tight awaiting his answer.

"No, just a human," he sighed, feeling guilty for ever having judged her the same as the rest of them. Even before he'd learnt what she was, he knew he wanted her, knew she was always meant to be his, but his hatred and prejudice against humans blinded him. What a fool he'd been. It no longer mattered to him who, or what she was. She was his, and he was never letting her go.

"I don't understand."

"The man was high on some restricted drugs, his mind lost."

"That's no excuse."

"No, but I only found out afterwards, learning he'd already killed several others in another town a few miles away."

"He killed them?" she whispered, her eyes already filling with unshed tears. If only it had been that simple. Things might have ended differently.

"No," Thane sighed, running his hand through his hair, "I chased after the sounds. Philip struggled to keep up behind me. I could still hear their screams, but they were growing faint, so I shifted. Something I was told never to do in front of a human, but I knew none of them were close enough to see, so I did it anyway."

Thane remembered the way his fur bristled underneath his skin before erupting and covering him from head to toe. The way his claws tingled and scraped at his fingertips, itching to spring free and cause some damage. The deafening growl that burst from his newly formed jaws. Even now he could feel his fur prickling beneath his skin. A powerful reminder of just how close he was to letting go.

"In my wolf form, I could run quicker, catch the smallest scent on the breeze and hear and see much further than when I was still human. It didn't take me long to find them. Lizzy was bruised and bloody, crying by the trees, holding herself close as the madman pinned my sister to the ground, his rifle digging into her throat."

He could hear the frantic beating of her heart and the blood rushing through the man's body as he looked down at Neela. She wouldn't cry, determined not to let him see she was afraid.

"He nudged at her skirt with his foot, lifting it high, pushing harder with his rifle, marking her neck. I saw red and jumped out of my hiding spot. Nobody was allowed to hurt my sister."

Anya gasped, knowing what he'd done. What a fool he was. Maybe if he'd shifted first they would've reacted differently, but then he'd never have beaten the man.

"I circled around him as he spun and saw me, now pointing his rifle in my direction. His hands were visibly shaking, his eyes fully dilated. It was no surprise really. He wouldn't have been expecting to come face to face with a wolf."

Thane turned away from Anya, looking off into the distance before he continued. He didn't want to see the disgust and fear in her eyes when she looked at him

"I killed him. I lunged at him and wrapped my jaws around his throat, starving him of air as he thrashed and kicked beneath me."

He didn't feel any guilt for killing the man who'd hurt his friend and was intent on doing the same to his sister. If he hadn't found them when he had, it could have ended a different story. The man was already a murderer, what was to stop him acting again? Thane just wished there was something he could've done to change the outcome.

"Lizzy began screaming again, but no longer because of the madman. She was looking at me. When the man took his last breath, I stepped toward her, blood dripping from my muzzle. Neela ran to her, trying to calm and reassure her, but all I could see was fear and loathing in her eyes as she looked at me."

He never would have hurt her. She was one of his closest friends, but she had no idea what he was.

Slowly she began to calm, looking into his eyes and seeing the resemblance of the boy in them. She'd turned to his sister then, asking her if she was the same.

"Philip finally caught up to us, waving a large branch through the air, trying to scare me away."

"People are fools and only see what they want to see," Anya commented, scowling and clenching her fists.

She was right. Philip saw the dead madman and assumed Thane was going to kill them next. He was wrong. All he'd wanted to do was protect the people he cared for.

"I understand she'd be scared after seeing you kill a man, but she should know you would never hurt her once she realised who you were."

Thane scoffed, shrugging his shoulder when she tried to turn him back to her. She still didn't understand. He wasn't finished yet, the worst was yet to come.

"Even though Neela told them who I was and that I wasn't going to hurt them, Philip dragged Lizzy away looking back at me in disgust and anger. We thought nothing more of it after hearing no word for days, but we were wrong."

His heart squeezed tight as the memories of what happened next flooded his mind. Tears building in his eyes before he clenched his jaw, ready to continue.

"A week or so later, some of the humans came onto our land, storming our homes and burning buildings to the ground, shouting we were dangerous and needed to die."

Even now Thane could hear their chants and the screams coming from his own family. His mother's and sister's cries piercing through him, making his heart ache.

"They pinned my father to the floor, stabbing him repeatedly as my mother and sister screamed, helpless. Then they turned to me, my mother's screams changed to sobs and pleas as she begged them to spare me."

They hadn't listened. He was responsible for killing a man, even if that man had been a murderer and a rapist, it didn't matter to them. Thane was dangerous.

"Four of them pinned me to the floor while another stabbed me between the ribs with a blunt kitchen knife."

Thane absently rubbed at his side, the feeling of his scar burning as he remembered the deep cut slicing through his skin and piercing his lung. Anya gently nudged his hand aside, holding hers against the spot that seemed to be throbbing now. He let her hold him, let her warmth and comfort anchor him.

Would she drop her hand when he'd finished?

"My mother and a few other females fought off the men, many of them dying in the process. My mother was stabbed and slashed before she managed to reach me, shielding me with her body as they continued their assault."

Thane clenched his fists tight, picturing each of their faces looming over him, killing his mother with each draw of their weapon.

He glanced across at Anya, wondering why she had gone silent. Her eyes were shining a brilliant green as she stared up at him, her bottom lip quivering.

"How could they?" she asked, noticing he was now watching her, "you were just saving her, and they treated you like—"

"Monsters," Thane finished for her, "that's what most people treat us as, Anya. It's something you'll find out for yourself, unfortunately."

"How did you survive?"

"I never realised until it was too late that my mother was pouring her energy into me before she died. She sacrificed herself in order to keep me alive, protected beneath her."

If he'd have known sooner, he might have told her to stop and keep fighting for herself. For years he'd wished he'd died along with them, only now he had someone else to fight for and protect.

"All the men attacking assumed I was dead. Philip's dad kicked me when he passed, grunting that I wouldn't be bothering them again," he sighed, cupping her cheek in his hand and never wanting to let go. But she had to know the truth. How else could she ever hope to accept him.

"What about your sister?"

"She managed to hide from them, running into the woods like she was told to do if anything ever went wrong."

Neela had always been a master of stealth, giving their parents a headache when she hid from them. Their father, Felan, always thought she would make a good soldier, but she wasn't cut out to be a fighter like him. She was submissive, like their mother, destined to be a healer; just like Anya.

Though Anya was in no way submissive, hers and Neela's personalities were so similar, it pained him to look at her right now as silent tears fell across her cheeks.

She moved to close the distance between them, attempting to wrap her arms around him in comfort, but he couldn't let her. Not yet. She needed to know what happened afterwards.

Thane held up his hand, keeping her at a distance even though inside he was screaming for her touch. She didn't fight him like he expected her to, just sat and cocked her head to one side, asking the one question he knew was coming.

"I don't understand why you feel like you're the one to blame here. It was them that attacked you. So why do you feel guilty?"

"I should never have let them see me transform. I'm the reason they attacked."

"They should have been grateful to you and your family for helping save one of them, not chase you away and destroy your lives," she paused, twiddling with her thumbs, glancing toward him for a second before staring at her hands, whispering her next question.

"What happened to your sister?"

Thane knew he'd have to explain, but he wasn't sure he could.

This time he pulled her close to him, needing her touch despite his fear that she'd push him away.

"After they all left," he began, squeezing her hand tight as he held it against his chest, easing the ache in his heart, "I followed her scent into the woods, shifting into the wolf knowing I'd be stronger."

It had been agony moving, but he pushed through it needing to know his sister had made it out, shifting and relying on the wolf's strength.

"It didn't take me long to pick up her trail, spotting her footprints in the dirt first, followed by her unique scent on the trees. Only the closer I got, the scent changed."

The metallic stench of blood made him pick up his pace, praying she was just injured and that he could help her heal. Moving as fast as his body would allow him.

"When I found her, she was laying on the floor in her wolf form, blood dripping from her side."

He raced toward her as fast as could, sniffing and nudging at her face, trying to wake her.

"S—she wouldn't wake up, no matter what I did," Thane whispered, his voice cracking as he tried to hold back his tears.

Neela had meant more to him than anyone else, and he

hadn't been able to protect her.

"They'd managed to get to her first, stabbing her multiple times in the side. Blood was pooling around her."

Thane didn't understand how they'd found her. She was always so well hidden, unless someone had followed her, or tricked her into coming out. It didn't even look like she'd had a chance to put up much of a fight; the slightest amount of blood on her claws and muzzle.

He heard a noise from beside him. When he turned, Anya's face was wet with fresh tears, her eyes red and bloodshot, her hands plastered over her mouth trying to hold back her sobs, but he had to continue.

"I was alone for a long time, but I never forgot what happened. Every year I went back to the same spot, paying respects to my parents, my sister, and my pack mates."

The town surrounding his old home never stopped growing, forming the town he was now in. Huge and busy, not one of its residents aware of the events that happened years ago.

Edwin, one of the few Guards who'd helped save him back then had built his home on the land, planting a small tree in the garden in the exact spot Thane had found Neela, helping him keep the place sacred.

"When I turned thirteen, I came back to place flowers on each of the graves I'd dug for my pack, honouring each of them in turn, but as I stood over Neela's grave, something inside me snapped," he sighed, rubbing a hand across his nape, eyes glued to the ceiling, trying to focus anywhere but Anya's eyes.

"I followed my feet and found myself standing in the middle of the human's town. Not one of them seemed to recognise me, but then, why would they? They all thought I was dead."

In some ways, he was grateful nobody knew him. It meant none of them were expecting it, but part of him still wanted them to run in fear when they saw him coming.

Anya gasped, gripping her hand tight around his forearm as he risked a glance toward her. He could see in the swirling depths of her eyes that she knew what he was about to say.

"I spotted Philip, and his dad, casually standing in the distance, laughing and joking to one another. I lost it, shifting I killed them both, but I didn't stop there."

The wolf had finally won the battle and took over his mind, eradicating all humanity and logical thought. He no longer cared who got in his way, he just wanted vengeance, wanted to make them all pay for taking away everything from him.

"I hunted for every one of the men that attacked our pack, and I slaughtered them. Destroying everything they had, but still I couldn't stop. I killed everyone in the village, old or young, guilty or innocent. It was just so easy to give myself over to the wolf, to wipe away all the pain and the sorrow I could feel with every inch of my humanity, surrendering to the blood lust and my need for revenge."

Thane turned away from her again, but not before he saw her hands trembling, and her eyes shift to a dark green. Was she now scared of him like so many others? Would she run away like she should've done all those months ago?

He couldn't allow her to. Not now that he had stopped denying what she was. He couldn't let her go no matter how much he knew he should. The need to keep her safe overwhelmed all his other instincts.

"For a time, I was lost to the wolf, no longer feeling the need to shift back into a human."

He had nothing to live for. All he wanted to do was stop hurting, and the wolf helped keep him numb, letting him live on instinct alone, killing anything that made him feel threatened. Taking what he needed to survive. More than once, he'd starved himself, his need to be reunited with his family overwhelming his need to live, but the wolf always won, gaining full control, not letting him give in.

"How long?"

"A few years."

It was such a long time not to change, his humanity all but wiped out. He still wasn't sure how he'd been saved.

"The Guardians came for me many times knowing I'd turned rogue; a monster that had lost his humanity. But even though I ended up killing many of them as they tried to calm me down, or take me out over the years, Lucas decided to spare me, insisting he could get through and train me as I was still so young."

Thane was much closer to the wolf than any other shifter he'd met, feeling more at ease alone than he did in groups. Even now he sometimes felt the urge to just give in to the wolf so he wouldn't have to remember all of the sorrow, or mourn for his family that he couldn't do a thing to protect.

Now he had someone who made him fight his urges in order to keep her safe. But what if she walked away? His heart skipped several beats waiting patiently for her to speak, afraid she would try to run from him. If she tried, what could he do? His humanity hung in the balance, just waiting for her to make a move. If she ran, his mind would be lost, turning him into the killer he feared he was.

"Lucas saw your potential to be something more," she commented, moving close to him now he wasn't holding her back.

She placed her hands on either side of his face, forcing him to turn to her, her eyes still shining that dark green they had done before.

"You may have killed a lot of people, Thane, but you did it out of love and grief, something we can all relate to. Especially me."

"Those who attacked us deserved to die and I do not mourn them, but all those innocents. Those Guards that tried to save me. I should have been stronger."

"You were so young when they were killed, with nobody to guide you grieving alone for years," she insisted, never allowing him to turn away from that impressive stare. "Stop blaming yourself for something that happened so long ago. Yes, you may have lost control, Thane, but you're the man you are today because of your past. You're the man I love."

He smiled at her then, his eyes filling with unshed tears as she accepted him, good and bad.

"Honestly, Thane. I was always more scared of your human self rather than the wolf," she laughed.

"Thanks," he huffed, nudging her gently with his shoulder. "He's only that way with you because he's always known who you were."

"You're not a monster, Thane. Nor is the wolf. People just fear you because you have a fiery temper, but now I know why. I understand."

How could he have ever thought she wouldn't? This woman was incredible with her huge heart that saw the best in everyone.

He took a hold of her, wrapping his arms around her waist, needing to touch her.

"I know you were trying to protect me, just like I know Edwin was, but you no longer need to worry about that," she said, smiling up at him, still stroking her hand over his cheek, "besides, who else can say they tamed the big bad wolf."

Thane laughed, pulling her on top of him as he lay back against the sheets, closing his eyes and luxuriating in her scent and warmth.

He knew that if he ever stepped out of line, this feisty little wolf would soon put him in his place. She always had.

"Thane?"

"Mm?" he groaned, opening up his eyes to see her leaning above him, staring down at his face with a wicked smile.

"Can you shift for me?"

# Chapter 37

Thane continued to stare up at her in disbelief. Of all the things he'd expected her to do or say, that was the last thing that crossed his mind. Though why it surprised him, he wasn't sure. Ever since he'd met her, she'd gone against the expected, standing her ground and actually putting him in his place. It made sense that now she would want to show him she wasn't scared of him, like she never had been.

"I know you're afraid you'll lose control, Thane, but I know you'd never hurt me," Anya began, resting her palms against his chest as she continued to gaze down at him, "I've never believed you would."

"I would never, and nor would the wolf. You're mine, and neither part of me would ever hurt you."

"I know. So please shift for me."

Thane wanted to change for her. He wanted to give her everything she wanted, but could he trust himself not to lose control and lose himself to the desires and blood lust of the wolf? He may never hurt her, but there were still so many people around him that he wasn't sure he trusted the wolf with right now. Would she really be able to tame him and keep the wolf in check?

"I want to feel your fur beneath my fingertips as I hold you. And I want to prove to you that you're not lost. Not yet. Not whilst I'm still here."

His heart clenched tight at her words. Could she really love him so much that she would risk all to save him from himself?

Thane closed his eyes and inhaled deeply, filling his lungs before he rolled her off of him, so he now sat staring down at her. She didn't fight him, neither did she look afraid. In fact, her heart raced, her eyes glinting with joy, smiling up at him, caressing his cheek tenderly. He leaned into her touch, closing his eyes once again to savour the feel of her skin against his, longing for it to last forever.

He heard her rustling beneath him and felt her pressing against the bed. She pushed up and brushed her lips against his in a fleeting kiss.

"All right," he sighed, hoping he had made the right choice.

Thane forced himself away from her and began to remove his clothing, piece by piece. Unable to keep the smile from his face. She watched, devouring every solid inch of him. Her eyes glowed so brightly, they made any gem look dull in comparison.

When she looked at him like that, it was even harder to rein the beast back in, but he must. He couldn't have her when she was still healing. He needed to be patient.

Anya smiled back at him, drawing his attention to her sinful mouth. A mouth he could envision wrapped around his ever-hardening length.

Thane growled deeply, his voice the first part of him to change, sounding more beast than man.

As quickly as the growl left his throat, the rest of his body began to transform. His nose and mouth elongated into a muzzle, filled with deadly canines that glinted in the light. His spine stretched and snapped into a new shape crouching over in front of her. Hands and feet shifting into paws with sharp claws that tapped on the wooden floor.

"Beautiful," Anya gasped, reaching her hand forward to brush it through the thick, midnight black fur that now covered every inch of his body.

He didn't hesitate. He jumped back onto the bed beside her, making her squeal like a little girl as he circled around her, lying close behind her, wrapping his paws around her middle. She leaned back against him, cuddling up close and burying her face in the thick fur around his neck.

"You smell like the woods," she sighed against him. Taking an indulgent breath she snuggled closer.

It felt right to hold her close like this. He never wanted it to end.

"Are you sure it's all right for me to stay here, in your room?" she asked, watching him with heavy eyes.

"I don't want you to leave. I want you by my side, always," he replied, nuzzling his head against her waist. He would never allow anyone to take her from him again.

Thane awoke as a human, surrounded by a delicious warmth he knew to be Anya snuggled against him.

He looked down at her with a smile. Her head resting against his chest, a hand delicately placed in front of her face. Long hair cascaded over his arm, spilling down onto the bed. She stirred, rubbing her legs against his, causing him to stifle a moan.

He wanted her more now than he had before, fearing he would never get enough of her body wrapped around his.

Thane stroked his fingers down her back, cupping her bottom in his hand, squeezing gently. This time he couldn't contain his groan as she writhed beneath his hands, her body rubbing against his. He nudged his hand lower, grazing the inside of her thigh.

Her eyes snapped open, glowing a dazzling green as she stared up at him through eyes half-mast.

Biting down on her lip, she traced her fingers across his chest, touching, learning every muscle across his front. She continued to stroke lower, gasping when she noticed he was naked beneath her. His fantasy of her mouth around him was making his body tremble as she licked her lips.

Thane dipped his hand lower, stroking the molten heat of her through her lace panties, causing him to shudder. She gasped, leaning into his touch. He smirked, taking full advantage of her offering, rubbing softly over the material until he had her moaning with pleasure.

Anya's hand skimmed lower too, rubbing at the hardness between his legs making her moan. The sound erotic to both their ears, spurring them on further.

Thane had planned on only pleasuring her, slowly easing her into the idea of being with him, but when she held him in her hand like that, rubbing and stroking like she was, he wasn't sure he could hold back the wolf. He'd been trying for so long, only making it more difficult the harder he tried. He wanted her, but he wasn't sure he should. Not when her bruising was still healing.

Thane took hold of her hand, tearing it away from his throbbing erection to hold against his chest.

"What's wrong?" she asked, her eyes still shining beautifully as her emotions got the better of her.

"I won't be able to stop if you keep doing that."

"Is that really such a bad thing?"

"I don't want to hurt you. You're not fully healed yet and the wolf's more in control than I am at the moment. He doesn't do gentle."

Anya bit down on her lip, her swollen red flesh beckoning him to do the same. He pushed up, taking her mouth in his, leaning his head to the side for a deeper, more passionate and possessive kiss. She moaned into his mouth, binding her arms behind his neck. She climbed onto his lap, her breasts bouncing beneath her nightdress as she moved. Thane shuddered as she lowered herself over him, the slickness between her thighs making him ache.

"Maybe I don't want gentle," she whispered in his ear, grinding her hips over his lap.

The friction was intense, making him clench his hands tight against her back.
He tilted his head back and roared.

She was driving him insane. The need for skin contact a scream inside his head.

He pulled at her panties, nudging them down her legs. When she refused to move, smiling against him, he growled, ripping the lace from her body, and made her gasp.

"I don't like to be teased," he grumbled, the sound deep and throaty.

"We'll see," she smirked against him, lifting herself back off his lap, kissing his neck and jaw. Her small, sharp teeth scraping his collarbone.

Sweat gleamed across his body as he tried to rein in the beast, to remain in control. Gripping hold of the bed sheets, his knuckles white from the pressure.

Anya placed her delicate hands on his torso, rubbing her way down and smiling wickedly, her claws now protruding from her fingertips. Bringing her hands back to his shoulders, she dug her nails in, scraping them across the smooth plains of his bare chest. He roared, snapping his eyes open to stare at her. How could she know to do something like that?

"Good?" she asked in a breathy voice.

Rather than answer her, Thane dipped his head into the crook of her neck, feasting on her sensitive flesh, making her tremble in his hands, but that didn't stop her teasing. She tried to push him back, using all of her force. He laughed at her pitiful attempts to move him, but he did what she wanted, lying back against the soft sheets, allowing her to take control.

He closed his eyes and waited eagerly for her to climb back over him, straddling his thighs once more, but nothing happened. Instead she placed her lips against his stomach, raking her nails down his sides.

She paused above him, licking her lips. Her green eyes tinged with amber specks. She gave him that same devilish smile as before.

Suddenly her head dipped out of sight, her mouth wrapping around his cock.

Thane growled, arching his back off of the bed, wrapping the sheets around his fingers.

He was wrong. He did like being teased by this woman.

As she stroked her mouth up and down his shaft, licking and sucking at his head, he throbbed, needing to be inside of her. He couldn't take it any longer. He lifted her with ease, flipping her over so she lay on her back before him like a treat ready to be devoured. She wiped at her mouth with the back of her hand and licked her lips.

"You're wearing too many clothes," he accused, tugging at the hem of her satin nightdress.

Anya gasped as he lifted it up over her head, discarding it on top of the t-shirt he shed last night. She tried to shy away from him, hiding her body beneath her shaky hands, but he wouldn't allow it.

"Don't hide yourself from me," he growled, pinning her arms above her head, feasting on her with his eyes, "you're perfect how you are. Every curve," he whispered, cupping her breast in one of his hands, "every freckle," he leaned forward and kissed her chest, lavishing at each and every mark across her skin. She squirmed beneath him, giggling when he kissed her ribs. The skin sensitive and ticklish.

"You're beautiful," he breathed, struggling to form coherent words.

He pressed his lips against hers, fisting his hand in her hair and holding her close. The need to be inside of her ruling him.

He positioned himself at her entrance and paused, waiting for her to accept him.

Her hand skirted down his stomach to his cock, squeezing him, pulling him forward as she lifted her hips up off of the sheets and took him inside of her, gasping loudly into the crook of his neck, making him roar with pleasure.

She was so tight, so wet and hot around him.

Her back arched, pressing her breasts forward, exposing her slender neck to him. His teeth itched with the need to mark her, claiming her for his own, but he couldn't, not yet.

Thane tilted his hips to thrust in deep, sweat beading on his skin. She moaned and wrapped her legs around his waist, rocking her hips up toward him, adjusting his angle inside of her. Thane groaned and pushed into her harder, pounding against her thighs. His body shaking as she matched his pace, rocking her hips in time with his thrusts.

His movements grew more urgent as he swelled inside of her, stretching her. The way she moved beneath his hands, breathtaking. The look in her eyes and their magnificent colour even more so.

Her scent surrounded him, turning him feral.

He wanted to plant his seed inside of her. This woman he loved, who loved him in return.

Thane lost control, seeing her now through the wolf's eyes. He leaned down and took her neck between his teeth, holding her in place, marking her as his. She squeezed her legs tighter, gasping out his name on a breathy whisper, her body shuddering as she fractured around him, her muscles squeezing so tight he almost came.

He rode her harder, feeding the fire that was building inside his veins. Plunging deep inside her with short, hard strokes. The silken tightness of her clenched around him, bringing him to a new level of pleasure he'd never felt before.

She was his. His mate. He was never going to push her away again.

Thane roared up to the skies, his muscles tightening as pleasure ripped through him. He dug his fingers into her rear, holding her to him as another orgasm hit her, taking him along with it.

He collapsed against her, his heart hammering inside his chest. He lay still for several minutes, regaining his energy.

This is how he wanted to spend the rest of his life, surrounded by her scent, her arms wrapped around him.

He pressed up on the bed and leaned forward for another kiss, nibbling at her bottom lip before he rolled off of her, concerned he could be crushing her beneath his weight.

She snuggled into him, curving her leg over his, absently stroking her hands across his chest.

"I wish we didn't have to move from here," she murmured against him.

"Me too," he whispered, pulling her closer with his hand on the small of her back.

"But we can't stay here, can we?"

Thane didn't answer. He didn't want to. All he wanted was to enjoy this moment and not think about what still had to be done.

"Where have you been the last few days?" Anya asked, leaning up on her elbows so she could look down at him. "I know you didn't leave my side once you'd freed Lucas and defeated the hunters, but since I've been awake, I haven't seen you before now."

"I wasn't avoiding you," Thane sighed, taking a loose strand of her silken hair between his thumb and fingers, "I've been trying to find Keri, hoping she hasn't had a chance to tell Richard what happened."

"Surely he already knows?"

"Unlikely," Thane grumbled, pulling her back down to lay her head against him. Even now, with her still within touching distance, he felt like she was too far away. He craved the skin contact he'd starved himself of these last few months, and every second counted.

"If Richard knew, he would attack now whilst we're weak, but he hasn't."

"You think Keri might have run away rather than going back to the hunters?"

"It's a possibility."

Thane hadn't thought of that. These last few days, Duncan, Hugh and himself had been checking all of Keri's usual hangouts hoping to catch a glimpse of her, or find someone who had, but nothing. What if Anya was right and she'd run away, scared Oleander wouldn't be so unlucky a second time? That would make things a lot more complicated.

"Where could she run too?" he found himself asking, curious whether Anya would have any more ideas.

"I'm not sure. It's not like we've spoken much over the last few years. Perhaps Oleander would know?"

"No he would've told me," Thane insisted.

Oleander understood Thane's need for vengeance. He'd even been willing to break the rules so he could get it. There was no way he would know where she was and not tell him, but perhaps the Council would. It wasn't like they would tell him if they did know. They dealt with their own, it was how the vampires managed their people.

Perhaps it was time to call upon Erebus once again. He

knew several powerful witches, one of them was sure to know how to cast a tracking spell.

"What are you thinking?" Anya asked, looking up at him with a frown, "I know you're planning something. I can tell by the look on your face."

"Maybe."

"Tell me," she demanded, shoving at his chest playfully.

Thane laughed, grabbing a hold of her wrists and rolling her over onto her back, pinning her hands above her head. He smiled down at her before leaning forward to kiss at her marked neck. He would never get enough of her.

"Really?" she gasped when she felt his erection pressing into her abdomen, "you can't be ready to go again. Not yet."

"I'll always be ready for you," he smirked, nuzzling at her neck once more.

# Chapter 38

After a quick shower, with Thane joining her, insisting she needed help scrubbing her back, his hands roaming over her body and caressing her skin; both of them dressed and made their way downstairs.

It didn't take them long to find Edwin and Tynan sitting in the kitchen, helping themselves to breakfast.

"Where's Lucas?" Thane asked, joining the others by the table.

"I'm here," he called from behind, wrapping his arms briefly around Anya's shoulders, kissing her cheek before joining the rest by the food.

It had only been a week or so since Lucas had been freed, yet he was already filling out his lean frame. His face was fuller and his body was more muscular than she remembered. He looked almost healthy.

Anya couldn't help but smile as she watched on. All those

she cared about huddled around one table, laughing and elbowing each other out of the way like a real family.

"What's for dessert?" Tynan asked around a mouthful of food.

"I've put some brownies in the oven, they'll be done soon. And Tynan—"

"Mm?"

"Don't talk with your mouth full dear," Heleana teased, hands on hips as she scolded him.

Anya laughed. All four men turned to her, handfuls of food paused halfway to their mouths.

"Not hungry, hunni?" Heleana asked, placing a hand on her shoulder as all the men turned back to their food.

Anya gasped from the unexpected contact, spinning and almost losing her footing.

"Sorry. I didn't mean to startle you, but you really should eat something before the boys devour it all," Heleana fussed, leaning in close to whisper in her ear, "you'll need to replenish your energy after all."

Anya's face turned scarlet, fiddling with the collar of her jumper, paranoid about the mark she'd spotted on her neck earlier as Heleana walked away with a huge smile on her face. She was over the moon that she was Thane's, but she didn't want everyone making a fuss about it.

"Heleana's brownies are to die for," Tynan announced, spraying the food still in his mouth, cringing when Heleana scowled at him over her shoulder.

"Sorry," he muttered, wiping the crumbs away from his mouth.

Of course they would have heard Heleana's question and would join in on the fussing, she was just surprised that Tynan had beaten the other three to the punch.

"I'm not that hungry," Anya replied, taking a seat away

from the table, sipping at some water, trying her best to ignore the glare Thane gave her. She knew she should listen and needed her energy to heal, but she didn't feel like eating. Her stomach was still churning from the poison. The smell of the food alone made her nauseous.

Silence fell in the room, their eyes all focused on something behind her, the sounds of footsteps approaching down the hall.

Anya spun around to see Hugh standing in the doorway looking exactly the same as he had when he took her. The only difference she could see was the look in his eyes as he stared back.

"I'm glad you've recovered," he spoke, clearing his throat and fiddling with the sleeves of his jacket.

"No thanks to you," she snapped, turning her back on him.

Edwin looked to the others and nodded his head toward the door, a signal for them to leave.

How could they leave her alone with him after what he'd done?

All of them filed out of the room; all except Thane. He remained propping himself against the counter.

Lucas paused to place a hand on her shoulder whispering, "Be careful," as he left.

"I didn't know about Keri. I never would have called her if I had," Hugh pleaded, realising that Thane didn't plan on leaving them alone like the others, "I thought she'd take care of you while I was gone."

"Then you're more of a fool than I am," she sighed, continuing not to look at him.

"I've been back a matter of months and even I noticed something different about her, but I put that down to the company she kept. What's your excuse?"

"She'd been that way since the moment I met her. I didn't

think anything of it."

Anya was aware that Keri had joined the hunters after she'd been changed into a vampire, but surely Hugh must have noticed the signs.

"I was never close to her. I was never close with any of them."

"You and Chase were always together, aside from when you babysat me and took me to see Lucas. To see my dad."

"Chase was just there to follow me. The only time I was alone was when I was with you or left on hunter's property. Richard doesn't trust me," Hugh continued, knitting his eyebrows together, stroking a hand through his short hair before taking a seat far away from her.

It irritated her to think he was afraid of her, that he no longer wanted to be near her. She was the same person she was when he met her.

"I knew who you were before I took you to Lucas, it's why I hesitated."

"If you knew, why didn't you tell me?" she fumed, spinning around to face him, knowing by his gasp that her eyes had changed, "why didn't you try and stop me from going there?"

"I did try, but you're so god damned stubborn. Besides if I told you, what would you have done?" he groaned, looking up to the ceiling. "You'd have laughed, or ran. And what if someone had heard me? You'd have been killed. I was trying to protect you the only way I knew how."

"Why?"

"There's something about you that I just couldn't ignore. No matter what punishment I received for helping you."

"You know your dad's not human, too right?" Anya asked, needing to change the subject when she noticed Thane's nostrils flare and his eyes turn to granite. She didn't know why she cared if Thane hurt him, he deserved it after what he'd done. Except, something inside told her to listen and give him the benefit of the doubt.

"Yes. I do, thanks to Thane."

"Then that means you're not either?"

"No," he sighed, looking from Thane back to her. "Richard isn't my real dad. He married my mum shortly after I was born, but when she died he kept me as his own, hoping to turn me into the perfect hunter that would jump to his every whim. He couldn't have been more wrong. I was always a disappointment to him."

"You want me to pity you?" she scoffed, slamming her water on the worktop, the contents sloshing over the rim.

"No," he muttered, pushing out of his chair to step toward her, pausing when Thane inched away from the counter he leaned upon. "I just want you to understand that I never chose to be a hunter. I was forced to be there."

Maybe he wasn't the monster she thought he was. He'd helped the Guards when the hunters had attacked after all. Thane had explained to her that he'd helped him, possibly even saved his life. He'd even freed Lucas when Thane was unable to pass the door to go to him, but did she trust him? He was the reason this all started in the first place. If he hadn't taken her, she wouldn't have been left with Keri to be poisoned. And now that Keri had escaped, she could have told all the hunters about Edwin and the rest of the Guards. Every one of them could now be in danger because of him. He was right to feel guilty.

If he wasn't like the rest of them as he claimed, why hadn't he done something sooner to help them? Why hadn't he released her dad when he had the chance? She couldn't afford to soften toward him. She needed to remain cautious until he proved to her that he could be trusted.

"I tried to run away several times, but each and every time Richard found me and punished me. I even released a prisoner once when I found her," Hugh admitted, taking another step toward her, despite Thane's growl. "I was disgusted that they had her locked away. I was only ten. So, I freed her. Richard found out and chained me in the same blood-soaked shackles that held her. Made me watch as he killed her before me."

Anya's heart skipped several beats. She knew that Richard was cruel, but she never thought he would be so vile to someone who was supposed to be his own child. But what if Hugh was lying? Just trying to make her feel sorry for him?

"Why would Richard trust you with the key to Lucas's cell if he knew you were a risk?" she asked, hoping to catch him in a trap.

"He wanted me to give it to you. To see what you'd do," he whispered, staring down at his feet. "I hesitated for as long as I could but figured it may actually help when you began to panic. If you'd tried to let him out, I would have stopped you, begged you to listen, but I don't think you ever realised the key unlocked the cell as well as the door."

"You knew it was a trap and still you gave it to me?" she snarled, her canines growing in her mouth. The sensation still shocked her as they tingled and prodded the inside of her lip.

"I know that was wrong, but you don't understand what happens when you go against Richard's wishes," he pleaded.

"Then enlighten me, Hugh. What did Richard do?"

He looked up at her then, tears forming in the corners of his chocolate eyes. She couldn't help but feel a pang of guilt for forcing him to tell her all the humiliating things Richard did to him, but she needed to know. How else could she ever expect to trust him?

"After the party, I tried to tell him he had to be wrong about you, but he got angry and threw me into one of the other cells whilst he went to see you," he turned away from her again, scratching a hand through his short hair.

"He soon learnt I had feelings for you and thought he could use them to his advantage. Then he told me to bring you to the hunters to see what you'd do. I refused again and he——" Hugh's voice shook, his hands tightening into fists that trembled by his sides.

She couldn't help it, she had to go to him and let him know that he wasn't alone. Crouching down in front of him, where he now sat on the floor holding his knees close to his chest, she placed a hand on his shoulder.

"It's OK, Hugh," she spoke softly, trying to soothe him.
"He branded me."
"What do you mean?"

Rather than trying to explain, Hugh spun around on the floor and removed his jacket, then lifted his shirt over his head. On his back was a scarred symbol she thought she recognized, still discoloured and raised.

"The hunter's mark," Thane breathed behind her, coming to a stop just inches from her back as she stretched her hand out to touch it, to prove to herself it was real.

"He told me there was no escaping what I was and this was a reminder, but it didn't work, I still refused. So he just asked Keri to fetch you instead. I mean, why would you refuse to go with someone you believed was your friend?" Hugh sighed, pulling his shirt back over his scarred body.

From the look of his back, all the welts, cuts and scars, Hugh had been fighting against Richard for years.

"You were right, Anya. I was stupid to think he hadn't gotten to her, but I thought she was different."

"Keri hates my kind. She blames us for what happened to her, but so far as I could tell, Keri had feelings for Richard and tried to impress him. That's why she wanted to take me back to him."

"A sacrifice to get in his good books," Hugh contemplated, nodding his head in agreement, "I can't believe I didn't see that before."

All this time Anya had despised Hugh for being a hunter, but the truth was, he didn't want to be there just as much as she didn't. She couldn't help but feel guilty for assuming the worst of him. In the end, she was just as bad as all those hunters and other humans Thane had mentioned, judging him for what he was instead of getting to know him.

"I'm sorry," she muttered under her breath, feeling a fool.

She'd argued with Richard and Hugh all those months ago saying Lucas was innocent before she learnt who he was, claiming there was good and bad in everyone, but she'd forgotten her own advice, never believing there could be hunters that didn't want to be there. Maybe if she'd gotten the chance to read the journal Hugh had given her, she might have realised sooner.

"I shouldn't have judged you just because you were a hunter."

"We all make mistakes. All we can do is learn from them. I can't help being brought up by a hunter, just like you can't change what you are."

"I know," she muttered, pushing to her feet and holding out her hand for him to take.

He looked up at her and gave a weak smile, taking hold of her hand and stepped toward her, pulling her in for a hug.

"Hold up, pretty boy," Thane growled, wrapping an arm around her waist from behind, moving her next to his side and holding her firm.

"Right. Sorry," Hugh sighed, taking a step back and dropping his arms back to his sides.

When Anya glanced up at Thane beside her, her breath caught in her throat. She was used to seeing his eyes change with his mood, but she'd never seen his eyes as dark as they were now.

Were all newly mated males this possessive and protective? Or was it the wolf being so close to the surface?

"Perhaps you should leave now," Anya suggested, noticing that Thane's fangs were now poking out from his mouth. The wolf was winning the battle, and it wanted Hugh's blood.

"I can forgive you for what you did, but it will take me awhile to trust you."

"I understand," he sighed, placing his hands in his pockets, headed for the door, "but I'll prove to you that you can trust me. Both of you."

Finally alone, Anya turned to Thane pulling at his collar to bring his lips to her own, a soft moan escaping his lips when she entwined her arms around his neck.

Before she realised it, she was in the air, her legs wrapped around his waist, Thane's hands cupping her buttocks as he deepened their kiss.

She couldn't help but smile against his mouth, wondering whether he'd always be this jealous of other males around her. Part of her knowing he always would be.

# The End

# Books by this Author

## The Otherworld Guardians
Reluctant Guardian

Hunter Guardian – Coming Soon

## Demon Warriors
Touch

Sight – Coming Soon

## The Dawnbury Shifters
To Catch an Alpha

## Stand Alone Books
The Wolves of Wulfric Manor

Printed in Great Britain
by Amazon